Blott on the Landscape

Tom Sharpe was born in 1928 and educated at Lancing College and at
Pembroke College, Cambridge. He did his National Service in the
Marines before going to South Africa in 1951, where he did social
work for the Non-European Affairs Department before teaching in
Natal. He had a photographic studio in Pietermaritzburg from 1957
until 1961, when he was deported. From 1963 to 1972 he was a lecturer
in History at the Cambridge College of Arts and Technology. He is
married and lives in Cambridge.

Tom Sharpe's novels *Indecent Exposure*, *Riotous Assembly* and *Porterhouse Blue* are also published in Pan.

Tom Sharpe

Blott on the Landscape

Pan Books London and Sydney

First published 1975 by Martin Secker & Warburg Ltd
This edition published 1977 by Pan Books Ltd,
Cavaye Place, London SW10 9PG
© Tom Sharpe 1975
ISBN 0 330 25080 9
Printed and bound in Great Britain by
Cox & Wyman Ltd, London, Reading and Fakenham

to Geoff Millard

1

Sir Giles Lynchwood, Member of Parliament for South Worfordshire, sat in his study and lit a cigar. Outside his window tulips and primroses bloomed, a thrush pecked at the lawn and the sun shone down out of a cloudless sky. In the distance he could see the cliffs of the Cleene Gorge rising above the river.

But Sir Giles had no thoughts for the beauties of the landscape. His mind was occupied with other things; with money and Mrs Forthby and the disparity between things as they were and things as they might have been. Not that the view from his window was one of uninterrupted beauty. It held Lady Maud, and whatever else she might be, nobody in his right mind would ever have described her as beautiful. She was large and ponderous and possessed a shape that someone had once aptly called Rodinesque – certainly Sir Giles, viewing her as dispassionately as six years of marriage allowed, found her monumentally unattractive. Sir Giles was not particularly fussy about external appearances. His fortune had been made by recognizing potential advantage in unprepossessing properties and he could justly claim to have evicted more impecunious tenants than any other anonymous landlord in London. Maud's appearance was the least of his marital problems. It was rather the cast of her mind, her outspoken self-assurance, that infuriated him. That, and the fact that for once in his life he was lumbered with a wife he could not leave and a house he could not sell.

Maud was a Handyman and Handyman Hall had always been her family home. A vast rambling building with twenty bedrooms, a ballroom with a sprung floor, a plumbing system that held fascinations for industrial archaeologists but which kept Sir Giles awake at night, and a central heating system that had been designed to consume coke by the ton, and now seemed to gulp oil by the megagallon, Handyman Hall had been built in 1899 to make manifest in bricks, mortar and the more hideous furnishings of the period the fact that the Handyman family had arrived. Theirs had been a brief social season. Edward the Seventh had twice paid visits to the house, on each occasion seducing Mrs Handyman in the mistaken belief that she was a chambermaid (a result of the diffidence which left her speechless in the presence of Royalty). In recompense for this royal gaffe, and for services rendered, her husband Bulstrode was raised to the Peerage. From that brief moment of social acceptance the Handymans had sunk to their present obscurity. Borne to prominence on a tide of ale – Handyman Pale, Handyman Triple XXX and Handyman West Country had been famous in their time – they had succumbed to a taste for brandy. The first earl of Handyman had died, a suspicious husband and an understandably ardent republican, in time to achieve posthumous fame as the first cadaver to incur Lloyd George's exorbitant death duties. He had been followed almost immediately by his eldest son Bartholomew, whose reaction to the taxman's summons had been to drink himself to death on two bottles of his father's Trois Six de Montpellier.

The outbreak of the First World War had completed the decline in the family fortunes. Boothroyd, the second son, had returned from France with his taste buds so irreparably impaired by taking a swig from a bottle of battery acid to steady his nerves before going over the top that his efforts to restore Handyman Ale to its pre-war quality and popularity had quite the contrary effect. For the first time the title 'Brewers Extraordinary to his Majesty the King' accurately reflected the character of the beer dispensed by the Handyman Brewery. During the twenties and thirties sales dropped until they were confined to a dozen tied houses in Worfordshire whose patrons were forced to consume Boothroyd's appalling concoctions out of a sense of loyalty to the family and by the refusal of the local magistrates (Boothroyd among them) to grant licences to sell spirituous liquors to anyone else. By that time the Handymans had been reduced to living in one wing of the great house and had celebrated the outbreak of the Second World War by offering the rest of their home to the War Office. Boothroyd had died on Home Guard duty to be succeeded by his brother Busby, Maud's father, and the Hall had served first as a home for General de Gaulle's chief of staff and the entire Free French army of that time and later as an Italian prisoner-of-war camp. The fourth Earl had done what he could to restore Handyman Ale to its previous popularity by reverting to the original recipe, and to restore the family fortune by using his influence to see that the War Office paid a quite disproportionately high rent for a building they didn't want.

It had been that influence, the Handyman influence, which had persuaded Sir Giles that he could do worse than marry Lady Maud and through her acquire a seat in Parliament. Looking back over the years Sir Giles was inclined to think that he had paid too high a price for the Hall and social acceptance. A marriage of convenience he had called it at the time, but the term had proved singularly inappropriate. Nothing about Maud's appearance had suggested an unduly fastidious attitude to sex and Sir Giles had been surprised, not to say pained, by her too literal interpretation of his suggestion on their honeymoon that she should tie him to the bed and beat him. Sir Giles' screams had been audible a quarter of a mile along the Costa Brava and had led to an embarrassing interview with the hotel manager. Sir Giles had stood all the way home and ever since had sought refuge in a separate bedroom and in Mrs Forthby, in whose flat in St John's Wood he could at least be assured of moderation. To make matters worse there was no possibility of a divorce. Their marriage settlement included a reversionary clause whereby the Hall and the Estate, for which he had had to pay one hundred thousand pounds to Maud, would revert to her in the event of his death without heirs or of misconduct on his part leading to a divorce case. Sir Giles was a rich man but one hundred thousand pounds was too high a price to pay for freedom.

He sighed and glanced out of the window. Lady Maud had disappeared but the scene was no pleasanter for her going. Her place had been taken by Blott, the gardener, who was plodding across the lawn towards the kitchen garden. Sir Giles studied the squat figure with distaste. For a gardener, for an Italian gardener *and* an ex PoW, Blott had an air of contentment that grated on Sir Giles' nerves. He liked his servants to be obsequious and there was nothing obsequious about Blott. The wretched fellow seemed to think he owned the place. Sir Giles watched him disappear through the door in the wall of the kitchen garden and considered ways and means of getting rid of Blott, Lady Maud and Handyman Hall. He had just had an idea.

*

So had Lady Maud. As she lumbered about the garden, uprooting here a dandelion and there a chickweed, her mind was occupied with thoughts of maternity.

'It's now or never,' she murmured as she squashed a slug. Between her legs she could see Sir Giles in his study and wondered once again why it was that she should have married a man with so little sense of duty. In her view there was no higher virtue. It was out of duty to her family that she had married him. Left to herself she would have chosen a younger, more attractive man, but young attractive men with fortunes were in short supply in Worfordshire and Maud too plain to seek them out in London.

'Coming out?' she had shouted at her mother when Lady Handyman had suggested she should be presented at court. 'Coming out? But I've already been.'

And it was true. Lady Maud's moment of beauty had been premature. At fifteen she had been lovely. At twenty-one the Handyman features, the prominent nose in particular, had made themselves and her plain. At thirty-five she was a Handyman all over and only acceptable to someone with Sir Giles' depraved taste and eye for hidden advantage. She had accepted his proposal without illusions, only to discover too late that his long bachelorhood had left him with a set of habits and fantasies which made it impossible for him to fulfil his part of the bargain. Whatever else Sir Giles was cut out for it was not paternity. After the unfortunate experience of their honeymoon, Maud had attempted a reconciliation, but without result. She had resorted to drink, to spicy foods, to oysters and champagne, to hard-boiled eggs, but Sir Giles had remained obdurately impotent. Now on this bright spring day when everything about her was breaking out or sprouting or proclaiming the joys of parenthood from every corner of the estate, Lady Maud felt distinctly wanton. She would make one more effort to make Sir Giles see reason. Straightening her back she marched across the lawn to the house and went down the passage.

'Giles,' she said entering the study without knocking, 'it's time we had this thing out.'

Sir Giles looked up from his *Times*. 'What thing?' he asked.

'You know very well what I'm talking about. There's no need to beat about the bush.'

Sir Giles folded the paper. 'Bush, dear?' he said doubtfully.

'Don't prevaricate,' said Lady Maud.

'I'm not prevaricating,' Sir Giles protested, 'I simply don't know what you are talking about.'

Lady Maud put her hands on the desk and leant forward menacingly. 'Sex,' she snarled.

Sir Giles curdled in his chair. 'Oh that,' he murmured. 'What about it?'

'I'm not getting any younger.'

Sir Giles nodded sympathetically. It was one of the few things he was grateful for.

'In another year or two it will be too late.'

Thank God, thought Sir Giles, but the words remained unspoken. Instead he selected a Ramon Allones from his cigarbox. It was an unfortunate move. Lady Maud leant forward and twitched it from his fingers.

'Now you listen to me, Giles Lynchwood,' she said, 'I didn't marry you to be left a childless widow.'

'Widow?' said Sir Giles flinching.

'The operative word is childless. Whether you live or die is of no great moment to me. What is important is that I have an heir. When I married you it was on the clear understanding that you would be a father to my children. We have been married six years now. It is time for you to do your duty.'

Sir Giles crossed his legs defiantly. 'We've been through all this before,' he muttered.

'We have never been through it at all. That is precisely what I am complaining about. You have steadfastly refused to act like a normal husband. You have—'

'We all have our little problems, dear,' Sir Giles said.

'Quite,' said Lady Maud, 'so we do. Unfortunately my problem is rather more pressing than yours. I am over forty and as I have already pointed out, in a year or two I will be past the childbearing age. My family has lived in the Gorge for five hundred years and I do not intend to go to my grave with the knowledge that I am the last of the Handymans.'

'I don't really see how you can avoid that whatever happens,' said Sir Giles. 'After all, in the unlikely event of our having any children, their name would be Lynchwood.'

'I have always intended,' said Lady Maud, 'changing the name by deed poll.'

'Have you indeed? Well then let me inform you that there will be no need,' said Sir Giles. 'There will be no children by our marriage and that's final.'

'In that case,' said Lady Maud, 'I shall take steps to get a divorce. You will be hearing from my solicitors.'

She left the room and slammed the door. Behind her Sir Giles sat in his chair shaken but content. The years of his misery were over. He would get his divorce and keep the Hall. He had nothing more to worry about. He reached for another cigar and lit it. Upstairs he could hear his wife's heavy movements in her bedroom. She was no doubt going out to see Mr Turnbull of Ganglion, Turnbull and Shrine, the family solicitors in Worford. Sir Giles unfolded *The Times* and read the letter about the cuckoo once again.

2

Mr Turnbull of Ganglion, Turnbull and Shrine was sympathetic but unhelpful. 'If you initiate proceedings on grounds as evidently insubstantial as those you have so vividly outlined,' he told Lady Maud, 'the reversionary clause becomes null and void. You might well end up losing the Hall and the Estate.'

'Do you mean to sit there and tell me that I cannot divorce my husband without losing my family home?' Lady Maud demanded.

Mr Turnbull nodded. 'Sir Giles has only to deny your allegations,' he explained, 'and frankly I can hardly see a man in his position admitting them. I'm afraid the Court would find for him. The difficulty about this sort of case is that you can't produce convincing proof.'

'I should have thought my virginity was proof enough,' Lady Maud told him bluntly. Mr Turnbull suppressed a shudder. The notion of Lady Maud presenting her maidenhead as Exhibit A was not one that appealed to him.

'I think we should need something a little more orthodox than that. After all, Sir Giles could claim that you had refused him his conjugal rights. It would simply be his word against yours. Of course, you could still get your divorce, but the Hall would remain legally his.'

'There must be something I can do,' Lady Maud protested. Looking at her, Mr Turnbull rather doubted it but he was tactful enough not to say so.

'And you say you have attempted a reconciliation?'

'I have told Giles that he must do his duty by me.'

'That's not quite what I meant,' Mr Turnbull told her. 'Marriage is after all a difficult relationship at the best of times. Perhaps a little tenderness on your part would . . .'

'Tenderness?' said Lady Maud. 'Tenderness? You seem to forget that my husband is a pervert. Do you imagine that a man who finds satisfaction in being—'

'No,' said Mr Turnbull hurriedly. 'I take your point. Perhaps tenderness is the wrong word. What I meant was . . . well . . . a little understanding.'

Lady Maud looked at him scornfully.

'After all *tout comprendre, c'est tout pardonner*,' continued Mr Turnbull, relapsing into the language he associated with sophistication in matters of the heart.

'I beg your pardon,' said Lady Maud.

'I was merely saying that to understand all is to pardon all,' Mr Turnbull explained.

'Coming from a legal man I find that remark astonishing,' said Lady Maud, 'and in any case I am not interested in either understanding or in pardon. I am simply interested in bearing a child. My family have lived in the Gorge for five hundred years and I have no intention of being responsible for their not living there for another five hundred. You may find my insistence on the importance of my family romantic. I can only say that I regard it as my duty to have an heir. If my husband refuses to do his duty by me I shall find someone who will.'

'My dear Lady Maud,' said Mr Turnbull, suddenly conscious that he might be in danger of becoming the first object of her extramarital attentions, 'I beg you not to do anything hasty. An act of adultery on your part would certainly allow Sir Giles to obtain a divorce on grounds which would invalidate the reversionary clause. Perhaps you would like me to have a word with him. It sometimes helps to have a third party, someone entirely impartial you understand, to bring about a reconciliation.'

Lady Maud shook her head. She was thinking about adultery.

'If Giles were to commit adultery,' she said finally, 'would I be right in supposing that the Estate would revert to me?'

Mr Turnbull beamed at the prospect. 'No difficulties at all in that case,' he said. 'You would have an absolute right to the Estate. It's in the settlement. No difficulties at all.'

'Good,' said Lady Maud, and stood up. She went downstairs, leaving Mr Turnbull with the distinct impression that Sir Giles Lynchwood was in for a nasty surprise and, better still, that the firm of Ganglion, Turnbull and Shrine could look forward to a protracted case with substantial fees.

Outside Blott was waiting in the car.

'Blott,' said Lady Maud climbing into the back seat, 'what do you know about telephone tapping?'

Blott smiled and started the car. 'Easy,' he said, 'all you need is some wire and a pair of headphones.'

'In that case stop at the first radio shop you come to and buy the necessary equipment.'

By the time they returned to Handyman Hall, Lady Maud had laid her plans.

*

So had Sir Giles. The first moment of elation at the prospect of a divorce had worn off and Sir Giles, weighing the matter up in his mind, had recognized some ugly possibilities. For one thing he did not relish the thought of being cross-examined about his private life by some eminent barrister. The newspapers, particularly one or two of the Sundays, would have a ball with Lady Maud's description of their honeymoon. Worse still, he would be unable to issue writs for libel. The story could be verified by the hotel manager and while Sir Giles might well win the divorce case and retain the Hall he would certainly lose his public reputation. No, the matter would have to be handled in some less conspicuous manner. Sir Giles picked up a pencil and began to doodle.

The problem was a simple one. The divorce, if and when it came, must be on grounds of his own choosing. He must be free from any breath of scandal. It was too much to hope that Lady Maud would find a lover, but desperation might drive her to some act of folly. Sir Giles rather doubted it, and besides, her age, shape and general disposition made it seem unlikely. And then there was the Hall and the one hundred thousand pounds he had paid for it. He drew a cat and was just considering that there were more ways of making a profit from property than selling it or burning it to the ground when the shape of his drawing, an eight with ears and tail, put him in mind of something he had once seen from the air. A flyover, a spaghetti junction, a motorway.

A moment later he was unfolding an ordnance survey map and studying it with intense interest. Of course. Why hadn't he thought of it before? The Cleene Gorge was the ideal route. It lay directly between Sheffingham and Knighton. And with motorways there came compulsory purchase orders and large sums paid in compensation. The perfect solution. All it needed was a word or two in the right ear. Sir Giles picked up the phone and dialled. By the time Lady Maud returned from Worford he was in excellent humour. Hoskins at the Worfordshire Planning Authority had been most helpful, but then Hoskins had always been helpful. It paid him to be and it certainly paid for a rather larger house than his salary would have led one to expect. Sir Giles smiled to himself. Influence was a wonderful thing.

'I'm going down to London this afternoon,' he told Lady Maud as they sat down to lunch. 'One or two business things to fix up. I daresay I shall be tied up for a couple of days.'

'I shouldn't be at all surprised,' said Lady Maud.

'If you need me for anything, leave a message with my secretary.'

Lady Maud helped herself to cottage pie. She was in a good humour. She had no doubt whatsoever that Sir Giles indulged his taste for restrictive practices with someone in London. It might take time to find out the name of his mistress but she was prepared to wait.

*

'Extraordinary woman, Lady Maud,' Mr Turnbull said as he and Mr Ganglion sat in the bar of the Four Feathers in Worford.

'Extraordinary family,' Mr Ganglion agreed. 'I don't suppose you remember her grandmother, the old Countess. No, you wouldn't. Before your time. I remember drawing up her will in . . . now when can it have been . . . must have been in March 1936. Let's see, she died in June of that year so it must have been in March. Insisted on my inserting the fact that her son, Busby, was of partially royal parentage. I did point out that in

16

that case he was not entitled to inherit but she was adamant. "Royal Blood," she kept saying. In the end I got her to sign several copies of the will but it was only in the top one that any mention was made of the royal bastardy.'

'Good Lord,' said Mr Turnbull, 'do you think there was anything in it?'

Mr Ganglion looked over the top of his glasses at him. 'Between ourselves, I must admit it was not outside the bounds of possibility. The dates did match. Busby was born in 1905 and the Royal visit took place in '04. Edward the Seventh had quite a reputation for that sort of thing.'

'It certainly goes some way to explain Lady Maud's looks,' Mr Turnbull admitted. 'And her arrogance, come to that.'

'These things are best forgotten,' said Mr Ganglion sadly. 'What did she want to see you about?'

'She's seeking a divorce. I dissuaded her, at least temporarily. Seems that Lynchwood has a taste for flagellation.'

'Extraordinary what some fellows like,' said Mr Ganglion. 'It's not as though he went to a public school either. Most peculiar. Still, I should have thought Maud could have satisfied him if anyone could. She's got a forearm like a navvy.'

'I got the impression that she had rather overdone it,' Mr Turnbull explained.

'Splendid. Splendid.'

'The main trouble seems to be non-consummation. She wants an heir before it's too late.'

'The perennial obsession of these old families. What did you advise? Artificial insemination?'

Mr Turnbull finished his drink. 'Certainly not,' he muttered. 'Apparently she's still a virgin.'

Mr Ganglion sniggered. 'There was an old virgin of forty, whose habits were fearfully naughty. She owned a giraffe whose terrible laugh . . . or was it distaff? I forget now.'

They went into lunch.

*

Blott finished his lunch in the greenhouse at the end of the kitchen garden. Around him early geraniums and chrysanthemums, pink and red, matched the colour of his complexion. This was the inner sanctum of Blott's world where he could sit surrounded by flowers whose beauty was proof to him that life was not entirely without meaning. Through the glass windows he could look down the kitchen garden at the lettuces, the peas and beans, the redcurrant bushes and the gooseberries of which he was so proud. And all around the old brick walls cut out the world he mistrusted. Blott emptied his thermos flask and stood up. Above his head he could see the telephone wires stretching from the house. He went outside and fetched a ladder and presently was busily engaged in attaching his wires to the line above. He was still there when Sir Giles left in the Bentley. Blott watched him pass without interest. He disliked Sir Giles intensely and it was one of the advantages of working in the kitchen garden that they seldom came into contact. He finished his work and fitted the headphones and bell. Then he went into the house. He found Lady Maud washing up in the kitchen.

'It's ready,' he said, 'we can test it.'

Lady Maud dried her hands. 'What do I do?'

'When the bell rings put the headphones on,' Blott explained.

'You go into the study and ring a number and I'll listen,' said Lady Maud. Blott went into the study and sat behind the desk. He picked up the phone and tried to think of someone to call. There wasn't anyone he knew to call. Finally his eye fell on a number written in pencil on the pad in front of him. Beside it there were some doodles and a drawing of a cat. Blott dialled the number. It was rather a long one and began with 01 and he had to wait for some time for an answer.

'Hullo, Felicia Forthby speaking,' said a woman's voice.

Blott tried to think of something to say. 'This is Blott,' he said finally.

'Blott?' said Mrs Forthby. 'Do I know you?'

'No,' said Blott.

'Is there anything I can do for you?'

'No,' said Blott.

There was an awkward silence and then Mrs Forthby spoke. 'What do you want?'

Blott tried to think of something he wanted. 'I want a ton of pig manure,' he said.

'You must have the wrong number.'

'Yes,' said Blott and put the phone down.

In the greenhouse Lady Maud was delighted with the experiment. 'I'll soon find out who's beating him now,' she thought and took the headphones off. She went back to the house.

'We shall take it in turns to monitor all telephone calls my husband makes,' she told Blott. 'I want to find out who he's visiting in London. You must write down the name of anyone he talks to. Do you understand?'

'Yes,' said Blott and went back to the kitchen garden happily. In the kitchen Lady Maud finished washing up. She'd meant to ask Blott who he had been talking to. Never mind, it wasn't important.

3

Sir Giles got back from London rather sooner than he had expected. Mrs Forthby's period had put her in a foul mood and Sir Giles had enough on his plate without having to put up with the side-effects of Mrs Forthby's menstrual tension. And besides, Mrs Forthby in the flesh was a different kettle of fish to Mrs Forthby in his fantasies. In the latter she had a multitude of perverse inclinations, which corresponded exactly with his own unfortunate requirements, while possessing a discretion that would have done credit to a Trappist nun. In the flesh she was disappointingly different. She seemed to think, and in Sir Giles' opinion there could be no greater fault in a woman, that he loved her for herself alone. It was a phrase that sent a shudder through him. If he loved her at all, and it was only in her absence that his heart grew even approximately fonder, it was not for Mrs Forthby's self. It was precisely because as far as he could make out she lacked *any* self that he was attracted to her in the first place.

Externally Mrs Forthby had all the attributes of desirable womanhood, rather too many for more fastidious tastes, and all confined within corsets, panties, suspender belts and bras that inflamed Sir Giles' imagination and reminded him of the advertisements in women's magazines on which his sexual immaturity had first cut its teeth. Internally Mrs Forthby was a void if her inconsequential conversation was anything to go by and it was this void that Sir Giles, ever hopeful of finding a lover with needs as depraved as his own, sought to fill. And here he had to admit that Mrs Forthby fell far short of his expectations. Broad-minded she might be, though he sometimes doubted that she had a mind, but she still lacked enthusiasm for the intricate contortions and strangleholds that constituted Sir Giles' notions of foreplay. And besides she had an unfortunate habit of giggling at moments of his grossest concentration and of interjecting reminiscences of her Girl Guide training while tightening the granny knots which so affected him. Worst of all was her absent-mindedness (and here he had no quarrel with the term). She had been known to leave him trussed to the bed and gagged for several hours while she entertained friends to tea in the next room. It was at such moments of enforced contemplation that Sir Giles was most conscious of the discrepancies between his public and his private posture and hoped to hell the two wouldn't be brought closer together by some damned woman looking for the lavatory. Not that he wouldn't have welcomed some intervention into his fantasy world if only he could be certain that he wouldn't be the laughing-stock of Westminster. After one such episode he had threatened to murder Mrs Forthby and had only been restrained by his inability to stand upright even after she had untied him.

'Where the hell have you been?' he shouted when she returned at one o'clock in the morning.

'Covent Garden,' Mrs Forthby said. 'The Magic Flute. A divine performance.'

'You might have told me. I've been lying here in agony for six hours.'

'I thought you liked that,' Mrs Forthby said. 'I thought that's what you wanted.'

'Wanted?' Sir Giles screamed. 'Six hours? Nobody in his right mind wants to be trussed up like a spring chicken for six hours.'

'No, dear,' Mrs Forthby said agreeably. 'It's just that I forgot. Shall I get you your enema now?'

'Certainly not,' shouted Sir Giles, in whom some measure of self-respect had been induced by his confinement. 'And don't meddle with my leg.'

'But it shouldn't be there, dear. It looks unnatural.'

Sir Giles stared violently out of the corner of his right eye at his toes. 'I know it shouldn't be there,' he yelled. 'And it wouldn't be if you hadn't been so damned forgetful.'

Mrs Forthby had tidied up the straps and buckles and had made a pot of tea. 'I'll tie a knot in my handkerchief next time,' she said tactlessly, propping Sir Giles up on some pillows so that he could drink his tea.

'There won't be a next time,' he had snarled and had spent a sleepless night trying desperately to assume a less contorted posture. It had been an empty promise. There was always a next time. Mrs Forthby's absent shape and her ready acceptance of his revolting foibles made good the lapses of her memory and Sir Giles returned to her flat whenever he was in London, each time with the fervent prayer that she wouldn't leave him hooded and bound while she spent a month in the Bahamas.

*

But if Sir Giles had difficulties with Mrs Forthby there were remarkably few as far as the motorway was concerned. The thing was already on the drawing board.

'It's designated the Mid-Wales Motorway, the M101,' he was told when he made discreet enquiries of the Ministry of the

Environment. 'It has been sent up for Ministerial approval. I believe there have been some doubts on conservation grounds. For God's sake don't quote me.' Sir Giles put the phone down and considered his tactics. Ostensibly he would have to oppose the scheme if only to keep his seat as member for South Worfordshire but there was opposition and opposition. He invested heavily in Imperial Cement, who seemed likely to benefit from the demand for concrete. He had lunch with the Chairman of Imperial Motors, dinner with the Managing Director of Motorway Manufacturers Limited, drinks with the Secretary of the Amalgamated Union of Roadworkers, and he pointed out to the Chief Whip the need to do something to lower the rate of unemployment in his constituency.

In short he was the catalyst in the chemistry of progress. And with it all no money passed hands. Sir Giles was too old a dog for that. He passed information. What companies were on the way to making profits, what shares to buy, and what to sell, these were the tender of his influence. And to insure himself against future suspicions he made a speech at the annual dinner of the Countryside Conservation League in which he urged eternal vigilance against the depredations of the property speculator. He returned to Handyman Hall in time to be outraged by the news of the proposed motorway.

'I shall demand an immediate enquiry,' he told Lady Maud when the requisition order arrived. He reached for the phone.

*

In the greenhouse Blott had his time cut out listening to Sir Giles' telephone calls. He had no sooner settled down to deal with some aphids on the ornamental apple trees that grew against the wall than the bell rang. Blott dashed in and listened to General Burnett fulminating from the Grange about blackguards in Whitehall, red tape, green belts and blue-stockings, none of which he fully understood. He went back to his aphids when the phone rang again. This time it was Mr Bullett-Finch phoning to find out what Sir Giles intended to do about stopping the motorway.

'It's going to take half the garden,' he said. 'We have spent the last six years getting things shipshape and now for this to happen. It's too much. It's not as though Ivy's nerves can stand it.'

Sir Giles sympathized unctuously. He was, he said, organizing a protest committee. There was bound to be an Enquiry. Mr Bullett-Finch could rest assured that no stone would be left unturned. Blott returned to the aphids puzzled. The English language still retained its power to baffle him, and Blott occasionally found himself trapped in some idiom. Shipshape? There was nothing vaguely in the shape of a ship about Mr Bullett-Finch's garden. But then Blott had to admit that the English themselves remained a mystery to him. They paid people more when they were unemployed than when they had to work. They paid bricklayers more than teachers. They raised money for earthquake victims in Peru while old-age pensioners lived on a pittance. They refused Entry Permits to Australians and invited Russians to come and live in England. Finally they seemed to take particular pleasure in being shot at by the Irish. All in all they were a source of constant astonishment to him and of reassurance. They were only happy when something dreadful happened to them, be it flood, fire, war or some appalling disaster, and Blott, whose early life had been a chapter of disasters, took comfort from the fact that he was living in a community that actually enjoyed misfortunes.

Born when, of whom, where, he had no idea. The date of his discovery in the Ladies Room in the Dresden railway station was as near as he could get to a birthday and since the lady cleaner had disclaimed any responsibility for his appearance there, although hard pressed by the authorities to do so, he had no idea who his mother was – let alone his father. He couldn't even be sure his parents had been Germans. For all he and the authorities knew they might have been Jews, though even the Director of the Race Classification Bureau had had the illogical grace to admit that Jews did not make a habit of abandoning their offspring in railway cloakrooms. Still, the notion lent a further element of uncertainty to Blott's adolescence in the Third Reich and he had got no help from his appearance. Dark, hook-nosed pure Aryans there doubtless were, but Blott, who had taken an obsessive interest in the question, found few who were happy to discuss their pedigree with him. Certainly no one was prepared to adopt him, and even the orphanage tended to push him into the background when there were visitors. As for the Hitler Youth ... Blott preferred to forget his adolescence and even the memory of his arrival in England still filled him with uneasiness.

It had been a dark night and Blott, who had been put in to stiffen the resolve of the crew of an Italian bomber, had taken the opportunity to emigrate. Besides, he had a shrewd suspicion that his squadron leader had ordered him to volunteer as navigator to the Italians in the hope that he would not return. It seemed the only explanation for his choice and Blott, whose previous experience had been as a rear-gunner where his only contribution to the war effort had been to shoot down two Messerschmidt 109s that were supposed to be escorting his bomber squadron, had fulfilled his squadron leader's expectations to the letter. Even the Italian airmen, pusillanimous to a man, had been surprised by Blott's insistence that Margate was situated in the heart of Worcestershire. After a heated argument they dropped their bombs over Exmoor and headed back for the Pas de Calais across the Bristol Channel before running out of fuel over the mountains of North Wales. It was at this point that the Italians decided to bale out and were attempting to explain the urgency of the situation to Blott, whose knowledge of Italian was negligible, when they were saved the bother by the intervention of a mountain which, according to Blott's bump of direction, should not have been there. In the ensuing holocaust Blott was the sole survivor and since he was discovered naked in the wreckage of an Italian bomber by a search party next morning it was naturally assumed that he must be Italian. The fact that he couldn't speak a word of his native tongue deceived nobody, least of all the Major in charge of the prisoner-of-war camp to which Blott was sent, for the simple reason that he couldn't speak Italian either and Blott was his first prisoner. It was only much later, with the arrival of some genuine Italian prisoners from North Africa, that doubts were cast on his nationality, but by that time Blott had established his bona fides by displaying no interest in the course of the war and by resolutely demonstrating a reluctance to escape that was authentically Italian. Besides, his claim to have been born the son of a shepherd in the Tyrol explained his lack of Italian.

In 1942 the camp had been moved to Handyman Hall and Blott had made the place his home. The Hall and the Handyman family appealed to him. They were both the epitome of Englishness and in Blott's view there could be no higher praise. To be English was the supreme virtue and being a prisoner in England was better than being free anywhere else. If he had had his way the war would have continued indefinitely. He lived in a great house, he had a park to walk in, a river to fish in, a kitchen garden to grow things in, and the run of an idyllic countryside full of woods and hills and fair women whose husbands were away fighting to save the world from people like Blott. Even at night when the camp gates were closed it was perfectly easy to scale the walls and go where he liked. There were no air-raids, no sudden alarms and the whole question of earning a living was taken care of. Even the food was good, supplemented as it was by his poaching and his husbandry in the kitchen garden. To Blott the place was paradise and his only worry was that Germany might win the war. It was an eventuality he dreaded. It had been bad enough being a German in Germany. He couldn't imagine what it would be like to be an Italian who was a German who looked like a Jew in conquered Britain, and the notion of trying to explain how he came to be what he was where he was to the German occupying authorities appalled him. It was one of the nicest things about the English that they didn't seem to worry about such details, but he knew his own countrymen too well to imagine that they would be satisfied with his evasions. Layer by layer, they would peel off his equivocations until the nothing that was the essential Blott was revealed quite naked and then they would shoot what was left for desertion. Blott had no doubt about his fate, and what made matters worse was that as far as he could tell the British were quite incapable of winning the war. Half the time they seemed oblivious of the fact that there was a war on, and for the rest conducted it with an inefficiency that astonished him. Shortly after his arrival at the Hall, Western Command had conducted manoeuvres in the Cleene Forest and Blott had watched the chaos that ensued with horror. If these were the men on whose fighting qualities he had to depend for his captivity, he would have to look for his salvation elsewhere. He found it in a nearby ammunition dump which was, quite typically, unguarded and Blott, determined that if the English wouldn't defend him he would, slowly acquired a small arsenal which he buried in the forest. Two-inch mortars, Bren guns, rifles, boxes of ammunition, all disappeared without notice and were cached, carefully greased and watertight, under the bracken in the hills behind the Hall. By 1945 Blott was in a position to fight a guerrilla war in South Worfordshire. And then the war ended and new problems arose.

The prospect of being repatriated to Italy was not one that appealed to him and he couldn't see himself settling down in Naples after so many agreeable years in England. On the other hand he had no intention of returning to what remained of Dresden. It was in the Russian Zone and Blott had no desire to swop the comforts of life in Worfordshire for the rigours of existence in Siberia. Besides, he rather doubted if even a defeated Fatherland would welcome home a man who had spent five years masquerading as an Italian PoW. It seemed far wiser to stay where he was, and here his devotion to the Handyman family paid off.

Lord Handyman had been a man of enthusiasms. Long before it was generally fashionable he had conceived the notion that the world's resources were on the verge of extinction and had sought to avoid the personal consequences by saving everything. He had been particularly keen on compost and Blott had dug enormous pits in the kitchen garden into which all household refuse of an organic sort was thrown.

'Nothing must be wasted,' the Earl had declared, and nothing was. Under his direction the Hall's sewage system had been diverted to empty into the compost pits and Blott and the Earl had spent happy hours observing the layers of cabbage stalks, potato peelings, and excrement which made up the day's leavings. As each pit filled Blott dug another one and the process began again. The results were quite astonishing. Enormous cabbages and alarming marrows and cucumbers proliferated. So, in summer, did the flies until the situation became intolerable and Lady Handyman, who had lost her appetite since the recycling began, put her foot down and insisted that either the flies went or she would. Blott diverted the sewage system back to its proper place while the Earl, evidently inspired by the rate of reproduction of the flies, turned his attention to rabbits. Blott had constructed several dozen hutches built one above the other on the lines of apartment buildings in which the Earl installed the largest rabbits he could buy, a breed called Flemish Giants. Like all the Earl's schemes, the rabbits had not been an unqualified success. They consumed enormous quantities of vegetation and the family had developed an aversion for rabbit pie, roast rabbit, rabbit stew and lapin à l'orange, while Blott had been driven to distraction trying to keep pace with their voracious appetites. To add to his problems Maud, then ten, had identified her father with Mr McGregor and had aided and abetted the rabbits to escape. As peace broke out in Europe the Gorge was overrun with Flemish Giants. By then Lord Handyman's enthusiasm had waned. He turned to ducks and particularly to Khaki Campbells, a species which had the advantage that they were largely self-supporting and produced an abundance of eggs.

'Can't go wrong with ducks,' he had said cheerfully as the family switched from a diet of rabbit to duck eggs. As usual with his prophecies this one had proved unfounded. It was all too easy to go wrong with ducks, as the family found out when the Earl succumbed to a lethal egg that had been laid too close to one of his old compost pits. Passing away as peacefully as ptomaine poisoning allowed, he had left Maud and her mother to manage alone. It was largely thanks to his death that Blott had been allowed to stay on at the Hall.

4

Over the next few weeks Lady Maud was intensely active. She took legal advice from Mr Turnbull daily. She canvassed opposition to the proposed motorway from every quarter of South Worfordshire and she sat almost continuously on committees. In particular she made her considerable presence felt on the Committee for the Preservation of the Cleene Gorge. General Burnett of the Grange, Guildstead Carbonell, was elected President but as Secretary Lady Maud was the driving force. Petitions were organized, protest meetings held, motions proposed, seconded and passed, money raised and posters printed.

'The price of justice is eternal publicity,' she said with an originality that startled her hearers, but which in fact she had found in *Bartlett's Familiar Quotations*. 'It is not enough to protest, we must make our protest known. If the Gorge is to be saved it will not be by words alone but by action.' On the platform beside her Sir Giles nodded his apparent approval, but inwardly he was alarmed. Publicity was all very well, and justice was fine when it applied to other people but he didn't want public attention focused too closely on his role in the affair. He had expected the motorway to upset Lady Maud; he had not foreseen that she would turn into a human tornado. He certainly hadn't supposed that his seat would be jeopardized by the uproar she seemed bent on provoking.

'If you don't see that the Hall is saved,' Lady Maud told him, 'I'll see to it that you don't sit for South Worfordshire at the next election.' Sir Giles took the threat seriously and consulted Hoskins at the Planning Authority in Worford.

'I thought you wanted the thing to go through the Gorge,' Hoskins told him as they sat in the bar of the Handyman Arms.

Sir Giles nodded unhappily. 'I do,' he admitted, 'but Maud has gone berserk. She's threatening . . . well, never mind.'

Hoskins was reassuring. 'She'll get over it. They always do. Got to give them time to get used to the idea.'

'It's all very well for you to talk,' said Sir Giles, 'but I have to live with the beastly woman. She's up half the night thundering about the bloody house and I'm having to cook for myself. Besides, I don't like the way she keeps cleaning her father's shotgun in the kitchen.'

'You know she took a potshot at one of the surveyors last week,' Hoskins said.

'Can't you have her charged?' Sir Giles asked eagerly. 'That would take the heat off for a bit. Haul her up before the local beaks.'

'She *is* a local magistrate,' Hoskins pointed out, 'and anyway there's no proof. She would just claim she was shooting rabbits.'

'And that's another thing. She's got the house full of bloody great Alsatians. Hired them from some damned security firm. I tell you I can't go down the passage for a pee in the night without running the risk of being bitten.' He ordered another two whiskies and considered the problem. 'There'll have to be an Enquiry,' he said finally. 'Promise them an Enquiry and they'll calm down a bit. Secondly, offer the Enquiry a totally unacceptable alternative. Like we did with the block of flats in Shrewton.'

'You mean give planning permission for a sewage farm?'

'That's what we did there. Worked like a charm,' Sir Giles said. 'Now if we could come up with an alternative route which nobody in his right mind would accept . . .'

'There's always Ottertown,' said Hoskins.

'What about Ottertown?'

'It's ten miles out of the way and you'd have to go through a council estate.'

Sir Giles smiled. 'Right through the middle?'

'Right through the middle.'

'It sounds promising,' Sir Giles agreed. 'I think I shall be the first to advocate the Ottertown route. You're quite sure it's unacceptable?'

'Quite sure,' said Hoskins. 'And, by the way, I'll take my fee in advance.'

Sir Giles looked round the bar. 'My advice is to buy . . .' he began.

'Cash this time,' said Hoskins, 'I lost on United Oils.'

Sir Giles returned to Handyman Hall in a fairly good humour. He disliked parting with money but Hoskins was worth it and the Ottertown idea was the sort of strategy he liked. It would take Maud's mind off eternal publicity. Tempers would cool and the Enquiry would decide in favour of the Gorge. By then it would be too late to inflame public opinion once again. Enquiries were splendid soporifics. He ran the gauntlet of the guard dogs and spent the evening in his study writing a letter to the Minister of the Environment demanding the setting up of an Enquiry. No one could say that the Member of Parliament for South Worfordshire had not got the interests of his constituents at heart.

*

While Sir Giles connived and Lady Maud committeed, Blott in the kitchen garden had his work cut out trying to do his conflicting duties. He would settle down to weed the lettuces only to be interrupted by the bell in the greenhouse. Blott spent hours listening to long conversations between Sir Giles and officials at the Ministry, between Sir Giles and members of his constituency or his stockbroker or his business partners, but never between Sir Giles and Mrs Forthby. Sir Giles had been forewarned. Mrs Forthby's remark that she had received a call from someone called Blott who had ordered a ton of pig manure had alarmed Sir Giles. There was obviously some mistake though how Blott could have got hold of the number in the first place he couldn't imagine. It wasn't in the telephone index on his desk. He kept it in his private diary and the diary was in his pocket. Sir Giles memorized the number and then erased it from the diary. There would be no more calls to Mrs Forthby from Handyman Hall.

When Sir Giles wasn't on the telephone, Lady Maud was, issuing orders, drumming up support or hurling defiance at the authorities with a self-assurance that amazed and delighted Blott. You knew where you were with her and Blott, who prized certainty above all else, emerged from the greenhouse after listening to her with the feeling that all was well with the world and would remain so. Handyman Hall, the Park, the Lodge, a great triumphal arch at the bottom of the drive where Blott lived, the kitchen garden, all those things to which he had grafted his own anonymity in a hostile world, would remain safe and secure if Lady Maud had anything to do with it. Sir Giles' calls left a different impression. His protests were muted, too polite and too equivocal to satisfy Blott; so that he came away with the feeling that something was wrong. He couldn't put his finger on it, but whenever he took the earphones off after listening to Sir Giles he felt uneasy. There was too much talk about money for Blott's liking, and in particular about ample compensation for the Hall. The sum most frequently mentioned was a quarter of a million pounds. As he went down the rows of lettuces with his hoe, Blott shook his head. 'Money talks,' Sir Giles had told his caller but it had said nothing to Blott. There were more important words in his vocabulary. On the other hand his hours of listening to Sir Giles had done wonders for his accent. With the headphones on Blott had sat practising Sir Giles' pronunciation. In his study Sir Giles said, 'Of course, my dear fellow, I absolutely agree with you . . .' In the greenhouse Blott repeated the words. By the end of a week his imitation was so exact that Lady Maud, coming into the kitchen garden to collect some radishes and spring onions for lunch one day, had been astonished to hear Sir Giles' voice issuing from among the geraniums. 'I looked upon the whole thing as an infringement of the rules of conservation,' he was saying. 'My dear General, I shall do my damnedest to see that the matter is raised in the House.' Lady

Maud stood and gazed into the greenhouse and was just considering the possibility that Blott had rigged up a loudspeaker there when he emerged, beaming triumphantly.

'You like it, my pronunciation?' he asked.

'Good heavens, was that you? You gave me quite a start,' Lady Maud said.

Blott smirked proudly. 'I have been practising correct English,' he said.

'But you speak English perfectly.'

'I don't. Not like an Englishman.'

'Well, I'd be glad if you didn't go round speaking like my husband,' said Lady Maud. 'It's bad enough having one of him about the place.'

Blott smiled happily. These were his sentiments exactly.

'Which reminds me,' she continued, 'I must see that the TV people cover the Enquiry. We must get the maximum publicity.'

Blott collected his hoe and went back to his lettuces while Lady Maud, having collected her radishes, returned to the kitchen. He was rather pleased with himself. It wasn't often he got a chance to demonstrate his ability to mimic people. It was a skill that had developed from his earliest days at the orphanage. Not knowing who he was, Blott had tried out other people's personalities. It had come in handy poaching, too. More than one gamekeeper had been startled to hear his employer's voice issuing from the darkness to tell him to stop making an ass of himself while Blott made good his escape. Now as he worked away at the weeds he tried out Sir Giles again. 'I demand that there be an Enquiry into this whole business,' he said. Blott smiled to himself. It sounded quite authentic. And there was going to be an Enquiry too. Lady Maud had said so.

5

The Enquiry was held in the Old Courthouse in Worford.
Everyone was there — everyone, that is, whose property stood
on the proposed route through the Cleene Gorge. General Burnett, Mr and Mrs Bullett-Finch, Colonel and Mrs Chapman,
Miss Percival, Mrs Thomas, the Dickinsons, all seven of them,
and the Fullbrooks who rented a farm from the General. There
were also a few other influential families who were quite
unaffected by the motorway but who came to support Lady
Maud. She sat in front with Sir Giles and Mr Turnbull and
behind them the seats were all filled. Blott stood at the back.
On the other side of the aisle the seats were empty except for a
solicitor representing the Ottertown Town Council. It was
quite clear that nobody seriously supposed that Lord Leakham
would decide in favour of Ottertown. The thing was a foregone
conclusion — or would have been but for the intervention of
Lady Maud and the intransigence of Lord Leakham, whose previous career as a judge had been confined to criminal cases in
the High Court. The choice of venue was unfortunate, too. The
Old Courthouse resembled too closely the courtrooms of Lord
Leakham's youth for the old man to deal at all moderately with
Lady Maud's frequent interruption of the evidence.

'Madam, you are trying the court's patience,' he told her
when she rose to her feet for the tenth time to protest that the
scheme as outlined by Mr Hoskins for the Planning Board was
an invasion of individual liberty and the rights of property.
Lady Maud bristled in tweeds.

'My family has held land in the Cleene Gorge since 1472,'
she shouted. 'It was entrusted to us by Edward the Fourth
who designated the Handyman family custodians of the
Gorge—'

'Whatever His Majesty Edward the Fourth may have done,'
said Lord Leakham, 'in 1472 has no relevance to the evidence
being presented by Mr Hoskins. Be so good as to sit down.'

Lady Maud sat down. 'Why don't you two men do something?' she demanded loudly. Sir Giles and Mr Turnbull shifted uncomfortably in their seats.

'You may continue, Mr Hoskins,' said the judge.

Mr Hoskins turned to a large relief model of the county which stood on a table. 'As you can see from this model South Worfordshire is a particularly beautiful county,' he began.

'Any fool with eyes in his head can see that,' Lady Maud commented loudly. 'It doesn't require a damnfool model.'

'Continue, Mr Hoskins, continue,' Lord Leakham said with a restraint that suggested he had in mind giving Lady Maud rope to hang herself with.

'Bearing this in mind the Ministry has attempted to preserve the natural amenities of the area to the greatest possible extent—'

'My foot,' said Lady Maud.

'We have here,' Mr Hoskins went on, pointing to a ridge of hills that ran north and south of the Gorge, 'the Cleene Forest, an area of designated natural beauty noted for its wild life . . .'

'Why is it,' Lady Maud enquired of Mr Turnbull, 'that the only species that doesn't seem to be protected is the human?'

By the time the Enquiry adjourned for lunch Mr Hoskins had presented the case for the Ministry. As they went downstairs Mr Turnbull had to admit that he was not optimistic.

'The snag as I see it lies in those seventy-five council houses in Ottertown. If it weren't for them I think we would stand a good chance, but quite frankly I can't see the Enquiry deciding in favour of demolishing them. The cost would be enormous and in any case there is the additional ten miles to be taken into account. Frankly, I am not hopeful.'

It was market day in Worford and the town was full. Outside the courtroom two TV cameras had been set up.

'I have no intention of being evicted from my home,' Lady Maud told the interviewer from the BBC. 'My family have lived in the Cleene Gorge for five hundred years and . . .'

Mr Turnbull turned away sadly. It was no good. Lady Maud might say what she liked, it would make no difference. The motorway would still come through the Gorge. In any case

Lady Maud had made a bad impression on Lord Leakham. He waited for her to finish and then they made their way through the market stalls to the Handyman Arms.

'I wonder where Giles has got to,' she said as they entered the hotel.

'I think he's gone over to the Four Feathers with Lord Leakham,' Mr Turnbull told her. 'He said something about putting him in a more mellow mood.'

Lady Maud looked at him furiously. 'Did he indeed? Well, I'll see about that,' she snapped and leaving Mr Turnbull in the foyer she went into the manager's office and phoned the Four Feathers. When she came out there was a new glint of malice in her eye.

They went into the dining-room and sat down.

*

At the Four Feathers Sir Giles ordered two large whiskies in the lounge before sending for the menu.

Lord Leakham took his whisky doubtfully.

'I really shouldn't at this time of the day,' he said. 'Peptic ulcer you know. Still, it's been a tiring morning. Who was that ghastly woman in the front row who kept interrupting?'

'I think I'll have prawns to start with,' said Sir Giles hurriedly.

'Reminded me of the assizes in Newbury in '28,' Lord Leakham continued. 'Had a lot of trouble with a woman there. Kept getting up in the dock and shouting. Now what was her name?' He scratched his head with a mottled hand.

'Lady Maud is rather outspoken,' Sir Giles agreed. 'She has something of a reputation in this part of the world.'

'I can well believe it,' said the Judge.

'She's a Handyman, you know.'

'Really?' said Lord Leakham indifferently. 'I should have thought she could have afforded to employ one.'

'The Handyman family have always been very influential,' Sir Giles explained. 'They own the brewery and a number of licensed premises. This is a Handyman House, as a matter of fact.'

'Elsie Watson,' said Lord Leakham abruptly. 'That's the name.' Sir Giles looked doubtful.

'Poisoned her husband. Kept shouting abuse from the dock. Didn't make the slightest difference. Hanged her just the same.' He smiled at the recollection. Sir Giles studied the menu wistfully and tried to think what to recommend for someone with a peptic ulcer. Oxtail à la Handyman or consommé? On the other hand, he was delighted at the way things had gone at the Enquiry. Maud's display had clinched the matter. Finally he ordered Tournedos Handyman for himself, and Lord Leakham ordered fish.

'Fish is off,' said the head waiter.

'Off?' said Sir Giles irritably.

'Not on, sir,' the man explained.

'What on earth is Bal de Boeuf Handyman?' asked the Judge.

'Faggot.'

'I beg your pardon.'

'Meatball.'

'And Brandade de Handyman?' Lord Leakham enquired.

'Cod balls.'

'Cod? That sounds all right. Yes I think I'll have that.'

'Cod's off,' said the waiter.

Lord Leakham looked desperately at the menu. 'Is anything on?'

'I can recommend the Poule au Pot Edward the Fourth,' said Sir Giles.

'Very appropriate,' said Lord Leakham grimly. 'Oh well I suppose I'd better have it.'

'And a bottle of Chambertin,' Sir Giles said indistinctly. He wasn't very happy with his French.

'Extraordinary way to run an hotel,' said Lord Leakham. Sir Giles ordered two more whiskies to hide his irritation.

*

In the kitchen the chef took their order. 'You can forget the chicken,' he said. 'He can have Lancashire hotpot or faggots à la me.'

'But it's Lord Leakham and he ordered chicken,' the waiter protested. 'Can't you do something?'

The chef took a bottle of chilli powder off the shelf. 'I'll fix something,' he said.

The wine waiter meanwhile was having difficulty finding a Chambertin. In the end he took the oldest bottle he could find. 'Are you sure you want me to serve him this?' he asked the manager, holding up a bottle filled with a purple cloudy fluid that looked like a post-mortem specimen.

'That's what her ladyship instructed,' said the manager. 'Just change the label.'

'It seems a bloody peculiar thing to do.'

The manager sighed. 'Don't blame me,' he muttered. 'If she wants to poison the old bugger that's her affair. I'm just paid to do what she tells me. What is it anyway?'

The wine waiter wiped the bottle. 'It says it's crusted port,' he said doubtfully.

'Crusted's about the word,' said the manager and went back to the kitchen, where the chef was crumbling some leftover faggots on to half a fried chicken. 'For God's sake don't let anyone else have a taste of that stuff,' he told the chef.

'Serve him right for poking his nose into our affairs,' said the chef, and poured sauce from the Lancashire hotpot on to the dish. The manager went upstairs and signalled to the head waiter. Sir Giles and Lord Leakham finished their whiskies and went through into the dining-room.

*

At the Handyman Arms Lady Maud finished her lunch and ordered coffee. 'One can place too much reliance on the law,' she said. 'My family didn't get where they did by appealing to the courts.'

'My dear Lady Maud,' said Mr Turnbull, 'I implore you not to do anything foolish. The situation is already fraught with difficulty and quite frankly your interruptions this morning didn't help. I'm afraid Lord Leakham may have been prejudiced against us.'

Lady Maud snorted. 'If he isn't he soon will be,' she said.

'You don't seriously suppose that I intend to accept his judgment? The man is a buffoon.'

'He is also a retired judge of considerable reputation,' said Mr Turnbull doubtfully.

'His reputation is only just beginning,' Lady Maud replied. 'It has been perfectly obvious from the beginning that he was going to decide to recommend that the motorway be put through the Gorge. The Ottertown route is not an alternative. It's a red herring. Well, I for one am not going to put up with that.'

'I don't really see what you can do.'

'That, Henry Turnbull, is because you are a lawyer and hold the law in high regard. I don't. And since the law is an ass I intend to see that everyone is aware of the fact.'

'I wish I could see some way out of the situation,' said Mr Turnbull sadly.

Lady Maud stood up. 'You will, Henry, you will,' she said. 'There are more ways of killing a cat than choking it with cream.' And leaving Mr Turnbull to meditate on the implications of this remark she stalked out of the dining-room.

*

At the Four Feathers Lord Leakham would have understood at once, though given the choice he would have chosen cream every time. The prawn cocktail which he had not ordered but which had been thrust on him by the head waiter appeared to have been marinated in tabasco, but it was as nothing to the Poule au Pot Edward the Fourth. His first mouthful left him speechless and with the absolute conviction that he had swallowed some appalling corrosive substance like caustic soda.

'That chicken looks good,' said Sir Giles as the Judge struggled to get his breath. 'It's a speciality of the maison, you know.'

Lord Leakham didn't know. With starting eyes he reached for his glass of wine and took a large swig. For a moment he cherished the illusion that the wine would help. His hope was short-lived. His palate, in spite of being cauterized by the Poule au Pot, was still sufficiently sensitive to recognize that whatever it was he was in the process of swallowing it most certainly wasn't Chambertin '64. For one thing it appeared to be filled with some sort of gravel which put him in mind of ground glass and for another what he could taste of the muck seemed to be nauseatingly sweet. Stifling the impulse to vomit he held the glass up to the light and stared into its opaque depths.

'Anything the matter?' asked Sir Giles.

'What did you say this was?' asked the Judge.

Sir Giles looked at the label on the bottle. 'Chambertin '64', he muttered. 'Is it corked or something?'

'It's certainly something,' said Lord Leakham who wished the stuff had never been bottled, let alone corked.

'I'll get another bottle,' said Sir Giles and signalled to the wine waiter.

'Not on my account I beg you.'

But it was too late. As the wine waiter hurried away Lord Leakham, distracted by the strange residue under his upper dentures, absent-mindedly took another mouthful of Poule au Pot.

'I thought it looked a bit dark myself,' said Sir Giles ignoring the desperate look in Lord Leakham's bloodshot eyes. 'Mind you I have to admit I'm not a connoisseur of wines.'

Still gasping for air, Lord Leakham pushed his plate away. For a moment he resisted the temptation to quench the flames with crusted port but the certain knowledge that unless he did something he would never speak again swept aside all considerations of taste. Lord Leakham drained his glass.

*

In the public bar of the Handyman Arms Lady Maud announced that drinks were on the house. Then she crossed the Market Square to the Goat and Goblet and repeated the order before making her way to the Red Cow. Behind her the bars filled with thirsty farmers and by two o'clock all Worford was drinking Lady Maud's health and damnation to the motorway. Outside the Old Courthouse she stopped to chat with the TV men. A crowd had assembled and Lady Maud was cheered as she went inside.

'I must say we do seem to have the public on our side,' said General Burnett as they went upstairs. 'Mind you I thought things looked pretty grim this morning.'

Lady Maud smiled to herself. 'I think you will find they liven up this afternoon,' she said and swept majestically into the courtroom where Colonel and Mrs Chapman were chattering with the Bullett-Finches.

'Leakham has a fine record as a judge,' Colonel Chapman was saying. 'I think we can rely on him to see our point of view.'

*

By the time he had finished his lunch Lord Leakham was incapable of seeing anyone's point of view but his own. What prawns tabasco and Poule au Pot had begun, the Chambertin '64 and its successor, a refined vinegar that Sir Giles chose to imagine was a Chablis, had completed. That and the Pêche Maud with which Lord Leakham had attempted to soothe the spasms of his peptic ulcer. The tinned peaches had been all right but the ice cream had been larded with a mixture of cloves and nutmeg, and as for the coffee . . .

As he hobbled down the steps of the Four Feathers in the vain hope of finding his car waiting for him – it had been moved on by a traffic warden – as he limped up Ferret Lane and across Abbey Close accompanied by his loathsome host, Lord Leakham's internal organs sounded the death knell of what little restraint he had shown before lunch. By the time he reached the Old Courthouse to be booed by a large crowd of farmers and their wives he was less a retired judge than an active incendiary device.

'Have those damned oafs moved on,' he snarled at Sir Giles. 'I will not be subject to hooliganism.'

Sir Giles phoned the police station and asked them to send some men over to the Courthouse. As he took his seat beside Lady Maud it was clear that things were not proceeding as he had expected. Lord Leakham's complexion was horribly mottled and his hand shook as he rapped the gavel on the bench.

'The hearing will resume,' he said huskily. 'Silence in court.' The courtroom was crowded and the Judge had to use his gavel a second time before the talking stopped. 'Next witness.'

Lady Maud rose to her feet. 'I wish to make a statement,' she said. Lord Leakham looked at her reluctantly. Lady Maud was not a sight for sore stomachs. She was large and her manner suggested something indigestible.

'We are here to take evidence,' said the Judge, 'not to listen to statements of opinion.'

Mr Turnbull stood up. 'My lord,' he said deferentially, 'my client's opinion is evidence before this Enquiry.'

'Opinion is not evidence,' said Lord Leakham. 'Your client whoever she may be . . .'

'Lady Maud Lynchwood of Handyman Hall, my lord,' Mr Turnbull informed him.

'. . . is entitled to hold what opinions she may choose,' Lord Leakham continued, staring at the author of Poule au Pot Edward the Fourth with undisguised loathing, 'but she may not express them in this court and expect them to be accepted as evidence. You should know the rules of evidence, sir.'

Mr Turnbull adjusted his glasses defiantly. 'The rules of evidence do not, with due deference to your lordship's opinion, apply in the present circumstances. My client is not under oath and—'

'Silence in court,' snarled the Judge, addressing himself to a drunken farmer from Guildstead Carbonell who was discussing swine fever with his neighbour. With a pathetic look at Lady Maud Mr Turnbull sat down.

'Next witness,' said Lord Leakham.

Lady Maud stood her ground. 'I wish to protest,' she said with a ring of authority that brought a hush to the courtroom. 'This Enquiry is a travesty . . .'

'Silence in court,' shouted the Judge.

'I will not be silenced,' Lady Maud shouted back. 'This is not a courtroom—'

'It most certainly is,' snarled the Judge.

Lady Maud hesitated. The courtroom was obviously a court-room. There was no denying the fact.

'What I meant to say . . .' she began.

'Silence in court,' screamed Lord Leakham whose peptic ulcer was in the throes of a new crisis.

Lady Maud echoed the Judge's private thoughts. 'You are not fit to conduct this Enquiry,' she shouted, and was supported by several members of the public. 'You are a senile old fool. I have a right to be heard.'

In his chair Lord Leakham's mottled head turned a plum colour and his hand reached for the gavel. 'I hold you in contempt of court,' he shouted banging the gavel. Lady Maud lurched towards him menacingly. 'Officer, arrest this woman.'

'My lord,' Mr Turnbull said, 'I beg you to . . .' but it was too late. As Lady Maud advanced two constables, evidently acting on the assumption that an ex-judge of the High Court knew his law better than they did, seized her arms. It was a terrible mistake. Even Sir Giles could see that. Beside him Mr Turnbull was shouting that this was an unlawful act, and behind him pandemonium had broken out as members of the public rose in their seats and surged forward. As his wife was frog-marched, still shouting abuse, from the courtroom, as Lord Leakham bellowed in vain for the court to be cleared, as fighting broke out and windows were broken, Sir Giles sat slumped in his seat and contemplated the ruin of his plans.

*

Downstairs the TV cameramen, alerted by the shouts and the fragments of broken glass raining on their heads from the windows above, aimed their cameras on the courtroom door as Lady Maud emerged dishevelled and suddenly surprisingly demure between two large policemen. Somewhere between the courtroom and the cameras her twinset had been quite obscenely disarranged, a shoe had been discarded, her skirt was torn suggestively and she appeared to have lost two front teeth. With a brave attempt at a smile she collapsed on the pavement, and was filmed being dragged across the market square to the police station. 'Help,' she screamed as the crowd parted. 'Please help.' And help was forthcoming. A small dark figure hurtled out of the Courthouse and on to the larger of the two policemen. Inspired by Blott's example several stallholders threw themselves into the fray. Hidden by the crowd from the cameras Lady Maud reasserted her authority. 'Blott,' she said sternly, 'let go of the constable's ears.' Blott dropped to the ground and the stallholders fell back obediently. 'Constables, do your duty,' said Lady Maud and led the way to the police station.

Behind her the crowd turned its attention to Lord Leakham's Rolls-Royce. Apples and tomatoes rained on the Old Courthouse. To roars of approval from the onlookers Blott attempted single-handed to turn the car over and was immediately joined by several dozen farmers. When Lord Leakham, escorted by a posse of policemen, emerged from the Courthouse it was to find his Rolls on its side. It took several baton charges to clear a way through the crowd and all the time the cameras recorded faithfully the public response to the proposed motorway through the Cleene Gorge. In Ferret Lane shop windows were broken. Outside the Goat and Goblet Lord Leakham was drenched with a pail of cold water. In the Abbey Close he was concussed by a portion of broken tombstone, and when he finally reached the Four Feathers the Fire Brigade had to be called to use their hoses to disperse the crowd that besieged the hotel. By that time the Rolls-Royce was on fire and groups of drunken youths roamed the streets demonstrating their loyalty to the Handyman family by smashing street lamps.

In her cell in the police station Lady Maud removed her dentures from her pocket and smiled at the sounds of revelry. If the price of justice was eternal publicity she was assured of a fair trial. She had done what she had set out to do.

In London the Cabinet, meeting to cope with yet another turn for the worse in the balance of payments crisis, greeted the news of the disturbances in Worford less enthusiastically. The evening papers had headlined the arrest of an MP's wife but it was left to the television news to convey to millions of homes the impression that Lady Maud was the victim of quite outrageous police brutality.

'Oh my God,' said the Prime Minister as he watched her on the screen. 'What the hell do they think they've been doing?'

'It rather looks as if she's lost a couple of teeth,' said the Secretary of State for Foreign Affairs. 'Is that a teat hanging out there?'

Lady Maud smiled bravely and collapsed on to the pavement.

'I shall institute a full investigation at once,' said the Home Secretary.

'Who the hell appointed Leakham in the first place?' snarled the Prime Minister.

'It seemed a suitably impartial appointment at the time,' murmured the Minister of the Environment. 'As I remember it was thought that an Enquiry would satisfy local opinion.'

'Satisfy . . .?' began the Prime Minister, only to be interrupted by a phone call from the Lord Chancellor who complained that the rule of law was breaking down and even after it was explained to him that Lord Leakham was a retired judge muttered mysteriously that the law was indivisible.

The Prime Minister put the phone down and turned on the Minister of the Environment. 'This is your pigeon. You got us into this mess. You get us out. Anyone would think we had an absolute majority.'

'I'll see what I can do,' said the Minister.

'You'll do better than that,' said the Prime Minister grimly. On the screen Lord Leakham's Rolls-Royce was burning brilliantly.

The Minister of the Environment hurried from the room and

phoned the home number of his Under-Secretary. 'I want a troubleshooter sent to Worford to sort this mess out,' he said.

'A troubleshooter?' Mr Rees, who was in bed with flu and whose temperature was 102, was in no fit state to deal with Ministerial requests for troubleshooters.

'Someone with a flair for public relations.'

'Public relations?' said Mr Rees, searching his mind for a subordinate who knew anything about public relations. 'Can I let you know by Wednesday?'

'No,' said the Minister, 'I need to be able to tell the Prime Minister that we have the situation in hand. I want someone despatched tomorrow morning by the latest. We need to have someone up there who will take charge of negotiations. I look to you to pick someone with initiative. None of your run-of-the-mill old fogies. Someone different.'

Mr Rees put the phone down with a sigh. 'Someone different indeed,' he muttered. 'Troubleshooters.' He felt aggrieved. He disliked being phoned at home, he disliked being ordered to make rapid decisions, he disliked the Minister and he particularly disliked the suggestion that his department consisted of run-of-the-mill old fogies.

He took another spoonful of cough mixture and considered a suitable candidate to send to Worford. Harrison was on leave. Beard was engaged on the Tanker Terminal at Scunthorpe. Then there was Dundridge. Dundridge was clearly unsuitable. But the Minister had specified someone different and Dundridge was decidedly different. There was no denying that. Mr Rees lay back in his bed, his head fuzzy with flu and recalled some of Dundridge's initiatives. There had been the one-way system for Central London, of an inflexibility that would have made it impossible to drive from Hyde Park Corner to Piccadilly except by way of Tower Bridge and Fleet Street. Then there was his pilot project for installing solid-state traffic lights in Clapham, a scheme so aptly named that it had isolated that suburb from the rest of London for almost a week. In practical terms Dundridge was clearly a disaster. On the other hand he did have a flair for public relations. His schemes good and year by year Dundridge had been promoted, ...ed upward by an ineluctable wave of inefficiency and the need to save the public the practical consequences of his latest idea until he had reached that rarefied zone of administration where, thanks to the inertia of his subordinates, his projects could never be implemented.

Mr Rees, semi-delirious and drugged with cough medicine, decided on Dundridge. He went downstairs and dictated his instructions by phone to the tape recorder on his secretary's desk at the Ministry. Then he poured himself a large whisky and drank to the thought of Dundridge in Worford. 'Trouble-shooter,' he said and went back to bed.

*

Dundridge travelled to work by tube. It was in his opinion the rational way to travel and one that avoided the harsh confusion of reality. Seated in the train he was able to concentrate on essentials and to find some sense of order in the world above by studying the diagram of the Northern Line on the wall opposite. Far above him there was chaos. Streets, houses, shops, blocks of flats, bridges, cars, people, a welter of disparate and perverse phenomena which defied easy categorization. By looking at the diagram he could forget that confusion. Chalk Farm followed Belsize Park and was itself followed by Camden Town in a perfectly logical sequence so that he knew exactly where he was and where he was going. Then again, the diagram showed all the stations as equidistant from their neighbours and while he knew that in fact they weren't, the schematic arrangement suggested that they should be. If Dundridge had had anything to do with it they would have been. His life had been spent in pursuit of order, an abstract order that would have supplanted the perplexities of experience. As far as he was concerned variety was not the spice of life but gave it a very bitter flavour. In Dundridge's philosophy everything conformed to a norm. On one side there was chance, nature red in tooth and claw and everything haphazard; on the other science, logic and numeration.

Dundridge particularly favoured numeration and his flat in

Hendon conformed to his ideal. Everything he possessed w
numbered and marked on a chart above his bed. His socks fo.
instance were 01/7, the 01 referring to Dundridge himself and
the 7 to the socks and were to be found in the top drawer left
(1) of his chest of drawers 23 against the wall 4 of his bedroom
3. By referring to the chart and looking for 01/7/1/23/4/3 he
could locate them almost immediately. Outside his flat things
were less amenable and his attempts to introduce a similar
system into his office at the Ministry had met with considerable
– grade 10 on the Dundridge scale – resistance and contributed
to his frequent transfers from one department to another.

He was therefore not in the least surprised to find that Mr
Joynson wanted to see him in his office at 9.15. Dundridge
arrived at 9.25.

'I got held up in the tube,' he explained bitterly. 'It's really
most irritating. I should have got here by 9.10 but the train
didn't arrive on time. It never does.'

'So I've noticed,' said Mr Joynson.

'It's the irregularity of the stops that does it,' said Dundridge. 'Sometimes it stops for half a minute and at other times
for a minute and a half. Really, you know, I do think it's time
we gave serious consideration to a system of continuous flow
underground transportation.'

'I don't suppose it would make any difference,' said Mr Joynson wearily. 'Why don't you just catch an earlier train?'

'I'd be early.'

'It would make a change. Anyway I didn't ask you here to
discuss the deficiencies of the Underground system.' He paused
and studied Mr Rees' instructions. Quite apart from the incred-
ible choice of Dundridge to handle a situation which demanded
intelligence, flexibility and persuasiveness, there was an un-
usually garbled quality about the syntax that surprised him.
Still, there was a lot to be said for getting Dundridge out of
London for a while and he couldn't be held personally responsible for his appointment.

'I have here,' he said finally, 'details of your new job. Mr Rees
wants you . . .'

v job?' said Dundridge. 'But I'm with Leisure Activi-

appropriate too,' said Mr Joynson. 'And now you
...n Motorways Midlands. Next month I daresay we'll be
able to find you a niche in Parks and Gardens.'

'I must say I find all this moving around very disturbing. I
don't see how I can be expected to get anything constructive
done when I'm being shifted from one Department to another
all the time.'

'There is that to be said for it,' Mr Joynson agreed. 'However, in this case there is nothing constructive for you to do.
You will merely be required to exercise a moderating influence.'

'A moderating influence?' Dundridge perked up.

Mr Joynson nodded. 'A moderating influence,' he said and
consulted his instructions again. 'You have been appointed the
Minister's troubleshooter in Worford.'

'What?' said Dundridge, now thoroughly alarmed. 'But
there's just been a riot in Worford.'

Mr Joynson smiled. He was beginning to enjoy himself. 'So
there has,' he said. 'Well now, your job is to see that there are
no more riots in Worford. I'm told it is a charming little town.'

'It didn't look very charming on the news last night,' said
Dundridge.

'Oh well, we mustn't go by appearances now, must we? Here
is your letter of appointment. As you can see it gives you full
powers to conduct negotiations—'

'But I thought Lord Leakham was heading the Enquiry,' said
Dundridge.

'Well, yes he is. But I understand he's a little indisposed just
at the moment and in any case he appears to be under some
misapprehension as to his role.'

'You mean he is in hospital, don't you?' said Dundridge.

Mr Joynson ignored the question. He turned to a map on the
wall behind him. 'The issue you will have to consider is really
quite simple,' he said. 'The M101, as you can see here, has two
possible routes. One through the Cleene Gorge here, the other
through Ottertown. The Ottertown route is out of the question

48

for a number of reasons. You will see to it that Leakham decides on the Cleene Gorge route.'

'Surely it's up to him to decide,' said Dundridge.

Mr Joynson sighed. 'My dear Dundridge, when you have been in public service as long as I have you will know that Enquiries, Royal Commissions and Boards of Arbitration are only set up to make recommendations that concur with decisions already taken by the experts. Your job is to see that Lord Leakham arrives at the correct decision.'

'What happens if he doesn't?'

'God alone knows. I suppose in the present climate of opinion we'll have to go ahead and build the bloody thing through Ottertown, and then there would be hell to pay. It is up to you to see it doesn't. You have full powers to negotiate with the parties involved and I daresay Leakham will cooperate.'

'I don't see how I can negotiate when I've got nothing to negotiate with,' Dundridge pointed out plaintively. 'And in any case what does it mean by troubleshooter?'

'Presumably whatever you choose to make it,' said Mr Joynson.

Dundridge took the file on the M101 back to his office.

'I'm the Minister's troubleshooter in the Midlands division,' he told his secretary grandly and phoned the transport pool for a car. Then he read his letter of authority once again. It was quite clear that his abilities had been recognized in high places. Dundridge had power, and he was determined to use it.

•

At Handyman Hall Lady Maud congratulated herself on her skill in disrupting the Enquiry. Released from custody against her own better judgment at the express command of the Chief Constable, she returned to the Hall to be deluged by messages of support. General Burnett called to offer her his congratulations. Mrs Bullett-Finch phoned to see if there was anything she needed after the ordeal of her confinement, a term Lady Maud found almost as offensive as Colonel Chapman's comment that she was full of spunk. Even Mrs Thomas wrote to thank her on behalf, as she modestly put it, of the common people. Lady Maud accepted these tributes abruptly. They were she felt quite unnecessary. She had only been doing her duty after all. As she put it to the reporter from the *Observer*, 'Local interests can only be looked after by local authorities,' a sufficiently ambiguous expression to satisfy the correspondent while stating very precisely Lady Maud's own view of her role in South Worfordshire.

'And do you intend to sue the police for unlawful arrest?' the reporter asked.

'Certainly not. I have the greatest respect for the police. They do a magnificent job. I hold Lord Leakham entirely responsible. I am taking legal counsel as to what action I should take against him.'

*

In the Worford Cottage Hospital Lord Leakham greeted the news that she was considering legal proceedings against him with a show of indifference. He had more immediate problems, the state of his digestive system for one thing, six stitches in his scalp for another, and besides he was suffering from concussion. In his lucid moments he prayed for death and in his delirium shouted obscenities.

*

But if Lord Leakham was too preoccupied with his own problems to think at all clearly about the disruption of the Enquiry, Sir Giles could think of little else.

'The whole situation is extremely awkward,' he told Hoskins when they conferred at the latter's office the next morning. 'That bloody woman has put the cat among the pigeons and no mistake. She's turned the whole thing into an issue of national interest. I've been inundated with calls from conservationists from all over the country, all supporting our stand. It's bloody infuriating. Why can't they mind their own confounded business?'

Hoskins lit his pipe moodily. 'That's not all,' he said, 'they're sending some bigwig up from the Ministry to take charge of the negotiations.'

'That's all we need, some damned bureaucrat to come poking his nose into our affairs.'

'Quite,' said Hoskins, 'so from now on no more phone calls to me here. I can't afford to be connected with you.'

'Do you think he's going to choose the Ottertown route?'

Hoskins shrugged. 'I've no idea. All I do know is that if I were in his shoes I'm damned if I'd recommend the Gorge.'

'Let me know what the blighter suggests,' said Sir Giles and went out to his car.

7

To Dundridge, travelling up the M1, the underlying complexities of the situation in South Worfordshire were quite unknown. For the first time in his life he was armed with authority and he intended to put it to good use. He would make a name for himself. The years of frustration were over. He would return to London with his reputation for swift, decisive action firmly established.

At Warwick he stopped for lunch, and while he ate he studied the file on the motorway. There was a map of the district, the outline of the alternative routes, and a list of those people through whose property the motorway would run and the sums they would receive as compensation. Dundridge concentrated his attention on the latter. A single glance was enough to explain the urgency of his appointment and the difficulty of his mission. The list read like a roll-call of the upper class in the county. Sir Giles Lynchwood, General Burnett, Colonel Chapman, Mr Bullett-Finch, Miss Percival. Dundridge peered uncomfortably at the names and incredulously at the sums they were being offered. A quarter of a million pounds for Sir Giles. One hundred and fifty thousand to General Burnett. One hundred and twenty thousand to Colonel Chapman. Even Miss Percival whose occupation was listed as schoolteacher was offered fifty-five thousand. Dundridge compared these sums with his own income and felt a surge of envy. There was no justice in the world and Dundridge (whose socialism was embodied in the maxim 'To each according to his abilities, from each according to his needs', the 'his' in both cases referring to Dundridge himself) found his thoughts wandering in the direction of money. It had been Dundridge's mother who had instilled in him the saying 'Don't marry money, go where money is' and since this had been easier said than done, Dundridge's sex life had been largely confined to his imagination. There, safe from the disagreeable complexities of real life, he had indulged his various passions. In his imagination Dundridge was rich, Dundridge was powerful and Dundridge was the possessor of an entourage of immaculate women – or to be precise of one woman, a composite creature made up of bits and pieces of real women who had once partially attracted him but without any of their concomitant disadvantages. Now for the first time he was going where money was. It was an alluring prospect. He finished his lunch and drove on.

And as he drove he became increasingly aware that the countryside had changed. He had left the motorway and was on a minor road that twisted and turned. The hedgerows grew taller and more rank. Hills rose up and fell away into empty valleys and woods took on a rougher, less domesticated air. Even the houses had lost the comfortable homogeneous look of the North London suburbs. They were either large and isolated, standing in their own grounds, or stone-built farmhouses surrounded by dark corrugated iron sheds and barns. Every now and again he passed through villages, strange conglomerations of cottages and shops, buildings that loomed misshapenly over the road or retreated behind hedges with an eccentricity of ornaments he found disturbing. And finally there were churches. Dundridge disliked churches most of all. They reminded him of death and burial, guilt and sin and the hereafter. Archaic reminders of a superstitious past. And since Dundridge lived if not for the present at least the immediate future, these memento mori held no attractions for him. They cast horrid doubts on the rational nature of existence. Not that Dundridge believed in reason. He placed his faith in science and numeration.

Now as he drove northwards he had to admit that he was entering a world far removed from his ideal. Even the sky had changed with the landscape and the shadows of large clouds slid erratically across the fields and hills. By the time he reached South Worfordshire he was distinctly perturbed. If Worford was anything like the surrounding countryside it must be a horrid place filled with violent, irrational creatures swayed by strange emotions. It was. As he drove over the bridge that spanned the Cleene he seemed to have moved out of the twentieth century into an earlier age. The houses below the town gate were huddled together higgledy-piggledy and only their scrubbed doorsteps redeemed their squalid lack of uniformity. The gate, a great stuccoed tower with a dark narrow entrance, loomed up before him. He drove nervously through and emerged into a street lined with eighteenth-century houses. Here he felt temporarily more at home but his relief evaporated when he reached the town centre. Dark narrow alleyways, half-timbered medieval houses jutting over the pavement, cobbled streets, and shopfronts which retained the format of an earlier age. Pots and pans, spades and sickles hung outside an ironmongers. Duffel coats, corduroy trousers and breeches were displayed outside an outfitters. A mackerel gleamed on a fishmonger's marble slab while a saddler's was adorned with bits and bridles and leather belts. Worford was in short a perfectly normal market town but to Dundridge, accustomed to the soothing anonymity of supermarkets, there was a disturbing, archaic quality about it. He drove into the Market Square and asked the car-park attendant for the Regional Planning Office. The attendant didn't know or if he did, Dundridge was none the wiser. The accents of Wales and England met in South Worfordshire, met and mingled incomprehensibly. Dundridge parked his car and went into a telephone kiosk. He looked in the Directory and found the Planning Office in Knacker's Yard.

'Where's Knacker's Yard?' he asked the car-park attendant.

'Down Giblet Walk.'

'Very informative,' said Dundridge with a shudder. 'And where's Giblet Walk?'

'Well now, let's see, you can go down past the Goat and Goblet or you can take a short cut through the Shambles,' said the old man and spat into the gutter.

Dundridge considered this unenticing alternative. 'Where are the Shambles?' he asked finally.

'Behind you,' said the attendant.

Dundridge turned round and looked into the shadow of a narrow alley. It was cobbled and led down the hill and out of sight. He walked down it uncomfortably. Several of the houses were boarded up and one or two had actually fallen down and the alleyway had a peculiar smell that he associated with footpaths and tunnels under railway lines. Dundridge held his breath and hurried on and came out into Knacker's Yard where a sign in front of a large red-brick building said Regional Planning Board. He opened an iron gate and went down a path to the door.

'Planning Board's on the second floor,' said a dentist's assistant who emerged from a room holding a metal bowl in which a pair of false teeth rested pinkly. 'You'll be lucky if you find it open though. You looking for anyone in particular?'

'Mr Hoskins,' said Dundridge.

'Try the Club,' said the woman. 'He's usually there this time of day. It's on the first floor.'

'Thank you,' said Dundridge and went upstairs. On the first landing there was a door marked Worford and District Gladstone Club. Dundridge looked at it doubtfully and went on up. As the woman had said, the Regional Planning Board was shut. Dundridge went downstairs and stood uncertainly on the landing. Then, reminding himself that he was the Minister's plenipotentiary and troubleshooter, he opened the door and looked inside.

'You looking for someone?' asked a large red-faced man who was standing beside a billiard table.

'I'm looking for Mr Hoskins, the Planning Officer,' said Dundridge. The red-faced man put down his cue and stepped forward.

'Then you've come to the right place,' he said. 'Bob, there's a bloke wants to see you.'

Another large red-faced man who was sitting at the bar in the corner turned round and stared at Dundridge. 'What can I do for you?' he asked.

'I'm from the Ministry of the Environment,' said Dundridge.

'Christ,' said Mr Hoskins and got down from his bar stool. 'You're early aren't you? Wasn't expecting you till tomorrow.'

'The Minister is most anxious that I should get down to work as rapidly as possible.'

'Quite right,' said Mr Hoskins more cheerfully now that he could see that Dundridge wasn't sixty, didn't wear gold-rimmed glasses and didn't carry an air of authority about him. 'What will you have?'

Dundridge hesitated. It wasn't his habit to drink in the middle of the afternoon. 'A half of bitter,' he said finally.

'Make it two pints,' Hoskins told the barman. They took their glasses across to a small table in the corner and sat down. At the billiard table the men resumed their game.

'Awkward business this,' said Mr Hoskins, 'I don't envy you your job. Local feeling's none too good.'

'So I've noticed,' said Dundridge sipping his beer. It tasted, as he had anticipated, both strong and unpleasantly organic. On the wall opposite a portrait of Mr Gladstone glared relentlessly down on this dereliction of the licensing laws. Spurred on by his example, Dundridge attempted to explain his mission. 'The Minister is particularly anxious that the negotiations should be handled tactfully. He has sent me to see that the outcome of these negotiations has the backing of all the parties involved.'

'Has he?' said Mr Hoskins. 'Well, all I can say is that you'll have your work cut out.'

'Now as I see it, the best approach would be to propose an alternative route,' Dundridge continued.

'We've done that already. Through Ottertown.'

'Out of the question,' said Dundridge.

'I couldn't agree more,' said Mr Hoskins. 'Which leaves the Cleene Gorge.'

'Or the hills to the south?' suggested Dundridge hopefully.

Mr Hoskins shook his head. 'Cleene Forest is an area of natural beauty, a designated area. Not a hope in hell.'

'Well that doesn't leave us with many alternatives, does it?'

'It doesn't leave us with any,' said Mr Hoskins.

Dundridge drank some more beer. The mood of optimism with which he had started the day had quite left him. It was all very well to talk about negotiating but there didn't seem any negotiations to conduct. He was faced with the unenviable task of enforcing a thoroughly unpopular decision on a group of extremely influential and hostile landowners. It was not a prospect he relished. 'I don't suppose there is any chance of persuading Sir Giles Lynchwood and General Burnett to drop their opposition,' he said without much hope.

'Not a hope in hell,' Hoskins told him, 'and anyway if they did it wouldn't make the slightest difference. It's Lady Maud you've got to worry about. And she isn't going to budge.'

'I must say you make it all sound extremely difficult,' said Dundridge and finished his beer. By the time he left the Gladstone Club he had a clear picture of the situation. The stumbling block was Handyman Hall and Lady Maud. He would explore the possibilities of that more fully in the morning. He walked back up the Shambles and Giblet Walk to the Market Square and booked in at the Handyman Arms.

*

At the Hall Sir Giles spent the day sequestered in his study. This seclusion was only partly to be explained by the presence in the house and grounds of half a dozen guard dogs who seemed to feel that he was an intruder in his own home. More to the point was the fact that Lady Maud had expressed herself very forcibly on the matter of his lunch with Lord Leakham. If the Judge regretted that lunch, and from the reports of the doctors at the Cottage Hospital he had cause to, so did Sir Giles.

'I was only trying to help,' he had explained. 'I thought if I gave him a good lunch he might be more prepared to see our side of the case.'

'Our side of the case?' Lady Maud snorted. 'If it comes to that we didn't have a case at all. It was perfectly obvious he was going to recommend the route through the Gorge.'

'There is the Ottertown alternative,' Sir Giles pointed out.

'Alternative my foot,' said Lady Maud. 'If you can't see a red herring when it's thrust under your nose, you're a bigger fool than I take you for.'

Sir Giles had retreated to his study cursing his wife for her perspicacity. There had been a very nasty look in her eye at the mention of Ottertown, and one or two unpleasant cracks about property speculators and their ways over breakfast had made him wonder if she had heard anything about Hoskins' new house. And now there was this damned official from Whitehall to poke his nose into the affair. Finally and most disturbing of all there had been the voices. Or rather one voice: his own. While putting the car away before lunch he had distinctly heard himself assuring nobody in particular that they could look to him to see that nothing was done that would in any way jeopardize . . . Sir Giles had stared round the yard with a wild surmise. For a moment he had supposed that he had been talking to himself but the presence in his mouth of a cigar had ended that explanation. Besides the voice had been quite distinct. It had been a most disturbing experience and one for which there was no rational explanation. It had taken two stiff whiskies to convince him that he had imagined the whole thing. Now to take his mind off the occurrence he sat at his desk and concentrated on the motorway.

'Red herring indeed,' he muttered to himself. 'I wonder what she would have said if Leakham had decided in favour of

Ottertown.' It was an idle thought and quite out of the question. They would never build a motorway through Ottertown. Old Francis Puckerington would have another heart attack. Old Francis Puckerington ... Sir Giles stopped in his tracks, amazed at his own intuitive brilliance. Francis Puckerington, the Member for Ottertown, was a dying man. What had the doctors said? That he'd be lucky to live to the next general election. There had been rumours that he was going to resign his seat. And his majority at the last election had been a negligible one, somewhere in the region of fifty. If Leakham had decided on the Ottertown route it would have killed old Francis. And then there would have to be a bye-election. Sir Giles' devious mind catalogued the consequences. A bye-election fought on the issue of the motorway and the demolition of seventy-five council houses with a previous majority of fifty. It wasn't to be thought of. The Chief Whip would go berserk. Leakham's decision would be reversed. The motorway would come through the Cleene Gorge after all. And best of all not a shred of suspicion would rest on Sir Giles. It was a brilliant stratagem. It would put him in the clear. He was about to reach for the phone to call Hoskins when it occurred to him that he had better wait to hear what the man from the Ministry had to say. There was no point in rushing things now. He would go and see Hoskins in the morning. Imbued with a new spirit of defiance he left the study and selecting a large walking-stick from the rack in the hall he went out into the garden for a stroll.

It was a glorious afternoon. The sun shone down out of a cloudless sky. Birds sang. The flowering cherries by the kitchen garden flowered and Sir Giles himself blossomed with smug self-satisfaction. He paused for a moment to admire the goldfish in the ornamental pond and was just considering the possibility of pushing up the compensation to three hundred thousand when for the second time that day he heard himself speaking. 'I'm damned if I'm going to allow the countryside to be desecrated by a motorway. I shall take the earliest opportunity of raising the matter in the House.' Sir Giles stared round the garden panic-stricken, but there was no one in sight. He turned and looked at the Hall but the windows were all shut. To his right was the wall of the kitchen garden. Sir Giles hurried across the lawn to the door in the wall and peered inside. Blott was busy in a cucumber frame.

'Did you say anything?' Sir Giles asked.

'Me?' said Blott. 'I didn't say anything. Did you?'

Sir Giles hurried back to the house. It was no longer a glorious afternoon. It was a quite horrible afternoon. He went into his study and shut the door.

8

Dundridge spent a perfectly foul night at the Handyman Arms. His room there had a sloping floor, a yellowed ceiling, an ochre chest of drawers and a wardrobe whose door opened of its own accord ten minutes after he had shut it. It did so with a hideous wheeze and would then creak softly until he got out of bed and shut it again. He spent half the night trying to devise some method of keeping it closed and the other half listening to the noises coming from the next room. These were of a most disturbing sort and suggested an incompatibility of size and temperament that played havoc with his imagination. At two o'clock he managed to get to sleep, only to be woken at three by a sudden eruption in the drainpipe of his washbasin which appeared to be most unhygienically connected to the one next door. At half past three a dawn breeze rattled the signboard outside his window. At four the man next door asked if someone wanted it again. 'For God's sake,' Dundridge muttered and buried his head under the pillow to shut out this evidence of sexual excess. At ten past four the wardrobe door, responding to the seismic tremors from the next room, opened again and creaked softly. Dundridge let it creak and turned for relief to his composite woman. With her assistance he managed to get back to sleep to be woken at seven by a repulsive-looking girl with a tea-tray.

'Is there anything else you wanted?' she asked coyly.

'Certainly not,' said Dundridge wondering what there was about him that led only the most revolting females to offer him their venereal services. He got up and went along to the bathroom and wrestled with the intricacies of a gas-fired geyser which had evidently set its mind on asphyxiating him or blowing him up. In the end he had a cold wash.

By the time he had finished breakfast he was in a thoroughly bad mood. He had been unable to formulate any coherent strategy and had no idea what to do next. Hoskins had advised him to have a word with Sir Giles Lynchwood and Dundridge decided he would do that later. To begin with he would pay a call on Lord Leakham at the Cottage Hospital.

After wandering down narrow lanes and up a flight of steps behind the Worford Museum he found the hospital, a grey gaunt stone building that looked as though it had once been a workhouse. It fronted on to the Abbey and in the small front garden a number of geriatric patients were sitting around in dressing-gowns. Stifling his disgust, Dundridge went inside and asked for Lord Leakham.

'Visiting hours are two to three,' said the nurse at Admissions.

'I'm here on Government business,' said Dundridge feeling that it was about time someone understood he was not to be trifled with.

'I'll have to ask Matron,' said the nurse. Dundridge went outside into the sunshine to wait. He didn't like hospitals. They were not, he felt, his forte, particularly hospitals which overlooked graveyards, stank of disinfectant and had the gall to call themselves Cottage Hospitals when they were situated in the middle of towns. He was just considering the awful prospect of being treated for a serious complaint in such a dead-and-alive hole when the Matron appeared. She was gaunt, grey-haired and grim.

'I understand you want to see Lord Leakham,' she said.

'On Government business,' said Dundridge pompously.

'You can have five minutes,' said the Matron and led the way down the passage to a private room. 'He's still suffering from concussion and shock.' She opened the door and Dundridge went inside. 'Now nothing controversial,' said the Matron. 'We don't want to have a relapse, do we?'

On the bed, ashen-faced and with his head swathed in bandages, Lord Leakham regarded her venomously. 'There's nothing the matter with me apart from food poisoning,' he said. Dundridge sat down beside his bed.

'My name is Dundridge,' he said. 'The Minister of the Environment has asked me to come up to see if I can do something to . . . er . . . well to negotiate some sort of settlement in regard to the motorway.'

Lord Leakham looked at him vindictively over the top of his glasses. 'Has he indeed? Well let me tell you what I intend to do about the motorway first and then you can inform him,' he said. He raised himself on his pillows and leant towards Dundridge. 'I was appointed to head the Enquiry into the motorway and I do not intend to relinquish my responsibility.'

'Oh quite,' said Dundridge.

'Furthermore,' said the Judge, 'I have no intention whatsoever of allowing myself to be influenced by hooliganism and riot from doing my duty as I see it.'

'Oh definitely,' said Dundridge.

'As soon as these damnfool doctors get it into their thick heads that there is nothing wrong with me except a peptic ulcer, I shall re-open the Enquiry and announce my decision.' Dundridge nodded.

'Quite right too,' he said. 'And what will your decision be? Or is it too early to ask that?'

'It most certainly isn't,' shouted Lord Leakham. 'I intend to recommend that the motorway goes through the Cleene Gorge, plumb through it, you understand. I intend to see that that damned woman's home is levelled to the ground, brick by brick. I intend . . .' He sank back on to the bed exhausted by his outburst.

'I see,' said Dundridge, wondering what possible use there was in trying to negotiate a compromise between an irresistible force and an immovable object.

'Oh no you don't,' said Lord Leakham. 'That woman deliberately sent her husband to poison me. She interrupted the proceedings. She insulted me in my own court. She incited to riot. She made a mockery of the legal process and she shall rue the day. The law shall not be mocked, sir.'

'Oh quite,' said Dundridge.

'So you go and negotiate all you want but just remember the decision to go through the Gorge is mine and I do not for one moment intend to forgo the pleasure of making it.'

Dundridge went out into the passage and conferred with the Matron.

'He seems to think someone tried to poison him,' he said carefully skirting the law of libel. The Matron smiled gently.

'That's the concussion,' she said. 'He'll get over that in a day or two.'

Dundridge went out into the Abbey Close past the geriatric patients and wandered disconsolately down the steps and out into Market Street. It didn't seem likely to him that Lord Leakham would get over his conviction that Lady Maud had tried to poison him and he had a shrewd suspicion that the Judge had in some perverse way enjoyed the contretemps in court and was looking forward to pursuing his vendetta as soon as he was up and about. He was just considering what to do next when he caught sight of his reflection in a shop window. It was not that of a man of authority. There was a sort of dispirited look about it, a hangdog look quite out of keeping with his role as the Minister's troubleshooter. It was time to take the bull by the horns. He straightened his back, marched across the road to the Post Office and telephoned Handyman Hall. He got Lady Maud and explained that he would like to see Sir Giles.

'I'm afraid Sir Giles is out just at present,' she said modulating her tone to suggest a secretary. 'He'll be back shortly. Would eleven o'clock be convenient?'

Dundridge said it would. He left the Post Office and threaded his way through the market stalls to the car park to collect his car.

*

At Handyman Hall Lady Maud congratulated herself on her performance. She was rather looking forward to a private chat with the man from the Ministry. Dundridge, he had said his name was. From the Ministry. Sir Giles had mentioned the fact that someone had been sent up from London on a fact-finding mission. And since Giles had said he would be out until late in the afternoon this seemed an ideal opportunity to provide this Mr Dundridge with facts that would suit her book. She went upstairs to change, and to consider her tactics. She had spiked Lord Leakham's guns by frontal assault but Dundridge on the phone had sounded far less self-assured than she had expected. It might be better to try persuasion, perhaps even a little charm. It would confuse the issue. Lady Maud selected a cotton frock and dabbed a little Lavender Water behind her ears. Mr Dundridge would get the meek treatment, the helpless little girl approach. If that didn't work she could always revert to sterner methods.

*

In the greenhouse Blott put down the earphones and went back to the broad beans. So an official was coming to see Sir Giles, was he? An official. Blott felt strongly about officials. They had made his early life a misery and he had no time for them. Still, Lady Maud had invited this one to the Hall so presumably she knew what she was doing. It was a pity. Blott would have liked to have been ordered to give this Dundridge the reception he deserved and he was just considering what sort of reception he would have organized for him when Lady Maud came into the garden. Blott straightened up and stared at her. She was wearing a cotton frock and to Blott at least she looked quite beautiful. It was not a notion anyone else would have shared but Blott's standards of beauty were not determined by fashion. Large breasts, enormous thighs and hips were attributes of a good or at least ample mother, and since Blott had never had a good, ample or even *any* mother in a post-natal sense he placed great emphasis on these outward signs of potential maternity. Now, standing among the broad beans, he was filled with a sudden sense of desire. Lady Maud in a cotton frock dappled with a floral pattern combined botany with biology. Blott goggled.

'Blott,' said Lady Maud, oblivious of the effect she was having, 'there's a man from the Ministry of the Environment coming to lunch. I want some flowers in the house. I want to make a good impression on him.'

Blott went into the greenhouse and looked for something suitable while Lady Maud bent low to select a lettuce for lunch. As she did so Blott glanced out of the greenhouse door. It was the turning point in his life. The silent devotion to the Handyman family which had been the passive mainspring of his existence for so long was gone, to be replaced by an active urgency of feeling.

Blott was in love.

9

Dundridge left Worford by the town gate, crossed the river and took the Ottertown road. On his left the Cleene wandered through meadows and on his right the Cleene Hills rose steeply to a wooded crest. He drove for three miles and turned up a side road that was signposted Guildstead Carbonell and found himself in evidently hostile territory. Every barn had the slogan 'Save the Gorge' whitewashed on it and there were similar sentiments painted on the road itself. At one point an avenue of beeches had been daubed with letters that spelt out 'No to the Motorway' so that as he drove down it Dundridge was left in no doubt that local feeling was against the scheme.

Even without the slogans Dundridge would have been alarmed. The Cleene Forest was nature undomesticated. There was none of that neatness that he found so reassuring in Middlesex. The hedges were rank, the few farmhouses he passed looked medieval, and the forest itself dense with large trees, humped and gnarled with bracken growing thickly underneath. He was relieved when the road ran into an open valley with hedges and little fields. The respite was brief. At the top of the next hill he came to a crossroads marked by nothing more informative than a decayed gibbet.

Dundridge stopped the car and consulted his map. According to his calculations Guildstead Carbonell lay to the left while in front was the Gorge and Handyman Hall. Dundridge wished it wasn't. Below him the forest lay thicker than before and the road less metalled, with moss and grass growing down the middle. He drove on for a mile and was beginning to wonder if the map had misled him when the trees thinned and he found himself looking down into the Gorge itself.

He stopped the car and got out. Below him the Cleene tumbled between cliffs overgrown with brambles, ivy and creepers. Ahead lay Handyman Hall. It stood, an amalgam in stone and brick, timber and tile and turret, a monument to all that was most eclectic and least attractive in English architecture. To Dundridge, himself a devotee of function, for whom simplicity was all, it was a nightmare. Ruskin and Morris, Gilbert Scott, Vanbrugh, Inigo Jones and Wren to name but a few had all lent their influence to a building that combined the utility of a water-tower with the homeliness of Wormwood Scrubs. Around it lay a few acres of parkland, a wall, and beyond the wall a circle of hills, heavily wooded. Over the whole scene there lay a sense of isolation. Somewhere to the west there were presumably towns and houses, shops and buses, but to Dundridge it seemed that he was standing on the very edge of civilization if not actually beyond it. With the sinking feeling that he was committing himself to the unknown he got back into the car and drove on, down the hill into the Gorge. Presently he came to a small iron suspension bridge across the river which rattled as he drove over. On the far side something large and strange loomed through the trees. It was the Lodge. Dundridge stopped the car and gaped at the building through the windshield.

Constructed in 1904 to mark the occasion of the visit of Edward the Seventh, the Lodge, in deference to the King's Francophilia, had been modelled on the Arc de Triomphe. There were differences. The Lodge was slightly smaller, its frieze did not depict scenes of battle, but for all that the resemblance was remarkable and to Dundridge its existence in the heart of Worfordshire came as final proof that whoever had built Handyman Hall had been an architectural kleptomaniac. Above all the Lodge bespoke a lofty arrogance which, coming so shortly after Lord Leakham's outburst, made a tactful approach all the more necessary. As he stood looking up at it Dundridge was recalled to his task. Some sort of compromise was clearly necessary to avoid his becoming embroiled in an extremely nasty situation. If the Ottertown route was out of the question and he had it on the highest authority that it was, and if the Gorge ... There was no if about the Gorge, Dundridge had seen enough to convince him of that, then a third route was imperative. But there was no third route. Dundridge got back into his car and drove thoughtfully through the great arch and as he did so a vision of the third route dawned upon him. A tunnel. A tunnel under the Cleene Hills. A tunnel had all the merits of simplicity, of straightness and, best of all, of leaving undisturbed the hideous landscape that so many irate and influential people inexplicably admired. There would be no more wrangles about property rights, no compensation, no trouble. Dundridge had discovered the ideal solution.

In the entrance hall Lady Maud, radiant in Tootal, lurked among the ferns. High above her head the stained-glass rooflight cast a reddish glow upon the marble staircase and lent a fresh air of apoplexy to the ruddy faces of her ancestors glowering down from the walls. Lady Maud patted her hair in readiness. She had laid her plans. Mr Dundridge would get the gracious treatment, at least to begin with. After that she would see how he responded. As his car crunched on the gravel outside she adjusted her step-in and gave a practice smile to a vase of snapdragons. Then she stepped forward and opened the door.

*

'Nincompoop? Nincompoop? Did you say nincompoop?' said Sir Giles. In his constituency office situated conveniently close to Hoskins' Regional Planning Board the word had a reassuring ring to it.

'A perfect nincompoop,' said Hoskins.

'Are you sure?'

'Positive. A first rate, Grade A nincompoop.'

'It sounds too good to be true,' said Sir Giles doubtfully. 'You can't always go by appearances. I've known some very slippery customers in my time who looked like idiots.'

'I'm not going by appearances,' Hoskins said. 'He doesn't look an idiot. He is one. Wouldn't know one end of a motorway from the other.'

Sir Giles considered the statement. 'I'm not sure I would come to that,' he said.

'You know what I mean,' said Hoskins. 'He's no more an expert on motorways than I am.'

Sir Giles pursed his lips. 'If he's such a dimwit why did the Minister send him up? He's given him full authority to negotiate.'

'Don't look a gift horse in the mouth, is what I say.'

'I daresay there's something in that,' said Sir Giles. 'So you don't think there's anything to worry about?'

Hoskins smiled. 'Not a thing in the world. He'll nosey around a bit and then he will do just what we want. I tell you this bloke takes the biscuit. Butter wouldn't melt in his mouth.'

Sir Giles considered this mixture of metaphors and found it to his taste. 'I hear Lord Leakham's still foaming at the mouth.'

'He can't wait to re-open the Enquiry. Says he's going to put the motorway through the Gorge if it's the last thing he does.'

'It probably will be if Maud has anything to do with it,' said Sir Giles. 'She's in a very nasty frame of mind.'

'There's nothing much she can do about it once the decision is taken,' said Hoskins.

'I wouldn't be too sure about that.'

Sir Giles got up and stared out of the window and considered his alternative plan. 'You don't think this fellow Dundridge will advise against the Gorge?' he asked finally.

'Lord Leakham wouldn't listen to him if he did. He's got it into his head you tried to poison him,' said Hoskins and went back to his office leaving Sir Giles to ponder on the best-laid plans of mice and men. It was all very well for Hoskins to talk confidently about nincompoops from the Ministry. He had nothing to lose. Sir Giles had. His seat in Parliament for one thing. Well, if the worst came to the worst and Maud carried out her threat he could always get another. It was worth the risk. Reassured by the thought that Lord Leakham had made up his mind to route the motorway through the Gorge Sir Giles went out to lunch.

•

At Handyman Hall Lady Maud's gracious approach had worked wonders. Like some delicate plant in need of water, Dundridge had blossomed out. He had come expecting to meet Sir Giles but, after the first shock of finding himself alone in a large house with a large woman had worn off, Dundridge began to enjoy himself. For the first time since he had arrived in Worfordshire he was being taken seriously. Lady Maud treated him as a person of consequence.

'It is so good to know that you have come to take over from Lord Leakham,' Lady Maud said as she led him down a corridor to the drawing-room.

Dundridge said he hadn't actually come to take over. 'I'm simply here in an advisory capacity,' he said modestly.

Lady Maud smiled knowingly. 'Oh quite, and we all know what that means, don't we?' she murmured, drawing Dunbridge into a warm complicity he found quite delightful.

Dundridge relaxed on the sofa. 'The Minister is most anxious that the proposed motorway should fit in with the needs of local residents as much as possible.'

Maud smothered a snarl with another smile. The notion that she was a local resident made her blood boil, but she had set out to humour this snivelling civil servant and humour him she would. 'And there is the landscape to consider too,' she said. 'The Cleene Forest is one of the few remaining examples of virgin woodland left in England. It would be a terrible shame to spoil it with a motorway, don't you think?'

Dundridge didn't think anything of the sort but he knew better than to say so, and besides this seemed as good an opportunity as any to test out his theory of a tunnel. 'I think I've found a solution to the problem,' he said. 'Of course it's only an idea, you understand, and it has no official standing, but it should be possible to build a tunnel under the Cleene Hills.' He stopped. Lady Maud was staring at him intently. 'Of course, as I say, it's only an idea . . .'

Lady Maud had risen and for one terrible moment Dundridge thought she was about to assault him. She lurched forward and took his hand. 'Oh how wonderful,' she said. 'How absolutely brilliant. You dear, dear man,' and she sat down beside him on the sofa and gazed into his face ecstatically. Dundridge blushed and looked down at his shoes. He was quite unused to married women taking his hand, gazing into his face ecstatically and calling him their dear, dear man. 'It's nothing. Only an idea.'

'A splendid idea,' said Lady Maud, engulfing him in a blast of Lavender Water. Out of the corner of his eye Dundridge could see her bosom quivering beneath a nosegay of marigolds. He shrank into the sofa.

'Of course, there would have to be a feasibility study . . .' he began but Lady Maud brushed his remark aside.

'Of course there would, but that would take time wouldn't it?'

'Months,' said Dundridge.

'Months!'

'Six months at least.'

'Six months!' Lady Maud relinquished his hand with a sigh and contemplated a respite of six months. In six months so much could happen and if she had anything to do with it a great deal would. Giles would throw his weight behind the tunnel or she would know the reason why. She would drum up support from conservationists across the country. In six months she would do wonders. And she owed it all to this insubstantial little man with plastic shoes. Now that she came to look at him she realized she had misjudged him. There was something almost appealing about his vulnerability. 'You'll stay to lunch,' she said.

'Well . . . er . . . I really . . .'

'Of course you will,' said Lady Maud. 'I insist. And you can tell Giles all about the tunnel when he gets back this afternoon.' She rose and, leaving Dundridge to wonder how it was that Sir Giles who had been coming back at eleven had delayed his return until the afternoon, Lady Maud swept from the room. Left to himself, Dundridge sat stunned by the enthusiasm his suggestion had unleashed. If Sir Giles' reaction was as favourable as that of his wife he would have made some influential friends. And rich ones. He ran his fingers appreciatively over the moulding of a rosewood table. So this was how the other half lived, he thought, before realizing that the cliché was inappropriate. The other two per cent. Useful people to know.

*

Sir Giles returned from Worford at four to find Lady Maud in a remarkably good mood.

'I had a visit from such a strange young man,' she told him when he enquired what the matter was.

'Oh really?'

'He was called Dundridge. He was from the Ministry of the—'

'Dundridge? Did you say Dundridge?'

'Yes. Such a very interesting man . . .'

'Interesting? I understood he was a nincom . . . oh never mind. What did he have to say for himself?'

'Oh, this and that,' said Lady Maud, gratified by her husband's agitation.

'What do you mean "this and that"?'

'We talked about the absurdity of putting a motorway through the Gorge,' said Lady Maud.

'I suppose he's in favour of the Ottertown route.'

Lady Maud shook her head. 'As a matter of fact he isn't.'

'He isn't?' said Sir Giles, now thoroughly alarmed. 'What the hell is he in favour of then?'

Lady Maud savoured his concern. 'He has in mind a third route,' she said. 'One that avoids both Ottertown and the Gorge.'

Sir Giles turned pale. 'A third route? But there isn't a third route. There can't be. He's not thinking of going through the Forest, is he? It's an area of designated public beauty.'

'Not through it. Under it,' said Lady Maud triumphantly.

'Under it?'

'A tunnel. A tunnel under the Cleene Hills. Don't you think that's a marvellous idea.'

Sir Giles sat down heavily. He was looking quite ill.

'I said "Don't you think that's a marvellous idea",' said Lady Maud.

Sir Giles pulled himself together. 'Er . . . What . . . oh yes . . . splendid,' he muttered. 'Quite splendid.'

'You don't sound very enthusiastic,' said Lady Maud.

'It's just that I wouldn't have thought it was financially viable,' Sir Giles said. 'The cost would be enormous. I can't see the Ministry taking to the idea at all readily.'

'I can,' said Lady Maud, 'with a little prodding.' She went out through the french windows on to the terrace and looked lovingly across the park. With Dundridge's help she had solved one problem. The house had been saved. There remained the question of an heir and it had just occurred to her that here again Dundridge might prove invaluable. Over lunch he had waxed quite eloquent about his work. Once or twice he had mentioned cementation. The word had struck a chord in her. Now as she leant over the balustrade and stared into the depths of the pinetum it returned to her insistently. 'Sementation,' she murmured, 'sementation.' It was a new word to her and strangely technical for such an intimate act, but Lady Maud was in no mood to quibble.

●

Sir Giles was. He waddled off to the study and phoned Hoskins. 'What's all this about that bastard Dundridge being a nincompoop?' he snarled. 'Do you know what he's come up with now? A tunnel. You heard me. A bloody tunnel under the Cleene Hills.'

'A tunnel?' said Hoskins. 'That's out of the question. They can't put a tunnel under the Forest.'

'Why not? They're putting one under the blasted Channel. They can put tunnels wherever they bloody well want to these days.'

'I know that, but it would be cost-prohibitive,' said Hoskins.

'Cost-prohibitive my arse. If this sod goes round bleating about tunnels he'll whip up support from every environmental crank in the country. He's got to be stopped.'

'I'll do my best,' said Hoskins doubtfully.

'You'll do better than that,' Sir Giles snarled. 'You get him on to the idea of Ottertown.'

'But what about the seventy-five council houses—'

'Bugger the seventy-five council houses. Just get him off the bloody tunnel.' Sir Giles put down the phone and stared out of the window vindictively. If he didn't do something drastic he would be saddled with Handyman Hall. And with Lady Maud to boot. He got up and kicked the wastepaper basket into the corner.

10

Dundridge drove back to Worford with no thought for the landscape. His encounter with Lady Maud had left him stunned and with his sense of self-importance greatly inflated. Lunch had been most enjoyable and Dundridge with two large gins inside him had found Lady Maud a most appreciative audience. She had listened to his exposition of the theory of non-interruptive constant-flow transportation with an evident fervour usually quite absent in his audience and Dundridge had found her enthusiasm extraordinarily refreshing. Moreover she exuded confidence, a supreme self-confidence which was contagious and which exerted an enormous fascination over him. In spite of her lack of symmetry, of beauty, in spite of the manifest discrepancy between her physique and that of the ideal woman of his imagination, he had to admit that she held charms for him. After lunch she had shown him over the house and garden and Dundridge had followed her from room to room with a quite inexplicable sense of weak-kneed excitement. Once when he had stumbled in the rockery Lady Maud had taken his arm and Dundridge had felt limp with pleasure. Again when he had squeezed past her in the doorway of the bathroom he had been conscious of a delicious passivity. By the time he left the house he felt quite childishly happy. He was appreciated. It made all the difference.

He got back to the Handyman Arms to find Hoskins waiting for him in the lounge.

'Just thought I'd drop in to see how you were getting on.'

'Fine. Fine. Just fine,' said Dundridge.

'Got on all right with Leakham?'

The warm glow in Dundridge cooled. 'I can't say I like his attitude,' he said. 'He seems determined to go ahead with the Gorge route. He has evidently developed a quite irrational hatred for Lady Maud. I must say I find his attitude inexplicable. She seems a perfectly charming woman to me.'

Hoskins stared at him incredulously. 'She does?'

'Delightful,' said Dundridge, the warm glow returning gently.

'Delightful?'

'Charming,' said Dundridge dreamily.

'Good God,' said Hoskins unable to contain his astonishment any longer. The notion that anyone could find Lady Maud charming and delightful was quite beyond him. He looked at

Dundridge with a new interest. 'She's a bit large, don't you think?' he suggested.

'Comely,' said Dundridge benevolently. 'Just comely.'

Hoskins shuddered and changed the subject. 'About this tunnel,' he began. Dundridge looked at him in surprise.

'How did you hear about that?'

'News travels fast in these parts.'

'It must,' said Dundridge, 'I only mentioned it this morning.'

'You're not seriously proposing to recommend the construction of a tunnel under the Cleene Hills, are you?'

'I don't see why not,' said Dundridge, 'it seems a sensible compromise.'

'A bloody expensive one,' said Hoskins, 'it would cost millions and take years to put through.'

'At least it would avoid another riot. I came up here to try to find a solution that would be acceptable to all parties. It seems to me that a tunnel would be a very sensible alternative. In any case the plan is still in the formative stage.'

'Yes, but . . .' Hoskins began but Dundridge had risen and with an airy remark about the need for vision had gone up to his room. Hoskins went back to the Regional Planning Board in a pensive mood. He had been wrong about Dundridge. The man wasn't such a nincompoop after all. On the other hand he had found Lady Maud charming and delightful. 'Bloody pervert,' Hoskins muttered as he picked up the phone. Sir Giles wasn't going to like this.

*

Nor was Blott. He had had a relatively phone-free day in the kitchen garden. There had been Dundridge's call in the morning but for the most part he had been left in peace. At half past four he had heard Sir Giles call Hoskins and tell him about the tunnel. At half past five he was watering the tomatoes when Hoskins called back to say that Dundridge was serious about the tunnel.

'He can't be,' Sir Giles snarled. 'It's an outrageous idea. A gross waste of taxpayers' money.'

Blott shook his head. The tunnel sounded a very good idea to him.

'You try telling him that,' said Hoskins.

'What about Leakham?' Sir Giles asked. 'He's not going to buy it, is he?'

'I wouldn't like to say. Depends what sort of weight this fellow Dundridge carries in London. The Ministry may bring pressure to bear on Leakham.'

There was a silence while Sir Giles considered this. In the greenhouse Blott wrestled with the intricacies of the English language. Why should Lord Leakham buy the tunnel? How could Dundridge carry weight in London? And in any case why should Sir Giles dislike the idea of a tunnel? It was all very odd.

'I've got another bit of news for you,' Hoskins said finally. 'He's keen on your missus.'

There was a strangled sound from Sir Giles. 'He's what?' he shouted.

'He has taken a fancy to Maud,' Hoskins told him. 'He said he found her charming and delightful.'

'Charming and delightful?' said Sir Giles. 'Maud?'

'And comely.'

'Good God. No wonder she's looking like the cat that's swallowed the canary,' said Sir Giles.

'I just thought you ought to know,' said Hoskins. 'It might give us some sort of lever.'

'Kinky?'

'Could be,' said Hoskins.

'Meet me at the Club at nine,' said Sir Giles, suddenly making up his mind. 'This needs thinking about.' He rang off.

*

In the greenhouse Blott stared lividly into the geraniums. If Sir Giles had been surprised, Blott's reaction was stronger still. The sudden discovery that he was in love with Lady Maud had coloured his day. The thought of Dundridge sharing his feelings for her infuriated him. Sir Giles he discounted. It was quite clear that Lady Maud despised her husband and from what she had said Blott had gathered that there was another woman in London. Dundridge was another matter. Blott left the greenhouse, tidied up and went home.

Home for Blott was the Lodge. The architect of the arch had managed to combine monumentality with utility and at one time the Lodge had housed several families of estate workers in rather cramped and insanitary conditions. Blott had the place to himself and found it quite adequate. The arch had its little inconveniences; the windows were extremely small and hidden among the decorations on the exterior; there was only one door so that to get from one side of the arch to the other one had to climb the staircase to the top and then cross over, but Blott had made himself very comfortable in a large room that spanned the arch. Through a circular window on one side he could keep an eye on the Hall and through another he could inspect visitors crossing the bridge. He had converted one small room into a bathroom and another into a kitchen, while he stored apples in some of the others so that the whole place had a pleasant smell to it. And finally there was Blott's library filled with books that he had picked up on the market stalls in Worford or in the second-hand bookshop in Ferret Lane. There were no novels in Blott's library, no light reading, only books on English history. In its way it was a scholar's library born of an intense curiosity about the country of his adoption. If the secret of being an Englishman was to be found anywhere it was to be found, Blott thought, in the past. Through the long winter evenings he would sit in front of his fire absorbed in the romance of England. Certain figures loomed large in his imagination, Henry VIII, Drake, Cromwell, Edward I, and he tended to identify if not himself at least other people with the heroes and villains of history. Lady Maud, in spite of her marriage, he saw as the Virgin Queen, while Sir Giles seemed to have the less savoury aspects of Sir Robert Walpole.

But that was for winter. During the summer he was out and about. Twice a week he cycled over to Guildstead Carbonell to the Royal George and sat in the bar until it was time for bed, the bed in question belonging to Mrs Wynn who ran the pub and whose husband had obligingly left her a widow as a result of enemy action on D-Day. Mrs Wynn was the last of Blott's wartime customers and the affair had lingered on owing more to habit than to affection. Mrs Wynn found Blott useful, he dried glasses and carried bottles, and Blott found Mrs Wynn comfortable, undemanding and accommodating in the matter of beer. He had a weakness for Handyman Brown.

But now as he washed his neck – it was Friday night and Mrs Wynn was expecting him – he was conscious that he no longer felt the same way about her. Not that he had ever felt very much, but that little had been swept aside by his sudden surge of feeling for Maud. He was sensible enough not to entertain any expectations of being able to do anything about it. It just didn't seem right to go off to Mrs Wynn any more. In any case it was all most peculiar. He had always had a soft spot for Lady Maud but this was different and it occurred to him that he might be sickening for something. He stuck out his tongue and studied it in the bathroom mirror but it looked all right. It might be the weather. He had once heard someone say something about spring and young men's fancies but Blott wasn't a young man. He was fifty. Fifty and in love. Daft.

He went downstairs and got on his bicycle and cycled off across the bridge towards Guildstead Carbonell. He had just reached the crossroads when he heard a car coming up fast behind him. He got off the bike to let it go by. It was Sir Giles in the Bentley. 'Going to the Golf Club to see Hoskins,' he thought, and looked after the car suspiciously. 'He's up to something.' He got back on to his bike and freewheeled reluctantly down the hill towards the Royal George and Mrs Wynn. Perhaps he ought to tell Maud what he had heard. It didn't seem a good idea and in any case he wasn't going to let her know that Dundridge fancied her. 'He can sow his own row,' he said to himself and was pleased at his command of the idiom.

*

In the Worford Golf Club, Sir Giles and Hoskins discussed tactics.

'He's got to have a weakness,' said Sir Giles. 'Every man has his price.'

'Maud?' said Hoskins.

'Be your age,' said Sir Giles. 'She isn't going to fartarse around with some tinpot civil servant with that reversionary clause in the contract at stake. Besides, I don't believe it.'

'I distinctly heard him say he found her charming. And comely.'

'All right, so he likes fat women. What else does he like? Money?'

Hoskins shrugged. 'Hard to tell. You need time to find that out.'

'Time is what we haven't got. He's only got to start blabbing about that bleeding tunnel and the fat's in the fire. No, we've got to act fast.'

Hoskins looked at him suspiciously. 'What's all this "We" business?' he asked. 'It's your problem, not mine.'

Sir Giles gnawed a fingernail thoughtfully. 'How much?'

'Five thousand.'

'For what?'

'Whatever you decide.'

'Make it five per cent of the compensation. When it's paid.'

Hoskins did a quick calculation and made it twelve and a half thousand. 'Cash on the nail,' he said.

'You're a hard man, Hoskins, a hard man,' Sir Giles said sorrowfully.

'Anyway what do you want me to do? Sound him out?'

Sir Giles shook his head. His little eyes glittered. 'Kinky,' he said. 'Kinky. What made you say that?'

'I don't know. Just wondered,' said Hoskins.

'Boys, do you think?'

'Difficult to know,' said Hoskins. 'These things take time to find out.'

'Drink, drugs, boys, women, money. There's got to be some damned thing he's itching for.'

'Of course, we *could* frame him,' said Hoskins. 'It's been done before.'

78

Sir Giles nodded. 'The unsolicited gift. The anonymous donor. It's been done before all right. But it's too risky. What if he goes to the police?'

'Nothing ventured nothing gained,' said Hoskins. 'In any case there would be no indication where it came from. My bet is he'd take the bait.'

'If he didn't we would have lost him. No, it's got to be something foolproof.'

They sat in silence and considered a suitably compromising future for Dundridge.

'Ambitious would you say?' Sir Giles asked finally. Hoskins nodded.

'Very.'

'Know any queers?'

'In Worford? You've got to be joking,' said Hoskins.

'Anywhere.'

Hoskins shook his head. 'If you're thinking what I'm thinking . . .'

'I am.'

'Photos?'

'Photos,' Sir Giles agreed. 'Nice compromising photos.'

Hoskins gave the matter some thought. 'There's Bessie Williams,' he said. 'Used to be a model, if you know what I mean. Married a photographer in Bridgeminster. She'd do it if the money was right.' He smiled reminiscently. 'I can have a word with her.'

'You do that,' said Sir Giles. 'I'll pay up to five hundred for a decent set of photos.'

'Leave it to me,' Hoskins told him. 'Now then, about the cash.'

By the time Sir Giles left the Golf Club the matter was fixed. He drove home in a haze of whisky. 'The stick first and then the carrot,' he muttered. Tomorrow he would go to London and visit Mrs Forthby. It was just as well to be out of the way when things happened.

11

Dundridge spent the following morning at the Regional Planning Board with Hoskins poring over maps and discussing the tunnel. He was rather surprised to find that Hoskins had undergone a change of heart about the project and seemed to favour it. 'It's a brilliant idea. Pity we didn't think of it before. Would have saved no end of trouble,' he said, and while Dundridge was flattered he wasn't so sure. He had begun to have doubts about the feasibility of a tunnel. The Ministry wouldn't exactly like the cost, the delay would be considerable and there was still Lord Leakham to be persuaded. 'You don't think we could find an alternative route,' he asked but Hoskins shook his head.

'It's either the Cleene Gorge or Ottertown or your tunnel.' Dundridge, studying the maps, had to concede that there wasn't any other route. The Cleene Hills stretched unbroken save for the Gorge from Worford to Ottertown.

'Ridiculous fuss people make about a bit of forest,' Dundridge complained. 'Just trees. What's so special about trees?'

They had lunch at a restaurant in River Street. At the next table a couple in their thirties seemed to find Dundridge quite fascinating and more than once Dundridge looked up to find the woman looking at him with a quiet smile. She was rather attractive, with almond eyes.

In the afternoon Hoskins took him on a tour of the proposed route through Ottertown. They drove over and inspected the council houses and returned through Guildstead Carbonell, Hoskins stopping the car every now and again and insisting that they climb to the top of some hill to get a better view of the proposed route. By the time they got back to Worford Dundridge was exhausted. He was also rather drunk. They had stopped at several pubs along the way and, thanks to Hoskins' insistence that pints were for men and that only boys drank halves — he put rather a nasty inflection on boys — Dundridge had consumed rather more Handyman Triple XXX than he was used to.

'We're having a little celebration party at the Golf Club tonight,' Hoskins said as they drove through the town gate. 'If you'd care to come over . . .'

'I think I'll get an early night,' said Dundridge.

'Pity,' Hoskins said. 'You'd meet a number of influential local people. Doesn't do to give the locals the idea you're hoity-toity.'

'Oh all right,' said Dundridge grudgingly. 'I'll have a bath and something to eat and see how I feel.'

'See you later, old boy,' said Hoskins as Dundridge got out of the car and went up to his room in the Handyman Arms. A bath and a meal and he'd probably feel all right. He fetched a towel and went down the passage to the bathroom. When he returned having immersed himself briefly in a lukewarm bath – the geyser still refused to operate at all efficiently – he was feeling better. He had dinner and decided that Hoskins was probably right. It might be useful to meet some of the more influential local people. Dundridge went out to his car and drove over to the Golf Club.

'Delighted you could make it,' said Hoskins when Dundridge made his way through the crush to him. 'What's your poison?'

Dundridge said he'd have a gin and tonic. He'd had enough beer for one day. Around him large men shouted about doglegs on the third and water hazards on the fifth. Dundridge felt out of it. Hoskins brought him his drink and introduced him to a Mr Snell. 'Glad to meet you, squire,' said Mr Snell heartily from behind a large moustache. 'What's your handicap?' Suppressing his immediate reaction to tell him to mind his own damned business, Dundridge said that as far as he knew he didn't have one. 'A Beginner, eh? Well, never mind. Give it time. We've all got to start somewhere.' He drifted away and Dundridge wandered in the opposite direction. Looking round the room at the veined faces of the men and the hennaed hair of the women Dundridge cursed himself for coming. If this was

Hoskins' idea of local influence he could keep it. Presently he went out on to the terrace and stared resentfully down the eighteenth. He'd finish his drink and then go home. He drained his glass and was about to go inside when a voice at his elbow said, 'If you're going to the bar, you could get me another one.' It was a soft seductive voice. Dundridge turned and looked into a pair of almond eyes. Dundridge changed his mind about leaving. He went through to the bar and got two more drinks.

'These affairs are such a bore,' said the girl. 'Are you a great golfer?'

Dundridge said he wasn't a golfer at all.

'Nor am I. Such a boring game.' She sat down and crossed her legs. They were really very nice legs. 'And anyway I don't like sporty types. I prefer intellectuals.' She smiled at Dundridge. 'My name is Sally Boles. What's yours?'

'Dundridge,' said Dundridge and sat down where he could see more of her legs. Ten minutes later he got another two drinks. Twenty minutes later two more. He was enjoying himself at last.

Miss Boles, he learnt, was visiting her uncle. She came from London too. She worked for a firm of beauty consultants. Dundridge said he could well believe it. She found the country so boring. Dundridge said he did too. He waxed lyrical about the joys of living in London and all the time Miss Boles' almond eyes smiled seductively at him and her legs crossed and recrossed in the gathering dusk. When Dundridge suggested another drink Miss Boles insisted on getting it.

'It's my turn,' she said, 'and besides I want to powder my nose.' She left Dundridge sitting alone on the terrace in a happy stupor. When she returned with the drinks she was looking thoughtful.

'My uncle's gone without me,' she said, 'I suppose he thought I had gone home already. Would it be too much for you to give me a lift?'

'Of course not. I'd be delighted,' said Dundridge and sipped his drink. It tasted extraordinarily bitter.

'I'm so sorry, I got Campari,' Miss Boles said by way of

explanation. Dundridge said it was quite all right. He finished his drink and they wandered off the terrace towards the car park. 'It's been such a lovely evening,' Miss Boles said as she climbed into Dundridge's car. 'You must look me up in London.'

'I'd like to,' said Dundridge. 'I'd like to see a lot more of you.'

'That's a promise,' said Miss Boles.

'You really mean that?'

'Call me Sally,' said Miss Boles and leant against him.

'Oh Sally . . .' Dundridge began, and suddenly felt quite extraordinarily tired, '. . . I do want to see so much more of you.'

'You will, my pet, you will,' said Miss Boles and took the car keys out of his inert fingers. Dundridge had passed out.

*

In London Sir Giles lay back supine on the bed while Mrs Forthby tightened the straps. Occasionally he struggled briefly for the look of the thing and whimpered hoarsely but Mrs Forthby was, at least superficially, implacable. The scenario of Sir Giles' fantasy called for a brutal implacability and Mrs Forthby did her best. She wasn't very good, being a kind-hearted soul and not given to tying people up and whipping them, and as a matter of fact she disapproved of corporal punishment on principle. It was largely because she was so progressive that she was prepared to indulge Sir Giles in the first place. 'If it gives the poor man pleasure who am I to say him nay,' she told herself. Certainly she had to say nay a great many times to Sir Giles in the throes of his ritual. But if Mrs Forthby wasn't naturally brutal, with the lights down low it was possible to imagine that she was and she had the merit of being strong and wearing her costume — there were several — most convincingly. Tonight she was Cat Woman, Miss Dracula, the Cruel Mistress Experimenting On Her Helpless Victim.

'No, no,' whimpered Sir Giles.

'Yes, yes,' insisted Mrs Forthby.

'No, no.'

'Yes, yes.'

Mrs Forthby's fingers forced his mouth open and inserted the gag. 'No ...' It was too late. Mrs Forthby inflated the gag and smiled maliciously down at him. Her breasts loomed above him, heavy with menace. Her gloved hands ...

Mrs Forthby went into the kitchen and made a pot of tea. While she waited for the kettle to boil she nibbled a digestive biscuit thoughtfully. There were times when she tired of Sir Giles' desultory attachment and longed for a more permanent arrangement. She would have to speak to him about it. She warmed the teapot, put in two teabags and then a third for the pot and poured the boiling water in. After all she was getting on and she rather fancied the idea of being Lady Lynchwood. She looked round the kitchen. Now where had she put the lid of the teapot?

On the bed Sir Giles struggled with his bonds and was still. He lay back happily exhausted and waited for his cruel mistress. He had to wait a long time. In between spasms of excitement his mind went back to Dundridge. He hoped Hoskins hadn't made a bloody mess of things. That was the trouble with subordinates, you couldn't trust them. Sir Giles preferred to attend to matters himself but he had too much to lose to be closely involved in the actual details of this particular operation. First the stick and then the carrot. He wondered how much the carrot would have to be. Two, three, four thousand pounds? Expensive. Add Hoskins' five thousand. Still, it was worth it. A profit of £150,000 was worth it. So was the prospect of Maud's fury when she realized that the motorway was coming through the Gorge. Teach the stupid bitch. But where was Mrs Forthby? Why didn't she come back?

Mrs Forthby finished her cup of tea and poured another. She was getting rather hot in her tight costume. Perhaps she would go and have a bath. She got up and went into the bathroom and turned on the tap before remembering that there was something she still had to do. 'Silly old me, talk about forgetful,' she said to herself and picked up the thin cane. The Cruel Mistress,

Miss Dracula, went through to the bedroom and closed the door.

*

In his library in the Lodge Blott sat reading Sir Arthur Bryant, but his mind wasn't on the Age of Elegance. It kept slipping away to Maud, Mrs Wynn, Dundridge, Sir Giles. Besides, he didn't much care for the Prince Regent. Nasty piece of goods in Blott's opinion. But then Blott had no time for any of the Georges. His sympathies were all with the Jacobites. The lost cause and Bonnie Prince Charlie. In his present mood of romantic devotion he felt a longing to kneel before Lady Maud and confess his love. It was an absurd notion. She would be furious with him. Worse still, she might laugh. The thought of her contemptuous laughter made him put the book down and go downstairs. It was a lovely evening. The sun had set over the hills to the west but the sky was still bright. Blott felt like a beer. He wasn't going over to Guildstead Carbonell for one. Mrs Wynn would expect him to spend the night and Blott didn't feel like another night with her. He had spent the previous evening wrestling with his conscience and trying to make up his mind to tell her it was all over between them. In the end his sense of realism had prevailed. Lady Maud wasn't for the likes of Blott. He would just have to dream about her. He had done so while making love to Mrs Wynn, who had been amazed at his renewed fervour. 'Just like the old days,' she had said wistfully as Blott got dressed to cycle back to the Lodge. No, he definitely didn't feel like another night at the Royal George. He would go for a walk. There were some rabbits over by the pinetum. Blott fetched his shotgun and set off across the Park. Beside him the river murmured gently and there was a smell of summer in the air. A blackbird called from a bush. Blott ignored his surroundings. He was dreaming of changed circumstances, of Lady Maud in peril, an act of heroism on his part that would reveal his true feelings for her and bring them together in love and happiness. By the time he reached the pinetum it was too dark to see any rabbits. But Blott wasn't

interested in rabbits any more. A light had come on in Lady
Maud's bedroom. Blott crept across the lawn and stood looking
up at it until it went out. Then he walked home and went to
bed.

12

Dundridge woke in a lay-by on the London road. He had a
splitting headache, he was extremely cold and the gear lever
was sticking into his ribs. He sat up, untangled his legs from
under the steering wheel and wondered where the hell he was,
how he had got there and what the devil had happened. He had
an extremely clear memory of the party at the Golf Club. He
could remember talking to Miss Boles on the terrace. He could
even recall walking back to his car with her. After that nothing.

He got out of the car to try to get the circulation moving in
his legs and discovered that his trousers were undone. He did
them up hurriedly and reached up automatically to tighten the
knot in his tie to hide his embarrassment only to find that he
wasn't wearing a tie. He felt his open shirt collar and the vest
underneath. It was on back to front. He pulled the vest out a
bit and looked down at the label. St Michael Combed Cotton it
said. It was definitely on back to front. Now he came to think
of it, his Y-fronts felt peculiar too. He took a step forward and
tripped over a shoelace. His shoes were untied. Dundridge
staggered against the car, seriously alarmed. He was in the
middle of nowhere at . . . He looked at his watch. At six a.m.
with his shoes untied, his vest and pants on back to front,
and his trousers undone, and all he could remember was
getting into the car with a girl with almond eyes and lovely
legs.

And suddenly Dundridge had a horrid picture of the night's
events. Perhaps he had raped the girl. A sudden brainstorm.
That would explain the headache. The years of self-indulgence

with his composite woman had come home to roost. He had gone mad and raped Miss Boles, possibly killed her. He looked down at his hands. At least there wasn't any blood on them. He could have strangled her. There was always that possibility. There were any number of awful possibilities. Dundridge bent over painfully and did up his shoes and then, having looked in the ditch to make sure that there was no body there, he got back into the car and wondered what to do. There was obviously no point in sitting in the lay-by. Dundridge started the car and drove on until he came to a signpost which told him he was going towards London. He turned the car round and drove back to Worford, parked in the yard of the Handyman Arms and went quietly up to his room. He was in bed when the girl brought him his tea.

'What time is it?' he asked sleepily. The girl looked at him with a nasty smile.

'You ought to know,' she said, 'you've only just come in. I saw you sneaking up the stairs. Been having a night on the tiles, have you?'

She put the tray down and went out, leaving Dundridge cursing himself for a fool. He drank some tea and felt worse. There was no point in doing anything until he felt better. He turned on his side and went to sleep. When he awoke it was midday. He washed and shaved, studying his face in the mirror for some sign of the sexual mania he suspected. The face that stared back at him was a perfectly ordinary face but Dundridge was not reassured. Murderers tended to have perfectly ordinary faces. Perhaps he had simply had a blackout or amnesia. But that wouldn't explain his vest being on back to front, nor his Y-fronts. At some time during the night he had undressed. Worse still, he had dressed in such a hurry that he hadn't noticed what he was doing. That suggested panic or at least an extraordinary urgency. He went downstairs and had lunch. After lunch he would get hold of a telephone directory and look up Boles. Of course her uncle might not be called Boles but it was worth a try. If that didn't work he would try Hoskins or the Golf Club. On second thoughts, that might not be such a good idea. There was no point in drawing attention to the fact that he had taken Miss Boles home. Or hadn't.

In the event there was no need to look in the telephone directory. As he passed the hotel desk, the clerk handed him a large envelope. It was addressed to Mr Dundridge and marked Private and Confidential. Dundridge took it up to his room before opening it and was extremely thankful that he hadn't opened it in the foyer. Dundridge knew now how he had spent the night.

He dropped the photographs on to the bed and slumped into a chair. A moment later he was up and locking the door. Then he turned back and stared at the pictures. They were 10 by 8 glossies and quite revolting. Taken with a flash, they were extremely clear and portrayed Dundridge with an unmistakable clarity, naked and all too evidently unashamed, engaged in a series of monstrous activities beyond his wildest imaginings with Miss Boles. At least he supposed it was Miss Boles. The fact that she seemed ... Not seemed, *was* wearing a mask, a sort of hood, made identification impossible. He thumbed through the pictures and came to the hooded man. Dundridge hurriedly put them back in the envelope and sat sweating on the edge of the bed. He'd been framed. The word seemed wholly inappropriate. Nothing on God's earth would get him to frame these pictures. Someone was trying to blackmail him.

Trying? They had bloody well succeeded, but Dundridge had no money. He couldn't pay anything. Dundridge opened the envelope again and stared at the evidence of his depravity. Miss Boles? Miss Boles? It obviously wasn't her real name. Sally Boles. He had heard that name before somewhere. Of course, Sally Bowles in *I am a Camera*. Dundridge didn't need telling. He'd been had in many more ways than one. In many more ways if the photos were anything to go by.

He was just wondering what to do next when the telephone rang. Dundridge grabbed it. 'Yes,' he said.

'Mr Dundridge?' said a woman's voice.

'Speaking,' said Dundridge shakily.

'I hope you like the proofs.'

'Proofs, you bitch?' Dundridge snarled.

'Call me Sally,' said the voice. 'There's no need to be formal with me now.'

'What do you want?'

'A thousand pounds . . . to be going on with.'

'A thousand pounds? I haven't got a thousand pounds.'

'Then you had better get it, hadn't you sweetie?'

'I'll tell you what I'm going to get,' shouted Dundridge, 'I'm going to get the police.'

'You do that,' said a man's voice roughly, 'and you'll end up with your face cut to ribbons. You're not playing with small fry, mate. We're bigtime, understand.'

Dundridge understood all too well. The woman's voice came back on the line. 'If you do go to the police remember we've had one or two customers there. We'll know. You just start looking for your thousand pounds.'

'I can't—'

'Don't call us. We'll call you,' said Miss Boles, and put the phone down. Dundridge replaced his receiver more slowly. Then he leant forward and held his head in his hands.

*

Sir Giles returned from London in excellent spirits. Mrs Forthby had excelled herself and he was still tingling with satisfaction. Best of all had been Hoskins' cryptic message over the phone. 'The fish is hooked,' he had said. All that was required now was to provide a net in which Mr Dundridge could flounder. Sir Giles parked his car and went up to his constituency office and sent for Hoskins.

'Here they are. As nice a set of prints as you could wish for,' Hoskins said, laying the photographs out on the desk.

Sir Giles studied them with an appreciative eye. 'Very nice,' he said finally. 'Very nice indeed. And what does lover-boy have to say for himself now?'

'They've asked him for a thousand pounds. He says he hasn't got it.'

'He'll have it, never fear,' said Sir Giles. 'He'll have his thousand pounds and we'll have him. There won't be any more talk about tunnels in future. From now on it's going to be Otter-town.'

'Ottertown?' said Hoskins, thoroughly puzzled. 'But I thought you wanted it through the Gorge. I thought—'

'The trouble with you, Hoskins,' said Sir Giles, putting the photographs back into the envelope and the envelope into his briefcase, 'is that you can't see further than the end of your nose. You don't really think I want to lose my lovely house and my beautiful wife, do you? You don't think I haven't got the interests of my constituents like General Burnett and Mr Bull-ett-Bloody-Finch at heart, do you? Of course I have. I'm honest Sir Giles, the poor man's friend,' and leaving Hoskins com-pletely confused by this strange change of tack, he went down-stairs.

There was nothing like throwing people off the scent. Killing two birds with one stone, he thought as he got into the Bent-ley. The decision to go through Ottertown would kill Puck-erington for sure. Sir Giles looked forward to his demise with relish. Puckerington was no friend of his. Snobby bastard. Well, he was bird number one. Then the bye-election in Ottertown and they would have to change the route to the Gorge and Handyman Hall would go. Bird number two. By that time he would be able to claim even more compensation and no one, least of all Maud, could say he hadn't done his damnedest. There was only one snag. That old fool Leakham might still insist on the Gorge route. It was hardly a snag. Maud would create a bit more. He might lose his seat in Parliament but he would be £150,000 richer and Mrs Forthby was waiting. Swings or roundabouts, Sir Giles couldn't lose. The main thing was to see that the tunnel scheme was scotched. Sir Giles parked out-side the Handyman Arms, went inside and sent a message up to Dundridge's room to say that Sir Giles Lynchwood was looking forward to his company in the lounge.

Dundridge went downstairs gloomily. The last person he wanted to see was the local MP. He could hardly consult him about blackmail. Sir Giles greeted him with a heartiness Dun-dridge no longer felt that his position warranted. 'My dear fellow, I'm delighted to see you,' he said shaking Dundridge's limp hand vigorously. 'Been meaning to look you up and have a chat about this motorway nonsense. Had to go to London unfortunately. Looking after you all right here? It's one of our houses, you know. Any complaints, just let me know and I'll see to it. We'll have tea in the private lounge.' He led the way up some steps into a small lounge with a TV set in the corner. Sir Giles plumped into a chair and took out a cigar. 'Smoke?'

Dundridge shook his head.

'Very wise of you. Still they do say cigars don't do one any harm and a fellow's entitled to one or two little vices, eh, what?' said Sir Giles and pierced the end of the cigar with a silver cutter. Dundridge winced. The cigar reminded him of something that had figured rather too largely in his activities with Miss Boles, and as for vices . . .

'Now then, about this business of the motorway,' said Sir Giles, 'I think it's as well to put our cards on the table. I'm a man who doesn't beat about the bush I can tell you. Call a spade a bloody shovel. I don't let the grass grow under my feet. Wouldn't be where I was if I did.' He paused briefly to allow Dundridge to savour this wealth of metaphors and the bluff dishonesty of his approach. 'And I don't mind telling you that I don't like this idea of your building a motorway through my damned land one little bit.'

'It was hardly my idea,' said Dundridge.

'Not yours personally,' said Sir Giles, 'but you fellows at the Ministry have made up your mind to slap the bloody thing smack through the Gorge. Don't tell me you haven't.'

'Well, as a matter of fact . . .' Dundridge began.

'There you are. What did I tell you? Told you so. Can't pull the wool over my eyes.'

'As a matter of fact I'm against the Gorge route,' Dundridge said when he got the opportunity. Sir Giles looked at him dubiously.

'You are?' he said. 'Damned glad to hear it. I suppose you favour Ottertown. Can't say I blame you. Best route by far.'

'No,' said Dundridge. 'Not through Ottertown. A tunnel under the Cleene Hills . . .'

Sir Giles feigned astonishment. 'Now wait a minute,' he said, 'the Cleene Forest is an area of designated public beauty. You can't start mucking around with that.' His accent, as variable as a weathercock, had veered round to Huddersfield.

'There's no question of mucking about . . .' Dundridge began but Sir Giles was leaning across the table towards him with a very nasty look on his face.

'You can say that again,' he said poking his forefinger into Dundridge's shirt front. 'Now you just listen to me, young man. You can forget all about tunnels and suchlike. I want a quick decision one way or t'other. I don't like to be kept hanging about while lads like you dither about talking a lot of airy twaddle about tunnels. That's all right for my missus, she being a gullible woman, but it won't wash with me. I want a straight answer. Yes or No. Yes to Ottertown and No to the Gorge.' He sat back and puffed his cigar.

'In that case,' said Dundridge stiffly, 'you had better have a word with Lord Leakham. He's the one who makes the final decision.'

'Leakham? Leakham? Makes the final decision?' said Sir Giles. 'Don't try to have me on, lad. The Minister didn't send you up so that that dry old stick could make decisions. He sent you up to tell him what to say. You can't fool me. I know an expert when I see one. He'll do what you tell him.'

Dundridge felt better. This was the recognition he had been waiting for. 'Well I suppose I do have some influence,' he conceded.

Sir Giles beamed. 'What did I say? Top men don't grow on trees and I've got a nose for talent. Well, you won't find me ungenerous. You pop round and see me when you've had your little chat with Lord Leakham. I'll see you right.'

Dundridge goggled at him. 'You don't mean—'

'Name your own charity,' said Sir Giles with a prodigious wink. 'Mind you, I always say "Charity begins at home". Eh? I'm not a mean man. I pays for what I gets.' He drew on his cigar and watched Dundridge through a cloud of smoke. This was the moment of truth. Dundridge swallowed nervously.

'That's very kind of you . . .' he began.

'Say no more,' said Sir Giles. 'Say no more. Any time you want me I'll be in my constituency office or out at the Hall. Best time to catch me is in the morning at the office.'

'But what am I going to say to Lord Leakham?' Dundridge said. 'He's adamant about the Gorge route.'

'You tell him from me that my good lady wife intends to take him to the cleaners about that unlawful arrest unless he decides for Ottertown. You tell him that.'

'I don't think Lord Leakham would appreciate that very much,' said Dundridge nervously. He didn't much like the idea of uttering threats against the old judge.

'You tell him I'll sue him for every brass farthing he's got. And I've got witnesses, remember. Influential witnesses who'll stand up in court and swear that he was drunk and disorderly at that Enquiry, and abusive too. You tell him he won't have a reputation and he won't have a penny by the time we've finished with him. I'll see to that.'

'I doubt if he'll like it,' said Dundridge, who certainly didn't.

'Don't suppose he will,' said Sir Giles, 'I'm not a man to run up against.'

Dundridge could see that. By the time Sir Giles left Dundridge had no doubts on that score at all. As Sir Giles drove away Dundridge went up to his room and looked at the photographs again. Spurred on by their obscenity he took an aspirin and went slowly round to the Cottage Hospital. He'd make Lord Leakham change his mind about the Gorge. Sir Giles had said he would pay for what he got and Dundridge intended to see that he got something to pay for. He didn't have any choice any longer. It was either that or ruin.

*

On the way back to Handyman Hall, Sir Giles stopped and unlocked his briefcase and took out the photographs. They were really very interesting. Mrs Williams was an imaginative woman. No doubt about it. And attractive. Most attractive. He might look her up one of these days. He put the photographs away and drove back to the Hall.

13

At the Cottage Hospital Dundridge had some difficulty in finding Lord Leakham. He wasn't in his room. 'It's very naughty of him to wander about like this,' said the Matron. 'You'll probably find him in the Abbey. He's taken to going over there when he shouldn't. Says he likes looking at the tomb-stones. Morbid, I call it.'

'You don't think his mind has been affected, do you?' Dundridge asked hopefully.

'Not so's you'd notice. All lords are potty in my experience,' the Matron told him.

In the end Dundridge found him in the garden discussing the merits of the cat o'nine tails with a retired vet who had the good fortune to be deaf.

'Well what do you want now?' Lord Leakham asked irritably when Dundridge interrupted.

'Just a word with you,' said Dundridge.

'Well, what is it?' said Lord Leakham.

'It's about the motorway,' Dundridge explained.

'What about it? I'm re-opening the Enquiry on Monday. Can't it wait till then?'

'I'm afraid not,' said Dundridge. 'The thing is that as a result of an in-depth on-the-spot investigative study of the socio-environmental and geognostic ancillary factors . . .'

'Good God,' said Lord Leakham, 'I thought you said you wanted a word . . .'

'It is our considered conclusion,' continued Dundridge, man-fully devising a jargon to suit the occasion, 'that given the—'

'Which is it to be? Ottertown or the Cleene Gorge? Spit it out, man.'

'Ottertown,' said Dundridge.

'Over my dead body,' said Lord Leakham.

'I trust not,' said Dundridge, disguising his true feelings. 'There's just one other thing I think you ought to know. As you are probably aware the Government is most anxious to avoid any further adverse publicity about the motorway . . .'

'You can't expect to demolish seventy-five brand-new council houses without attracting adverse publicity,' Lord Leakham pointed out.

'And,' continued Dundridge, 'the civil action for damages which Lady Lynchwood intends to institute against you is bound—'

'Against *me*?' shouted the Judge. 'She intends to—'

'For unlawful arrest,' said Dundridge.

'That's a police matter. If she has any complaints let her sue those responsible. In any case no sane judge would find for her.'

'I understand she intends to call some rather eminent people as witnesses,' said Dundridge. 'Their testimony will be that you were drunk.'

Lord Leakham began to swell.

'And personally abusive,' said Dundridge gritting his teeth. 'And disorderly. In fact that you were not in a fit state . . .'

'WHAT?' yelled the Judge, with a violence that sent several elderly patients scurrying for cover and a number of pigeons fluttering off the hospital roof.

'In short,' said Dundridge as the echo died away across the Abbey Close, 'she intends to impugn your reputation. Naturally the Minister has to take all these things into account, you do see that?'

But it was doubtful if Lord Leakham could see anything. He had slumped on to a bench and was staring lividly at his bedroom slippers.

'Naturally too,' continued Dundridge, pursuing his advantage, 'there is a fairly widespread feeling that you might be biased against her in the matter of the Gorge.'

'Biased?' Lord Leakham snuffled. 'The Gorge is the logical route.'

'On the grounds of the civil action she intends to take. Now if you were to decide on Ottertown ...' Dundridge left the consequences hanging in the air.

'You think she might reconsider her decision?'

'I feel sure she would,' said Dundridge. 'In fact I'm positive she would.'

Dundridge walked back to the Handyman Arms rather pleased with his performance. Desperation had lent him a fluency he had never known before. In the morning he would go and see Sir Giles about a thousand pounds. He had an early dinner and went up to his room, locked the door and examined the photographs again. Then he turned out the light and considered several things he hadn't done to Miss Sally Boles but which on reflection he wished he had. Strangled the bitch for one thing.

•

At Handyman Hall Sir Giles and Lady Maud dined alone. Their conversation seldom sparkled and was usually limited to an exchange of acrimonious opinions but for once they were both in a good mood at the same time. Dundridge was the cause of their good humour.

'Such a sensible young man,' Lady Maud said helping herself to asparagus. 'I'm sure that tunnel is the right answer.'

Sir Giles rather doubted it. 'My bet is he'll go for Ottertown,' he said.

Lady Maud said she hoped not. 'It seems such a shame to turn those poor people out of their homes. I'm sure they would feel just as strongly as I do about the Hall.'

'They build them new houses,' said Sir Giles. 'It's not as if they turn them out into the street. Anyway, people who live on council estates deserve what they get. Sponging off public money.'

Lady Maud said some people couldn't help being poor. They were just built that way like Blott. 'Dear Blott,' she said. 'You know he did such a strange thing this morning, he brought me a present, a little figure he had carved out of wood.'

But Sir Giles wasn't listening. He was still thinking about

people who lived in council houses. 'What the man in the street doesn't seem to be able to get into his thick head is that the world doesn't owe him a living.'

'I thought it was rather sweet of him,' said Lady Maud.

Sir Giles helped himself to cheese soufflé. 'What people don't understand is that we're just animals,' he said. 'The world is a bloody jungle. It's dog eat dog in this life and no mistake.'

'Dog?' said Lady Maud, roused from her reverie by the word. 'That reminds me. I suppose I'll have to send all those Alsatians back now. Just when I was getting fond of them. You're quite sure Mr Dundridge is going to advise Ottertown?'

'Positive,' said Sir Giles, 'I'd stake my life on it.'

'Really,' said Lady Maud wistfully, 'I don't see how you can be so certain. Have you spoken to him?'

Sir Giles hesitated. 'I have it on the best authority,' he said.

'Hoskins,' said Lady Maud, 'that horrid man. I wouldn't trust him any further than I could throw him. He'd say anything.'

'He also says that this fellow Dundridge has taken a fancy to you,' Sir Giles said. 'It seems you had a considerable effect on him.'

Lady Maud considered the remark and found it intriguing. 'I'm sure that can't be true. Hoskins is making things up.'

'It might explain why he is in favour of the Ottertown route,' Sir Giles said. 'You bowled him over with your charm.'

'Very funny,' said Lady Maud.

But afterwards as she washed up in the kitchen she found herself thinking about Dundridge, if not fondly, at least with a renewed interest. There was something rather appealing about the little man, a vulnerability that she found preferable to Sir Giles' disgusting self-sufficiency . . . and Dundridge had taken a fancy to her. It was useful to know these things. She would have to cultivate him. She smiled to herself. If Sir Giles could have his little affairs in London, there was no reason why she shouldn't avail herself of his absence for her own purposes. But above all there was an anonymity about Dundridge that appealed to her. 'He'll do,' she said to herself and dried her hands.

*

Next morning Dundridge went round to Sir Giles' constituency office at eleven. 'I've had a word with Lord Leakham and I think he'll be amenable,' he said.

'Splendid, my dear fellow, splendid. Delighted to hear it. I knew you could do it. A great weight off my mind, I can tell you. Now then is there anything I can do for you?' Sir Giles leant back in his chair expansively. 'After all, one good turn deserves another.'

Dundridge braced himself for the request. 'As a matter of fact, there is,' he said, and hesitated before going on.

'I'll tell you what I'll do,' said Sir Giles coming to his rescue. 'I don't know if you're a betting man but I am. I'll bet you a thousand pounds to a penny that old Leakham says the motorway has to go through Ottertown. How about that? Couldn't ask for anything fairer, eh?'

'A thousand pounds to a penny?' said Dundridge, hardly able to believe his ears.

'That's right. A thousand pounds to a penny. Take it or leave it.'

'I'll take it,' said Dundridge.

'Good man. I thought you would,' said Sir Giles, 'and just to show my good faith I'll put the stake up now.' He reached down to a drawer in the desk and took out an envelope. 'You can count it at your leisure.' He put the envelope on the desk. 'No need for a receipt. Just don't spend it until Leakham gives his decision.'

'Of course not,' said Dundridge. He put the envelope in his pocket.

'Nice meeting you,' said Sir Giles. Dundridge went out and down the stairs. He had accepted a bare-faced bribe. It was the first time in his life. Behind him Sir Giles switched off the tape recorder. It was just as well to have a receipt. Once the Enquiry was over he would burn the tape but in the meantime better safe than sorry.

14

Lord Leakham's announcement that he was recommending the Ottertown route provoked mixed reactions. In Worford there was open rejoicing and the Handyman pubs dispensed free beer. In Ottertown the Member of Parliament, Francis Puckerington, was inundated with telephone calls and protest letters and suffered a relapse as a result. In London the Prime Minister, relieved that there hadn't been another riot in Worford, congratulated the Minister of the Environment on the adroit way his department had handled the matter, and the Minister congratulated Mr Rees on his choice of a troubleshooter. No one in the Ministry shared his enthusiasm.

'That bloody idiot Dundridge has dropped us in it this time,' said Mr Joynson. 'I knew it was a mistake to send him up there. The Ottertown route is going to cost an extra ten million.'

'In for a penny in for a pound,' said Rees. 'At least we've got rid of him.'

'Got rid of him? He'll be back tomorrow crowing about his success as a negotiator.'

'He won't you know,' Rees told him. 'He got us into this mess, he can damned well get us out. The Minister has approved his appointment as Controller Motorways Midlands.'

'Controller Motorways Midlands? I didn't know there was such a post.'

'There wasn't. It's been specially created for him. Don't ask me why. All I know is that Dundridge has found favour with one or two influential people in South Worfordshire. Wheels within wheels,' said Mr Rees.

*

In Worford Dundridge greeted the news of his appointment with consternation. He had spent an anxious weekend confined to his room at the Handyman Arms partly because he was afraid of missing the telephone call from Miss Boles and partly because he had no intention of leaving the money he had received from Sir Giles in his suitcase or of carrying it around on his person. But there had been no phone call. To add to his troubles, there was the knowledge that he had accepted a bribe. He tried to persuade himself that he had merely taken a bet on, but it was no use.

'I could get three years for this,' he said to himself, and seriously considered handing the money back. He was deterred by the photographs. He couldn't imagine how many years he could get for doing what they suggested he had done.

By the time the Enquiry re-opened on Monday, Dundridge's nerves were frayed to breaking point. He had taken his seat inconspicuously at the back of the courtroom and had hardly listened to the evidence. The presence of a large number of policemen, brought in to ensure that there was no further outbreak of violence, had done nothing to reassure him. Dundridge had misconstrued their role and had finally left the courtroom before Lord Leakham announced his decision. He was standing in the hall downstairs when a burst of cheering indicated that the Enquiry was over.

Sir Giles and Lady Maud were the first to congratulate him. They issued from the courtroom and down the stairs followed by General Burnett and Mr and Mrs Bullett-Finch.

'Splendid news,' said Sir Giles. Lady Maud seized Dundridge's hand.

'I feel we owe you a great debt of gratitude,' she said staring into his face significantly.

'It was nothing,' murmured Dundridge modestly.

'Nonsense,' said Lady Maud, 'you have made me very happy. You must come and see us before you leave.'

Sir Giles had winked prodigiously – Dundridge had come to loathe that wink – and had whispered something about a bet being a bet and Hoskins had insisted on their going to have a drink together to celebrate. Dundridge couldn't see anything to celebrate about.

'You've got friends at court,' Hoskins explained.

'Friends at court?' said Dundridge. 'What on earth do you mean?'

'A little bird has told me that someone has put in a good word for you. You wait and see.'

Dundridge had waited in the hope (though that was hardly the right word) that Miss Boles would call but instead of a demand for a thousand pounds he had received a letter of appointment. 'Controller Motorways Midlands with responsibility for co-ordinating . . . Good God!' he muttered. He made a number of frantic phone calls to the Ministry threatening to resign unless he was brought back to London, but the enthusiasm with which Mr Rees endorsed his decision was enough to make him retract it.

Even Hoskins, who might have been expected to resent Dundridge's appointment as his superior, seemed relieved. 'What did I tell you, old boy,' he said when Dundridge told him the news. 'Friends at court. Friends at court.'

'But I don't know anything about motorway construction. I'm an administrator not an engineer.'

'All you have to do is see that the contractors keep to schedule,' Hoskins explained. 'Nothing to it. You leave all the rest of it to me. Basically yours is a public-relations role.'

'But I'm responsible for coordinating construction work. It says so here,' Dundridge protested, waving his letter of appointment, ' "and in particular problems relating to environmental factors and human ecology". I suppose that means dealing with the tenants of those council houses in Ottertown.'

'That sort of thing,' said Hoskins. 'I shouldn't worry about that too much. Cross your bridges when you come to them is my motto.'

'Oh well, I suppose I'll just have to get used to the idea.'

'I'll fix you up an office here. You'd better set about finding somewhere to live.'

Dundridge had spent two days looking at flats in Worford before settling on an apartment overlooking Worford Castle. It wasn't a prospect he found particularly pleasing, but the flat had the merit of being comparatively modern and was certainly better than some of the squalid rooms he had looked at elsewhere. And besides it had a telephone and was partly furnished. Dundridge placed particular emphasis upon the telephone. He didn't want Miss Boles to get the false idea that he wasn't prepared to pay a thousand pounds for the photographs and negatives. But as the days passed and there was still no demand from her he began to relax. Perhaps the whole thing had been some sort of filthy practical joke. He even asked Hoskins if he knew anything about the girl at the party but Hoskins said he couldn't remember much about the evening and hadn't known half the people who were there.

'My mind's a blank on the whole evening, old chap,' he said. 'Had a good time, though. I do remember that. Why? Are you thinking of looking her up again?'

'Just wondered who she was,' said Dundridge and went back to his office to draw up plans for the opening ceremony to mark the start of the construction of the motorway. It was going to be a grand affair, he had decided.

*

So had Lady Maud, though the affair she had in mind was of quite a different sort. She waited until Sir Giles said he was going to spend a fortnight in London before inviting Dundridge to dinner. She sent a formal invitation.

Dundridge hired a dinner-jacket and expected to find a number of other guests. He was extremely nervous and had fortified himself in advance with two stiff gins. In the event he need not have bothered. He arrived to find Lady Maud dressed, if not to kill, at least to seriously endanger anyone who came near her.

'I'm so glad you could come,' she said taking his arm almost as soon as he had entered the front door. 'I'm afraid my husband has had to go to London on business. I hope you don't mind having to put up with me.'

'Not at all,' said Dundridge, conscious once again of that weakness in his legs that Lady Maud's presence seemed to induce in him. They went into the drawing-room and Lady Maud mixed drinks. 'I did think of inviting General Burnett and the Bullett-Finches but the General does tend to monopolize the conversation and Ivy Bullett-Finch is a bit of a wet blanket.'

Dundridge sipped his drink and wondered what the hell she had put into it. It looked innocuous, but clearly wasn't. Lady Maud's dress, on the other hand, practised no such deception. A thing of silk designed to emphasize the curvature of the female form, it had evidently been created with someone more lissom in mind. It bulged where it should have hung and wheezed when it should have rustled. Above all it was so clearly breathtaking in its constriction that Dundridge found himself almost panting in empathy. Besides Lady Maud's voice had undergone a strange alteration. It was curiously husky.

'How do you like your new flat?' she asked, sitting down beside him with a squeak of pre-stressed silk.

'Flat?' said Dundridge momentarily unable to make the transition between adjective and noun. 'Oh flat. Yes. Very pleasant.'

'You must let me come up and see it some time,' said Lady Maud. 'Unless you feel I might be compromising you.' She sighed, and her great bosom heaved like an approaching breaker.

'Compromising?' said Dundridge, who couldn't imagine that he was likely to be compromised by being alone in his flat with her any more than he was already by those beastly photographs. 'I'd be delighted to have you.'

Lady Maud tittered coyly. 'I'm afraid you're going to miss the excitement of life in London,' she murmured. 'We must do what we can to see that you don't get bored.'

It seemed a remote prospect to Dundridge. He sat rigid on the sofa and tried to keep his eyes averted from the incomprehensible fascinations of her body.

'Let me get you another drink,' she breathed softly, and once again he was conscious of a feeling of being overcome. It was partly the drink, partly the waft of perfume, but it was mostly the strength of her self-assurance that held him fascinated. In spite of her size, in spite of her assertiveness, in spite of everything about her that conflicted with his idea of a beautiful woman, Lady Maud was wholly confident. And Dundridge, who wasn't (or at best only partially and whose completeness, depending on achievement and money, lay in the future) was intoxicated by her presence. If the past could confer such assurance there was more to be said for it than Dundridge had previously admitted. Dundridge sipped his drink and smiled at her. Lady Maud smiled back.

By the time they went in to dinner, Dundridge was incongruously gay. He opened the door for her; he held her arm; he pulled back her chair and nudged it forward against her thighs meaningfully; he opened the champagne with a nonchalance that suggested he seldom drank anything else and laughed debonairly as the cork tinkled among the glass lustres of the chandelier. And through the meal, oysters followed by cold duck, Dundridge no longer cared what the world might think of him. Lady Maud's appreciative smile, half yawn and half abyss, beckoned him on to be himself. And Dundridge was. For the first time in his life he lived up to his own expectations, up to and far beyond. The champagne cork flew a second time into the upper reaches of the room, the duck disappeared to be followed by strawberries and cream, and Dundridge lost the last vestiges of inhibition or even the apprehension that there was anything at all unusual about dining alone with a married woman whose husband was away on business. All such considerations vanished in the bubble of his gaiety and in the light of Lady Maud's approval. Under the table her knee confirmed the implications of her smile; on top her hand lay heavily on his and traced the contours of his fingers; and when, their coffee finished, she took his arm and suggested that they dance Dundridge heard himself say he would be delighted to. Arm-in-arm they went down the passage to the ballroom with the sprung floor. Only then, with the chandeliers lighting the great room brilliantly and a record on the turntable, did he realize what he had let himself in for. Dundridge had never danced in his life.

*

Blott walked down the hill from Wilfrid's Castle. For a week he had been avoiding the Royal George in Guildstead Carbonell and Mrs Wynn's favours. He had taken to going over to a small pub on the lane leading from the church to the Ottertown Road. It wasn't up to the standard of the Royal George, merely a room with benches round the walls and a barrel of Handyman beer in one corner, but its dismal atmosphere suited Blott's mood. By the time he had silently consumed eight pints he was ready for bed. He wobbled up the hill past the church and stood gazing down at the Hall in amazement. The great ball-room lights were on. Blott couldn't remember when he had last seen them on, certainly not since Lady Maud's marriage. They cast yellow rectangles on to the lawn, and the conservatory which opened out of the ballroom glowed green with ferns and palms. He stumbled down the path and across the bridge into the pinetum. Here it was pitch-dark but Blott knew his way instinctively. He came out at the gate and crossed the lawn to the terrace. Music, old-fashioned music, floated out towards him. Blott went round the corner and peered through the window.

Inside Lady Maud was dancing. Or learning to dance. Or teaching someone to dance. Blott found difficulty in making up his mind. Under the great chandeliers she moved with a tender gracelessness that took his breath away. Up and down, round and about, in great sweeps and double turns she went, the floor moving visibly beneath her, and in her arms she held a small thin man with an expression of intense concentration on his face. Blott recognized him. He was the man from the Ministry who had stayed to lunch the previous week. Blott hadn't liked the look of him then and he liked it even less now. And Sir Giles was away. Sick with disgust Blott blundered off the flower bed and away from the window. He had half a mind to go in and say what he thought. It wouldn't do any good. He walked unsteadily round the front of the house. There was a car standing there. He peered at it. The man's car. Serve him right if he had to walk home, the bastard. Blott knelt by the front tyre and undid the valve. Then he went round to the boot and let the air out of the spare tyre. That would teach the swine to come messing about with other people's wives. Blott staggered off down the drive to the Lodge and climbed into bed. Through the circular window he could see the lights of the Hall. They were still on when he fell asleep and through the night air there came the faint sound of trombones.

15

What drinks, dinner and Lady Maud's assiduous coquetry had done for Dundridge, dancing had undone. In particular her interpretation of the hesitation waltz – Dundridge considered the probability of a slipped disc – while her tango had threatened hernia. All his attempts to get her to do something a little less complicated had been ignored.

'You're doing splendidly,' she said treading on his toes. 'All you need is a little practice.'

'What about something modern?' said Dundridge.

'Modern dancing is so unromantic,' said Maud, changing the record to a quickstep. 'There's no intimacy in it.'

Intimacy was not what Dundridge had in mind. 'I think I'll sit this one out,' he said limping to a chair. But Lady Maud wouldn't hear of it. She whirled him on to the floor and strode off through a series of half-turns clasping him to her bosom with a grip that brooked no argument. When the record stopped Dundridge put his foot down politely.

'I really think it is time I was off,' he said.

'What? So early? Just one more teeny weeny glass of champers,' said Lady Maud, relapsing rather prematurely into the language of the nursery.

'Oh all right,' said Dundridge choosing the devil of drink to the deep blue sea of the dance floor. They took their glasses through to the conservatory and stood for a moment among the ferns.

'What a wonderful night. Let's go out on the terrace,' said Lady Maud and took his arm. They leant on the stone balustrade and looked into the darkness of the pinetum.

'All we need now is a lovers' moon,' Lady Maud murmured and turned to face him. Dundridge looked up into the night sky. It was long past his bedtime and besides not even the champagne could disguise the fact that he was in an ambiguous situation. He had had enough of ambiguous situations lately to last him a lifetime and he certainly didn't relish the thought of Sir Giles returning home unexpectedly to find him on the terrace drinking champagne with his wife at one o'clock in the morning.

'It looks as if it's going to rain,' he said to change the topic from lovers' moons.

'Silly boy,' cooed Lady Maud. 'It's a lovely starlit night.'

'Yes. Well, I really do think I must be getting along,' Dundridge insisted. 'It's been a lovely evening.'

'Oh well if you must go . . .' They went indoors again.

'Just one more glass . . .?' Lady Maud said but Dundridge shook his head and limped on down the passage.

'You must look me up again,' said Lady Maud as he climbed into his car. 'The sooner the better. It's been ages since I had so much fun.' She waved goodbye and Dundridge drove off down the drive. He didn't get very far. There was something dreadfully wrong with the steering. The car seemed to veer to the left all the time and there was a thumping sound. Dundridge stopped and got out and went round to the front.

'Damn,' said Dundridge feeling the flat tyre. He went to the boot and got the jack out. By the time he had jacked the car up and taken the left front wheel off, the lights in the Hall had gone out. He fetched the spare wheel from the boot and bolted it into place. He let the jack down and stowed it away. Then he got back into the car and started the engine and drove off. There was a thumping noise and the car pulled to the left. Dundridge stopped with a curse.

'I must have put the flat tyre on again,' he muttered and got out the jack.

*

In the Hall Lady Maud switched off the ballroom lights sadly. She had enjoyed the evening and was sorry it had ended so tamely. There had been a moment earlier in the evening when she had thought Dundridge was going to prove amenable to her few charms.

'Men,' she said contemptuously as she undressed and stood looking at herself dispassionately in the mirror. She was not, and she was the first to admit it, a beautiful woman by contemporary standards of beauty but then she didn't pay much heed to contemporary standards of any sort. The world she lived for had admired substantial things, large women, heavy furniture, healthy appetites and strong feelings. She had no time for the present with its talk of sex, its girlish men and boyish women, and its reducing diets. She longed to be swept off her feet by a strong man who knew the value of bed, board and babies. She wasn't going to find him in Dundridge.

'Silly little goose doesn't know what he's missing,' she said, and climbed into bed.

*

Outside the silly little goose knew only too well what he was missing. An inflated tyre. He had changed the wheel again and had let down the jack only to find that his spare tyre had been flat after all. He got back into the car and tried to think what to do. Nearby something moved heavily through the grass and a night bird called. Dundridge shut the door. He couldn't sit there all night. He got out of the car and trudged back up the drive to the house and rang the doorbell.

Upstairs Lady Maud climbed out of bed and turned on the light. So the silly little goose had come back after all. He had caught her unprepared. She grabbed a lipstick and daubed her lips hastily, powdered her face and put a dollop of Chanel behind each ear. Finally she changed out of her pyjamas and slid into a see-through nightdress and went downstairs and opened the door.

'I'm sorry to bother you like this but I'm afraid I've had a puncture,' said Dundridge nervously. Lady Maud smiled knowingly.

'A puncture?'

'Yes, two as a matter of fact.'

'Two punctures?'

'Yes. Two,' said Dundridge conscious that there was something rather improbable about having two punctures at the same time.

'You had better come in,' said Lady Maud eagerly. Dundridge hesitated.

'If I could just use the phone to call a garage . . .'

But Lady Maud wouldn't hear of it. 'Of course you can't,' she said, 'it's far too late for anyone to come out now.' She took his arm and led him into the house and closed the door.

'I'm terribly sorry to be such a nuisance,' said Dundridge but Lady Maud shushed him.

'What a silly boy you are,' she cooed. 'Now come upstairs and we'll see about a bed.'

'Oh really . . .' Dundridge began but it was no good. She turned and led the way, a perfumed spinnaker, up the marble staircase. Dundridge followed miserably.

'You can have this room,' she said as they stood on the landing and she switched on the light. 'Now you go down to the bathroom and have a wash and I'll make the bed up.'

'The bathroom?' said Dundridge gazing at her astonished. In the dim light of the hall Lady Maud had been a mere if substantial shape but now he could see the full extent of her abundant charms. Her face was extraordinary too. Lady Maud smiled, a crimson gash with teeth. And the perfume!

'It's down the corridor on the left.'

Dundridge stumbled down the corridor and tried several doors before he found the bathroom. He went inside and locked the door. When he came out he found the corridor in darkness. He groped his way back to the landing and tried to remember which room she had given him. Finally he found one that was open. It was dark inside. Dundridge felt for the switch but it wasn't where he had expected.

'Is there anyone there?' he whispered but there was no reply. 'This must be the room,' he muttered and closed the door. He edged across the room and felt the end of the bed. A faint light came from the window. Dundridge undressed and noticed that Lady Maud's perfume still lingered heavily on the air. He went across to the window and opened it and then, moving carefully so as not to stub his toes, he went back and got into bed. As he did so he knew there was something terribly wrong. A blast of Chanel No. 5 issued from the bedclothes overpoweringly. So did Lady Maud. Her arms closed round him and with a husky, 'Oh you wicked boy,' her mouth descended on his. The next moment Dundridge was engulfed. Things seemed to fold round him, huge hot terrible things, legs, arms, breasts, lips, noses, thighs, bearing him up, entwining him, and bearing him down again in a frenzy of importunate flesh. He floundered frantically while the waves of Lady Maud's mistaken response broke over him. Only his mind remained untrammelled, his mind and his inhibitions. As he writhed in her arms his thoughts raced to a number of ghastly conclusions. He had chosen the wrong room; she was in love with him; he was in bed with a nymphomaniac; she was providing her husband with grounds for divorce; she was seducing him. There was no question about the last. She was seducing him. Her hands left him in no doubt about that, particularly her left hand. And Dundridge, accustomed to the wholly abstract stimulus of his composite woman, found the inexperience of a real woman – and Lady Maud was both real and inexperienced – hard to put up with.

'There's been a terr—' he managed to squeak as Lady Maud surfaced for air, but a moment later her mouth closed over his, silencing his protest while threatening him with suffocation. It was this last that gave him the desperation he needed. With a truly Herculean revulsion Dundridge hurled himself and Lady Maud, still clinging limpetlike to him, out of the bed. With a crash the bedside table fell to the floor as Dundridge broke free and leapt to his feet. The next moment he was through the door and running down the corridor. Behind him Lady Maud staggered to the bed and pulled the light cord. Stunned by the vigour of his rejection and by the bedside table which had caught her on the side of the head, she lumbered into the corridor and turned on the light but there was no sign of Dundridge.

'There's no need to be shy,' she called but there was no reply. She went into the next room and switched on the light. No Dundridge. The next room was empty too. She went from room to room switching on lights and calling his name, but Dundridge had vanished. Even the bathroom was unlocked and empty and she was just wondering where to look next when a sound from the landing drew her attention. She went back and switched on the hall light and caught him in the act of tiptoeing down the stairs. For an instant he stood there, a petrified satyr, and turned pathetic eyes towards her and then he was off down the stairs and across the marble floor, his slender legs and pale feet twinkling among the squares. Lady Maud leant over the balustrade and laughed. She was still laughing as she went down the staircase, laughing and holding on to the banister to keep herself from falling. Her laughter echoed in the emptiness of the hall and filtered down the corridors.

In the darkness by the kitchen Dundridge listened to it and shuddered. He had no idea where he was and there was a demented quality about that laughter that appalled him. He was just wondering what to do when, silhouetted against the hall light at the end of the passage he saw her bulky outline. She had stopped laughing and was peering into the gloom.

'It's all right, you can come out now,' she called, but Dundridge knew better. He understood now why his car had two flat tyres, why he had been invited to the Hall when Sir Giles was away. Lady Maud was a raving nymphomaniac. He was alone in a huge house in the middle of the back of beyond with no clothes on, a disabled car and an enormously powerful and naked female lunatic. Nothing on God's earth would induce him to come out now. As Lady Maud lumbered down the passage Dundridge turned and fled, collided with a table, lurched into some iron banisters and was off up the servants' stairs. Behind him a light went on. As he reached the landing he glanced back and saw Lady Maud's face staring up at him. One glance was enough to confirm his fears. The smudged lipstick, the patches of rouge, the disordered hair . . . mad as a hatter. Dundridge scampered down another corridor and behind him came the final proof of her madness.

'Tally ho,' shouted Lady Maud. 'Gone away.' Dundridge went away as fast as he could.

*

In the Lodge, Blott woke up and stared out through the circular window. Dimly below the rim of the hills he could see the dark shape of the Hall and he was about to turn over and go back to sleep when a light came on in an upstairs room to be followed almost immediately by another and then a third. Blott sat up in bed and watched as one room after another lit up. He glanced at his clock and saw it was ten past two. He looked back towards the house and saw the stained glass roof-light above the hall glowing. He got up and opened the window and stared out and as he did so there came the faint sound of hysterical laughter. Or crying. Lady Maud. Blott pulled on a pair of trousers, put on his slippers, took his twelve-bore and ran downstairs. There was something terribly wrong up at the house. He ran up the drive, almost colliding in the darkness with Dundridge's car. The bastard was still around. Probably chasing her from room to room. That would explain the lights going on and the hysterical laughter. He'd soon put a stop to that. Clutching his shotgun he went through the stable yard and in the kitchen door. The lights were on. Blott went across to the passage and listened. There was no sound now. He went down the passage to the hall and stood there. Must be upstairs. He was halfway up when Lady Maud emerged from a corridor on to the landing breathlessly. She ran across the landing to the top of the stairs and stood looking down at Blott naked as the day she was born. Blott gaped up at her open mouthed. There above him was the woman he loved. Clothed she had been splendid. Naked she was perfection. Her great breasts, her stomach, her magnificent thighs, she was everything Blott had ever dreamed of and, to make matters even better, she was clearly in distress. Tear-stains ran down her daubed cheeks. His moment of heroism on her behalf had arrived.

'Blott,' said Lady Maud, 'what on earth are you doing here? And what are you doing with that gun?'

'I am here at your service,' said Blott gallantly assuming the language of history.

'At my service?' said Lady Maud, oblivious of the fact that she wasn't exactly dressed for discussions about service with her gardener. 'What do you mean by my service? You're here to look after the garden, not to wander about the house in the middle of the night in your bedroom slippers armed with a shotgun.'

On the staircase Blott bowed before the storm. 'I came to protect your honour,' he murmured.

'My honour? You came to protect my honour? With a shotgun? Are you out of your mind?'

Blott was beginning to wonder. He had come up expecting to find her lying raped and murdered, or at least pleading for mercy, and here she was standing naked at the top of the stairs dressing him down. It didn't seem right. It didn't seem exactly right to Lady Maud now that she came to think of it. She turned and went into her bedroom and put on a dressing-gown.

'Now then,' she said with a renewed sense of authority, 'what's all this nonsense about my honour?'

'I thought I heard you call for help,' Blott mumbled.

'Call for help indeed,' she snorted. 'You heard nothing of the sort. You've been drinking. I've spoken to you about drinking before and I don't want to mention it again. And what's more when I need any help protecting my so-called honour, which God knows I most certainly don't, I won't ask you to come up here with a twelve-bore. Now then go back to the Lodge and go to bed. I don't want to hear any more about this nonsense, do you understand?'

Blott nodded and slunk down the staircase.

'And you can turn the lights off down there as you go.'

'Yes, ma'am,' said Blott and went down the passage to the kitchen filled with a new and terrible sense of injustice. He turned the kitchen light off and went back to the ballroom and switched off the chandeliers. Then he made his way through the conservatory to the terrace and was about to shut the door when he glimpsed a figure cowering among the ferns. It was the man from the Ministry, and like Lady Maud he was naked. Blott slammed the door and went off down the terrace steps, his mind seething with dreams of revenge. He had come up to the house with the best of intentions to protect his beloved mistress from the sexual depravity of that beastly little man and instead he had been blamed and abused and told he was drunk. It was all so unfair. In the middle of the park he paused and aimed the shotgun into the air and fired both barrels. That was what he thought of the bloody world. That was all that the bloody world understood. Force. He stamped off across the field to the Lodge and went upstairs to his room.

*

To Dundridge, still cowering in the conservatory, the sound of the shotgun came as final proof that Lady Maud's intentions towards him were homicidal. He had been lured to the Hall, his tyres had been punctured, he had suffered attempted rape, he had been chased naked around the house by a laughing and demented woman and now he was being hunted by a man with a gun. And finally he was in danger of freezing to death. He stayed in the conservatory for twenty minutes anxiously listening for any sounds that might indicate pursuit, but the house was silent. He crept out from his hiding-place and went through the door to the terrace and peered outside. There was no sign of the man with the gun. He would have to take a chance. There was a light look about the eastern sky which suggested the coming of dawn and he had to get away while it was still dark. He ran across the terrace and scampered down the steps towards his car.

Two minutes later he was in the driver's seat and had started the engine. He drove off as fast as the flat tyre would allow, crouching low and waiting for the blast of the shotgun. But nothing came and he passed under the Lodge and into the darkness of the wood. He switched on the headlights, negotiated the suspension bridge and headed up the hill, his flat tyre thumping on the road and the steering pulling violently to the left. Around him the Cleene Forest closed in, his headlights picked out monstrous shapes and weird shadows but Dundridge had lost his terror of the wild landscape. Anything was preferable to the human horrors he had left behind and even when two miles further on the tyre finally came away from the rim and he had to jack the car up and change it for the other flat spare he did so without hesitation. After that he drove more slowly and reached Worford as dawn broke. He parked his car on the double yellow line outside his flat, made sure there was nobody about and flitted across the pavement and down the alley to the outside stairs that led up to his apartment. Even here he was baulked. The key of his flat was in the pocket of his dinner-jacket.

Dundridge stood on the landing outside his door, naked, shivering and livid. Deprived of dignity, pretensions, authority and reason, Dundridge was almost human. For a moment he hesitated and then with a sudden ferocity he hurled himself against the door. At the second attempt the lock gave. He went inside slamming it to behind him. He had made up his mind. Come hell or high water he would do his damnedest to see that the route of the motorway was changed. They could bribe him and blackmail him for all they were worth but he'd get his own back. By the time he had finished that fat insane bitch would laugh on the other side of her filthy face.

16

His opportunity came sooner than he had expected and from an unforeseen quarter. Overwhelmed by the volume of complaints arriving at his office from the tenants of the seventy-five council houses due for demolition, harried by the Ottertown Town Council, infuriated by the refusal of the Minister of the

Environment to re-open the Enquiry, and warned by his doctors that unless he curtailed most of his activities his heart would end them all, Francis Puckerington resigned his seat in Parliament. Sir Giles was the first to congratulate him on the wisdom of his withdrawal from public life. 'Wish I could do the same myself,' he said, 'but you know how things are.'

Mr Puckerington didn't but he had a shrewd idea that lurking behind Sir Giles' benevolent concern there was financial advantage. Lady Maud shared his suspicion. Ever since the Enquiry there had been something strange about Giles' manner, an air of expectation and suppressed excitement about him which she found disturbing. Several times she had noticed him looking at her with a smile on his face and when Sir Giles smiled it usually meant that something unpleasant was about to happen. What it was she couldn't imagine and since she took no interest in politics the likely consequences of Mr Puckerington's resignation escaped her. Hoskins was understandably more informed. He realized at once why Sir Giles had agreed so readily to the Ottertown route. 'Brilliant,' he told him when he saw him at the Golf Club. Sir Giles looked mystified.

'I don't know what you're talking about. I had no idea the poor fellow was so ill. A great loss to the party.'

'My eye and Betty Martin,' said Hoskins.

'I'd rather have your Bessie Williams myself,' Sir Giles said, relaxing a little. 'I trust she is keeping well?'

'Very well. She and her husband took a holiday in Majorca I believe.'

'Sensible of them,' Sir Giles said. 'So our young friend Dundridge must be a little puzzled by now. No harm in keeping him hanging in the wind, as someone once put it.'

'He's probably blown that money you gave him.'

'I gave him?' said Sir Giles who preferred not to let his right hand know what his left was doing.

'Say no more,' said Hoskins. 'I'll tell you one thing though. He's lost all interest in your wife.'

Sir Giles sighed. 'Such a pity,' he said. 'There was a time

when I entertained the hope that he would . . . One can't expect miracles. Still, it was a nice thought.'

'He's got it in for her now, anyway. Hates her guts.'

'I wonder why,' said Sir Giles thoughtfully. 'Ah well, it happens to us all in the end. Still, it couldn't have come at a better time.'

'That's what I thought,' said Hoskins. 'He's already sent three memoranda to the Ministry asking for the motorway to be re-routed through the Gorge.'

'Quite the little weathercock, isn't he? I trust you tried to dissuade him.'

'Every time. Every time.'

'But not too hard, eh?'

Hoskins smiled. 'I try to keep an open mind on the matter.'

'Very wise of you,' said Sir Giles. 'No point in getting yourself involved. Well, things seem to be moving.'

*

Things certainly were. In London Francis Puckerington's resignation had immediate repercussions.

'Seventy-five council houses due for demolition in a constituency with a bye-election pending?' said the Prime Minister. 'And what did you say his last majority was?'

'Forty-five,' said the Chief Whip. 'A marginal seat.'

'Marginal be damned. It's lost.'

'It does rather look that way,' the Chief Whip agreed. 'Of course if the motorway could be re-routed . . .'

The Prime Minister reached for the phone.

*

Ten minutes later Mr Rees sent for Mr Joynson.

'Done it,' he said beaming delightedly.

'Done what?'

'Pulled the fat out of the fire. The Ottertown scheme is dead and buried. The M101 is going ahead through the Cleene Gorge.'

'Oh, that is good news,' said Mr Joynson. 'How on earth did you do it?'

'Just a question of patience and gentle persuasion. Ministers may come and Ministers may go but in the end they do tend to see the errors of their ways.'

'I suppose this means you'll be recalling Dundridge,' said Mr Joynson, who was inclined to look on the dark side of things.

'Not on your Nelly,' said Mr Rees, 'Dundridge is coping very well. I look forward to his perpetual absence.'

*

Dundridge received the news with mixed emotions. On the one hand here was his golden opportunity to teach that bitch Lady Maud a lesson. On the other the knowledge that he had accepted a bribe from Sir Giles bothered him. He looked forward to Lady Maud's misery when she learnt that Handyman Hall was going to be demolished after all but he didn't relish the thought of her husband's reaction. He need not have worried. Sir Giles, anxious to be out of the way when the storm broke, had taken the precaution of being tied up in London in advance of the announcement. In any case Hoskins was reassuring.

'You don't have to worry about Giles,' he told Dundridge. 'It's Maud who'll be out for blood.'

Dundridge knew exactly what he meant. 'If she calls I'm not in,' he told the girl on the switchboard. 'Remember that. I am never in to Lady Maud.'

While Hoskins concentrated on the actual details of the new route and arranged for the posting of advance notices of compulsory purchase, Dundridge spent much of his time on field work, which meant in fact sitting in his flat and not answering the telephone. To occupy his mind and to lend some sort of credence to his title of Controller Motorways Midlands, he set about devising a strategy for dealing with the campaign to stop construction which he was convinced Lady Maud would initiate.

'Surprise is of the essence,' he explained to Hoskins.

'She's had that already,' Hoskins pointed out. He had in his time supervised the eviction of too many obstinate householders to be daunted by the threat of Lady Maud, and besides he was relying on Sir Giles to undermine her efforts. 'She's not going to give us any trouble. You'll see. When it comes to the push she'll go. They all do. It's the law.' Dundridge wasn't convinced. From his personal experience he knew how little the law meant to Lady Maud.

'The thing is to move quickly,' he explained.

'Move quickly?' said Hoskins. 'You can't move quickly when you're building a motorway. It's a slow process.'

Dundridge waved his objections aside. 'We must hit at key objectives. Seize the commanding heights. Maintain the initiative,' he said grandly.

Hoskins looked at him doubtfully. He wasn't used to this sort of military language. 'Look, old boy, I know how you feel and all that but . . .'

'You don't,' said Dundridge vehemently.

'But what I was going to say was that there's no need to go in for anything complicated. Just let things take their natural course and you'll find people will get used to the idea. It's amazing how adaptable people are.'

'That's precisely what's worrying me,' said Dundridge. 'Now then the essence of my plan is to make random sorties.'

'Random sorties?' said Hoskins. 'What on earth with?'

'Bulldozers,' said Dundridge and spread out a map of the district.

'Bulldozers? You can't have bulldozers roaming the countryside making random sorties,' said Hoskins, now thoroughly alarmed. 'What the hell are they going to randomly sort?'

'Vital areas of control,' said Dundridge, 'lines of communication. Bridgeheads.'

'Bridgeheads? But—'

'As I see it,' Dundridge continued implacably, 'the main centre of resistance is going to be here.' He pointed to the Cleene Gorge. 'Strategically this is the vital area. Seize that and we've won.'

'Seize it? You can't suddenly go in and seize the Cleene Gorge!' shouted Hoskins. 'The motorway has to proceed by deliberate stages. Contractors work according to a schedule and we have to keep to that.'

'That is precisely the mistake you're making,' said Dundridge. 'Our tactics must be to alter the schedule just when the enemy least expects it.'

'But that's impossible,' Hoskins insisted. 'You can't go about knocking people's houses down without giving them fair warning.'

'Who said anything about knocking houses down?' said Dundridge indignantly. 'I certainly didn't. What I have in mind is something entirely different. Now then what we'll do is this.'

For the next half hour he outlined his grand strategy while Hoskins listened. When he had finished Hoskins was impressed in spite of himself. He had been quite wrong to call Dundridge a nincompoop. In his own peculiar way the man had flair.

'All the same I just hope it doesn't have to come to that,' he said finally.

'You'll see,' said Dundridge. 'That bitch isn't going to sit back and let us put a motorway through her wretched house without putting up a struggle. She's going to fight to the bitter end.'

Hoskins went back to his office thoughtfully. There was nothing illegal about Dundridge's plan in spite of the military jargon. In a way it was extremely shrewd.

*

The Committee for the Preservation of the Cleene Gorge met under the Presidency of General Burnett at Handyman Hall. Lady Maud was the first speaker.

'I intend to fight this project to the bitter end,' she said, fulfilling Dundridge's prediction. 'I have no intention of being driven from my own home simply because a lot of bureaucratic dunderheads in London take it into their thick skulls to ignore the recommendations of a properly constituted Enquiry. It's outrageous.'

'It's so unfair,' said Mrs Bullett-Finch, 'particularly after what Lord Leakham said about preserving the wildlife of the area. What I can't understand is why they changed their minds so suddenly.'

'As I see it,' said General Burnett, 'the change is a direct consequence of Puckerington's resignation. I have it on the highest authority that the Government felt that the new candidate was bound to lose the bye-election if they went ahead with the route through Ottertown.'

'Why did Puckerington resign?' asked Miss Percival.

'Ill-health,' said Colonel Chapman. 'He's got a dicky heart.'

Lady Maud said nothing. What she had just heard explained a great many things and suggested more. She knew now why Sir Giles had smiled so secretively at her and why he had had that air of expectation. Everything suddenly fell into place in her mind. She understood why he had been so alarmed about the possibility of a tunnel, why he had insisted on Ottertown, why he had been so pleased at Lord Leakham's decision. Above all, she realized for the first time the full enormity of his betrayal. Colonel Chapman put her thoughts into numbers.

'I suppose there is this to be said for it. I've heard a rumour that we are going to get increased compensation,' he said. 'The figure mentioned was twenty per cent. That makes your sum, Lady Maud, something in the region of three hundred thousand pounds.'

Lady Maud sat rigid in her chair. Three hundred thousand pounds. It was not her share. Sir Giles owned the Hall. Owned it and had put it up for sale in the only way legally available to him. Faced with such treachery there was nothing left for her to say. She shook her head wearily and while the discussion continued round her she stared out of the window to where Blott was mowing the lawn.

The meeting broke up without any decision being taken on the next move.

'Poor old Maud seems quite broken up about this dreadful business,' General Burnett said to Mrs Bullett-Finch as they walked across the drive to their cars. 'It's knocked all the spirit out of her. Bad business.'

'One does feel so terribly sorry for her,' Mrs Bullett-Finch agreed.

*

Lady Maud watched them leave and then went back into the

house to think. Committees would achieve nothing now. They would talk and pass resolutions but when the time for taking action came they would still be talking. Colonel Chapman had given the game away by talking about money. They would settle.

She went down the passage to the study and stood there looking round the room. It was here that Giles had thought the whole thing out, in this sanctum, at this desk where her father and grandfather had sat, and it was here that she would sit and think until she had planned some way of stopping the motorway and of destroying him. In her mind the two things were inextricably linked. Giles had conceived the idea of the motorway, he would be broken by it. There was no compunction left in her. She had been outwitted and betrayed by a man she had always despised. She had sold herself to him to preserve the house and the family and the knowledge of her own guilt added force to her determination. If need be she would sell herself to the devil to stop him now. Lady Maud sat down behind the desk and stared at the filigree of her grandfather's silver ink-stand for inspiration. It was shaped like a lion's head. An hour later she had found the solution she was looking for. She reached for the phone and was about to pick it up when it rang. It was Sir Giles calling from London.

'I just thought I had better let you know I shan't be back this weekend,' he said. 'I know it is a damned inconvenient time for me to be away with all this motorway business going on, but I really can't get away.'

'That's all right,' said Lady Maud, feigning her usual degree of indifference, 'I daresay I'll be able to cope without you.'

'How are things going?'

'We've just had a committee meeting to discuss the next move. We are thinking of organizing protest meetings round the county.'

'That's the sort of thing we need,' said Sir Giles. 'I'm doing my damnedest down here to get the Ministry to reconsider. Keep up the good work at your end.' He rang off. Lady Maud smiled grimly. She would keep up the good work all right. And he could go on doing his damnedest. She picked up the phone and dialled. In the next two hours she spoke to her bank manager, the Head Keeper at Whipsnade Zoo, the Game Warden at Woburn Wildlife Park, the managers of five small private zoos and a firm of fencing experts in Birmingham. Finally she went outside to look for Blott.

Ever since the night of Dundridge's visit she had been worried by Blott's attitude. It hadn't been like him to behave like that and she had been alarmed by the sound of the shotgun going off outside. She rather regretted what she had said about his drinking too. It certainly hadn't had any good effect. If anything he had taken to going off to the Royal George more often and late one night she had heard him singing in the pinetum. 'Typically Italian,' she thought, confusing 'Wir Fahren Gegen England' with *La Traviata*. 'Probably pining for Naples.' But Blott stumbling through the park was merely drunk and if he was pining for anything it was for her innocence which Dundridge's visit had destroyed.

She found him, as she had expected, in the kitchen garden. 'Blott,' she said, 'I want you to do something for me.'

Blott grunted morosely. 'What?'

'You know the wall safe in the study?' Blott nodded. 'I want you to open it for me.'

Blott shook his head and went on weeding the onion bed. 'Not possible without the combination,' he said.

'If I had the combination I wouldn't have to ask you to open it,' Lady Maud said tartly. Blott shrugged. 'If I don't know the combination,' he said, 'how do I open it?'

'You blow it open,' said Lady Maud. Blott straightened up and looked at her.

'Blow it open?'

'With explosive. Use a . . . what are those things with flames . . . oxy . . .'

'Acetylene torch,' said Blott. 'It wouldn't work.'

'I don't mind how you do it. You can pull it out of the wall

123

and drop it from the roof for all I care but I want that safe opened. I've got to know what is inside it.'

Blott pushed back his hat and scratched his head. This was a new Lady Maud speaking. 'Why don't you ask him for the combination?' he said.

'Him?' said Lady Maud with a new contempt. 'Because I don't want him to know. That's why.'

'He'll know it if we blow it open,' Blott pointed out.

Lady Maud thought for a moment. 'We can always say it was burglars,' she said finally.

Blott considered the implications of this remark and found them to his liking. 'Yes, we could do that. Let's go and have a look at it.'

They went into the house and stood in the study examining the safe which was set into the wall behind some books.

'Difficult,' said Blott. He went into the dining-room next door and looked at the wall on that side. 'It's going to do a lot of damage,' he said when he came back.

'Do whatever damage you have to. The house is coming down if we don't do something. What does it matter if we do some damage to it now? It can always be repaired.'

'Ah,' said Blott, who had begun to understand. 'Then I'll use a sledgehammer.' He went round to the workshop in the yard and returned with a sledgehammer, a metal wedge and a crowbar.

'You're quite sure?' he asked. Lady Maud nodded. Blott swung the sledgehammer against the dining-room wall. Half an hour later the safe was out of the wall. Together they carried it outside and laid it on the drive. It was quite small. Blott twiddled the knob idly and tried to think what next to do.

'What we need is some high-explosive,' he said. 'Dynamite would do it.'

'We haven't got any dynamite,' Lady Maud pointed out. 'And you can't go into a shop and buy it. You couldn't bore a hole in it and hoik things out with a wire?'

'Too thick and the steel is too hard,' said Blott. 'It's like armour-plate on a tank.' He stopped. Like a tank. Somewhere among the armoury of weapons he had collected during the war there was a rocket-launcher. It was in a long wooden box and labelled PIAT. Projectile Infantry Anti-Tank. Now where had he buried it?

17

As dusk fell over the Cleene Gorge Blott left the Lodge with a spade. He had had his supper, sausages and mashed potatoes, and was comfortably full. Above all he was happy. As he followed the park wall round to the west and found the exact spot where he had climbed over as a prisoner of war he was boyishly excited. There had been a piece of iron fencing which he had propped against the wall to give himself a leg-up. It was still there, rusting in a patch of stinging-nettles. Blott dragged it out and leant it against the wall and climbed up. The barbed-wire had gone but as he straddled the top of the wall and dropped down on the other side he had the same feeling of freedom he had experienced night after night over thirty years before. Not that he had disliked life in the camp. He had felt freer then than at any time before. To sneak out at night and roam the woods on his own was to escape from the orphanage in Dresden and all the petty restrictions of his dreadful childhood. It had been to cock a snook at authority and to be himself.

And so it was now as he pushed through the bracken and began to climb through the trees. He was doing the forbidden thing again and he exulted in it. Half a mile up the hillside he came to a clearing. You turned left here. Blott turned left, following the old instinct as surely as if there had been a path there, and came out into the setting sunlight behind a mound of stones that had once been a cottage. Here he turned up the hill again until he found the tree he was looking for. It was a large old oak. Blott went round the trunk and found the slash he had made in the bark. He walked away from the tree, counting his paces. Then he took off his jacket and began to dig. It

125

took him an hour to get down to the cache but it was there exactly where he had recalled. He pulled out a box and prised the lid open with a hammer. Inside caked in grease and wrapped in oilskin was a two-inch mortar. He dragged out another box. Mortar bombs. Finally he found what he was looking for. The long box and the four cases of armour-piercing rockets. He sat down on the box and wondered what to do next. Now that he came to think about it, all he needed were the rockets. All he had to do was to tie a piece of string to the fin and drop it from a height on to the safe. That would do the trick just as well as firing the rocket at the safe.

Still, he had come so far, he might as well take the PIAT home with him and clean it up. It would make an interesting souvenir. Blott put the mortar back with the cases of bombs, and covered them with earth. Then he went back down the hill with the long box. It was very heavy and he had to stop fairly frequently to rest. By the time he got back to the Lodge it was dark. He humped the box up to his room and went back for the rockets. He didn't take those up to his room but left them in the grass outside. He didn't feel like sleeping beside some rockets that were thirty years old.

In the morning he was up early and busy in the Gorge. He fetched the safe down on a wheelbarrow and stood it upright at the bottom of the cliff. Then he took a long piece of twine and tied it to the knob of the combination lock before going back up the cliff with it and attaching it to an overhanging branch so that it ran in a straight line some fifty feet down to the safe. Finally he fetched two of the finned projectiles and tied a short length of string to the fin of the first. At the other end of the string he tied a small ring, undid the twine and fitted the ring over it and tied it back on to the branch. Then he lay down at the top of the cliff and removed the cap from the detonator on the nose of the rocket. Blott peered over the edge. There was the safe directly below. He held the PIAT bomb out and let go and watched as it plummeted down the twine. The next moment there was a flash and a roar. Blott shut his eyes and pulled his head back and as he did so something hurtled past him into the air above. He looked up. The fin of the rocket reached its peak, curved over and fell into the road behind him. Blott got up and went down to the safe. The bomb had missed the combination lock but it had done its job. A small hole the size of a pencil was blown in the front of the safe and the door was loose.

Lady Maud was having breakfast when the blast came. For a moment she thought Blott was out shooting rabbits but there had been a concussion and an echo about the explosion that had suggested something more powerful than a shotgun. She went outside and saw Blott coming down the cliff path on the other side of the river. Of course, the safe. He had sworn he would blow it open and that's what he had done. She ran across the lawn and through the pinetum and over the footbridge.

Blott was bending over the safe when she came up.

'Have you done it?' she asked.

'Yes, it's open,' said Blott, 'but there's nothing much in it.' Lady Maud could see that. The safe was much smaller inside than she had expected and it appeared to be filled with burnt, charred and torn fragments of paper. She reached in and picked one out. It was a portion of what had once been a photograph. She held it up and looked at it. It appeared to be the legs of a naked man. She reached in and took out another piece, this time an arm, a bare arm and what looked like a woman's breast. She peered into the safe again but apart from the shreds of photographs there was nothing inside.

'I'll go and get an envelope,' Lady Maud said. 'Don't touch anything until I get back.' She walked off thoughtfully towards the Hall while Blott went back to the top of the cliff and collected the unused PIAT bomb. At least he knew now that they worked. 'Might come in handy,' he said to himself and took it back to the Lodge.

An hour later the safe was buried under some bushes at the base of the cliff and Blott had gone back to the kitchen garden. In the study Lady Maud sat at the desk and examined the fragments of photographs, trying to sort out which portion of anatomy fitted the next. It was a difficult task and an un-edifying one. The photographs were too charred and torn to be reassembled properly and besides the force of the explosion had decapitated the participants in what even on this slender evidence appeared to be a series of extremely unnatural acts. And slender was the word. Certainly in the case of the man. That ruled out Sir Giles. It was a pity. She could have done with some photographic proof of his obscene habits. She picked up another fragment and was about to look for the appropriate place in the jigsaw puzzle where it would fit when she suddenly realized where she had seen those slender legs and pale feet. Of course. Twinkling across the marble floor of the hall. She looked again at the portion of leg, at the arm. She was certain now. Dundridge. Dundridge engaged in . . . It was unthinkable. She was just trying to work out what this extraordinary idea implied when the front doorbell rang. She went out and opened the door. It was the manager of the high-security fencing company.

'Ah, good,' said Lady Maud. 'Now then, to business. I'll show you exactly what I want.' They went inside to the billiard room and Lady Maud unrolled a map of the estate. 'I am opening a wildlife park,' she explained. 'I want a fence extending the entire perimeter of the park. It must be absolutely secure and proof against any sort of animal.'

'But I understood . . .' the manager began.

'Never mind what you understood,' said Lady Maud. 'Just understand that I am opening a wildlife park in three weeks' time.'

'In three weeks? That's out of the question.'

Lady Maud rolled up the map. 'In that case I shall employ someone else,' she said. 'Some enterprising firm that can erect a suitable fence . . .'

'You won't get any firm to do it in three weeks,' said the manager. 'Not unless you pay a fortune.'

'I am prepared to pay a fortune,' said Lady Maud.

The manager looked at her and rubbed his jaw. 'Three weeks?' he said.

'Three weeks,' said Lady Maud.

The manager took out a notebook and made some calculations. 'This is simply a rough estimate,' he said finally, 'but I would say somewhere in the region of twenty-five thousand pounds.'

'Say thirty and be done with it,' said Lady Maud. 'Thirty thousand pounds for the fence to be completed in three weeks from today with a bonus of one thousand a day for every day under three weeks and a penalty clause of two thousand pounds for every day after three weeks.'

The manager gaped at her. 'I suppose you know what you're doing,' he muttered.

'I know precisely what I'm doing, thank you very much,' said Lady Maud. 'What is more you will work day and night. You will bring your materials in at night. I don't want any lorries coming here during the day and you will house your men here. I will provide accommodation. You will see to their bedding and their food. This whole operation must be done in the strictest secrecy.'

'If you don't mind,' said the manager and sat down in a chair. Lady Maud sat down opposite him.

'Well?'

'I don't know,' said the manager. 'It *can* be done . . .'

'It will be,' Lady Maud assured him. 'Either by you or someone else.'

'You realize that if we were to finish the job in a fortnight the cost would have risen to thirty-seven thousand pounds.'

'And I should be delighted. And if you can finish in a week I shall be happy to pay forty-two thousand pounds,' she said. 'Are we agreed?' The manager nodded. 'Right, in that case I shall make out a cheque to you for ten thousand now and two post-dated cheques for the same amount. I trust that will be a sufficient earnest of my good faith.' She went through to the study and wrote out the cheques. 'I shall expect the arrival of materials tonight and work to begin at once. You can bring the contract tomorrow for me to sign.'

The manager went out and got into his car in a state of

shock. 'Mad as a March bloody hare,' he muttered as he drove down the drive.

Behind him Lady Maud went back to the study and sat down. It was costing more than she had anticipated but it was worth every penny. And then there was the price of the animals. Lions didn't come cheap. Nor did a rhinoceros. And finally there was the puzzle of the photographs. What were obscene pictures of Mr Dundridge doing in Giles' safe? She got up and went out into the garden and walked up and down the path by the wall of the kitchen garden. And suddenly it dawned on her. It explained everything and in particular why Dundridge had changed his mind about the tunnel. The wretched little man had been blackmailed. Well, two could play at that game. By God they could. She went through the door into the kitchen garden.

'Has my husband ever put through a call to a woman in London?' she asked Blott.

'His secretary,' said Blott. Lady Maud shook her head. Sir Giles' secretary wasn't the sort of woman who would take kindly to the suggestion that she should tie her employer to a bed and beat him and in any case she was happily married.

'Anyone else?'

'No.'

'Has he ever mentioned a woman in any of his conversations on the phone?'

Blott tried to remember. 'No, I don't think so.'

'In that case, Blott,' she said, 'you and I are going to London tomorrow.'

Blott gazed at her in astonishment. 'To London?' He had never been to London.

'To London. We shall be away for a few days.'

'But what shall I wear?' said Blott.

'A suit of course.'

'I haven't got one,' said Blott.

'Well then,' said Lady Maud, 'we had better go into Worford and get you one. And while we're about it we'll get a camera as well. I'll pick you up in ten minutes.'

She went back into the house and put the photographs into an envelope and hid it behind a set of Jorrocks on the bookshelf. It might be worth paying Mr Dundridge a visit while she was in Worford.

18

But Dundridge was not to be found in Worford. 'He's out,' said the girl at the Regional Planning Board.

'Where?' said Lady Maud.

'Inspecting the site,' said the girl.

'Well, kindly tell him when he comes back that I have some sights I would like him to inspect.'

The girl looked at her. 'I'm sure I don't know what you mean,' she said nastily. Lady Maud suppressed the reaction to tell the little hussy exactly what she did mean.

'Tell Mr Dundridge that I have a number of photographs in which I feel sure he will take a particular interest. You had better write it down before you forget it. Tell him that. He knows where he can find me.'

She went back to the outfitters where Blott was trying on a salmon-pink suit of Harris Tweed. 'If you think I'm going to be seen with you in London in that revolting article of menswear, you've got another think coming,' she snorted. She ran an eye over a number of less conspicuous suits and finally selected a dark grey pinstripe. 'That'll do.' By the time they left the shop Blott was fitted out with shirts, socks, underwear and ties. They called at a shoe shop and bought a pair of black shoes.

'And now all we need is a camera,' said Lady Maud as they stowed Blott's new clothes in the back of the Land-Rover. They went into a camera shop.

'I want a camera with an excellent lens,' she told the assistant, 'one that can be operated by a complete idiot.'

'You need an automatic camera,' said the man.

'No, she doesn't,' said Blott who resented being called a complete idiot in front of strangers. 'She means a Leica.'

'A Leica?' said the man. 'But that's not a camera for a novice. That's a . . .'

'Blott,' said Lady Maud, taking him out on to the pavement, 'do you mean to say that you know how to take photographs?'

'In the Luft . . . before the war I was trained in photography. I was . . .'

Lady Maud beamed at him. 'Oh Blott,' she said, 'you're a godsend. An absolute godsend. Go and buy whatever you need to take good clear photographs.'

'What of?' asked Blott. Lady Maud hesitated. Oh well, he would have to know sooner or later. She took the plunge. 'Him in bed with another woman.'

'Him?'

'Yes.'

It was Blott's turn to beam now. 'We'll need flash and a wide-angle lens.' They went back into the shop and came out with a second-hand Leica, an enlarger, a developing tank, an electronic flash, and everything they needed. As they drove back to Handyman Hall Blott was in his seventh heaven.

*

Dundridge, on the other hand, was in the other place. The girl at the switchboard had phoned him as soon as Lady Maud had left.

'Lady Maud's been,' she told him. 'She left a message for you.'

'Oh yes,' said Dundridge. 'I hope you didn't tell her where I was.'

'No, I didn't,' said the girl. 'She's a horrid old bag isn't she? I wouldn't wish her on my worst enemy.'

'You can say that again,' Dundridge agreed. 'What was the message?'

'She said "Tell Mr Dundridge that I have a number of photographs in which I feel sure he will take a particular interest". She made me write it down. Hullo, are you still there? Mr Dundridge. Hullo. Hullo. Mr Dundridge, are you there?' But there was no reply. She put the phone down.

In his flat Dundridge sat in a state of shock. He still clutched the phone but he was no longer listening. His thoughts were concentrated on one terrible fact, Lady Maud had those ghastly photographs. She could destroy him. There was nothing he could do about it. She would use them if the motorway went ahead and there was absolutely no way he could stop it now. The fucking bitch had arranged the whole thing. First the photographs, then the bribe, and finally the attempt to murder him. The woman was insane. There could be no doubt about it now. Dundridge put down the phone and tried desperately to think what to do. He couldn't even go to the police. In the first place they would never believe him. Lady Maud was a Justice of the Peace, a respected figure in the community and what had that Miss Boles told him? 'We'll know if you tell the police. We've had customers in the police.' And in any case he had no proof that she was involved. Only the word of the girl at the Planning Board and Lady Maud would claim she had been talking about photographs of the Hall or something like that. He needed proof but above all he needed legal advice. A good lawyer.

He picked up the telephone directory and looked in the yellow pages under Solicitors. 'Ganglion, Turnbull and Shrine.' Dundridge dialled and asked to speak to Mr Ganglion. Mr Ganglion would see him in the morning at ten o'clock. Dundridge spent the evening and most of the night pacing his room in an agony of doubt and suspense. Several times he picked up the phone to call Lady Maud only to put it down again. There was nothing he could say to her that would have the slightest effect and he dreaded what she would have to say to him. Towards dawn he fell into a restless sleep and awoke exhausted at seven.

*

At Handyman Hall Lady Maud and Blott slept fitfully too; Blott because he was kept awake by the rumble of lorries through the arch; Lady Maud because she was superintending the whole operation and explaining where she wanted things put.

'Your men can sleep in the servants' quarters,' she told the manager. 'I shall be away for a week. Here is the key to the back door.'

When she finally got to bed in the early hours Handyman Hall had assumed the aspect of a construction camp. Concrete mixers, posts, lorries, fencing wire, bags of cement and gravel were arranged in the park and work had already begun by the light of lamps and a portable generator.

She lay in bed listening to the voices and the rumble of the machines and was well satisfied. When money was no object you could still get things done quickly even in England. 'Money no object,' she thought and smiled to herself at the oddity of the phrase. She would have to do something about money before very long. She would think about it in the morning.

At seven she was up and had breakfasted. Through the window of the kitchen she was pleased to note that several concrete posts had already been installed and that a strange machine that looked like a giant corkscrew was boring holes for some more. She went along to the study and spent an hour going through Sir Giles' filing-cabinets. She paid particular attention to a file marked Investments and took down the details of his shareholdings and the correspondence with his stockbroker. Then she went carefully through his personal correspondence, but there was no indication to be found there of any mistress with a penchant for whips and handcuffs.

At nine she signed the contract and went up to her room to pack and at ten she and Blott, now dressed in his pinstripe suit and wearing a blue polka-dot tie, drove off in the Land-Rover for Hereford and the train to London. Behind them in the study the phone was off the stand. There would be no phone calls to Handyman Hall from Sir Giles.

*

Dundridge arrived promptly at the offices of Ganglion, Turnbull and Shrine and was kept waiting for ten minutes. He sat in an outer office clutching his briefcase and looking miserably at the sporting prints on the walls. They didn't suggest the sophisticated modern approach to life that he felt an understanding of his particular case required. Nor did Mr Ganglion, who finally deigned to see him. He was an elderly man with gold-rimmed glasses over which he looked at Dundridge critically. Dundridge sat down in front of his desk and tried to think how to begin.

'And what did you wish to consult me about, Mr Dundridge?' Mr Ganglion enquired. 'I think you should know in advance that if this has anything to do with the motorway we are not prepared to handle it.'

Dundridge shook his head. 'It hasn't got anything to do with the motorway, well not exactly,' he said. 'The thing is that I'm being blackmailed.'

Mr Ganglion put the tips of his fingers together and tapped them. 'Blackmailed? Indeed. An unusual crime in this part of the world. I can't remember when we last had a case of blackmail. Still it does make a change, I must say. Yes, blackmail. You interest me, Mr Dundridge. Do go on.'

Dundridge swallowed nervously. He hadn't come to interest Mr Ganglion or at least not in the way his smile suggested. 'It's like this,' he said. 'I went to a party at the Golf Club and I met this girl ...'

'A girl, eh?' said Mr Ganglion and drew his chair up to the desk. 'An attractive girl I daresay.'

'Yes,' said Dundridge.

'And you went home with her, I suppose,' said Mr Ganglion, his eyes alight with a very genuine interest now.

'No,' said Dundridge. 'At least I don't think so.'

'You don't think so?' said Mr Ganglion. 'Surely you know what you did?'

'That's the whole point,' Dundridge said, 'I don't know what I did.' He stopped. He did know what he had done. The photographs proclaimed his actions all too clearly. 'Well actually ... I know what I did and all that ...'

'Yes,' Mr Ganglion said encouragingly.

'The thing is I don't know where I did it.'

'In a field perhaps?'

Dundridge shook his head. 'Not in a field.'

'In the back of a car?'

'No,' said Dundridge. 'The thing is that I was unconscious.'

'Were you really? Extraordinary. Unconscious?'

'You see, I had a Campari before we left. It tasted bitter but then Campari does, doesn't it?'

'I have no idea,' said Mr Ganglion, 'what Campari tastes like but I'll take your word for it.'

'Very bitter,' said Dundridge, 'and we got into the car and that's the last thing I remember.'

'How very unfortunate,' said Mr Ganglion, clearly disappointed that he wasn't going to hear the more intimate details of the encounter.

'The next thing I knew I was sitting in my car in a lay-by.'

'A lay-by. Very appropriate. And what happened next?'

Dundridge shifted nervously in his chair. This was the part he had been dreading. 'I got some photographs.'

Mr Ganglion's flagging interest revived immediately. 'Did you really? Splendid. Photographs indeed.'

'And a demand for a thousand pounds.'

'A thousand pounds? Did you pay it?'

'No,' said Dundridge. 'No I didn't.'

'You mean they weren't worth it?'

Dundridge chewed his lip. 'I don't know what they're worth,' he muttered bitterly.

'Then you've still got them,' said Mr Ganglion. 'Good. Good. Well I'll soon tell you what I think of them.'

'I'd rather . . .' Dundridge began but Mr Ganglion insisted.

'The evidence,' he said, 'let's have a look at the evidence of blackmail. Most important.'

'They're pretty awful,' said Dundridge.

'Bound to be,' said Mr Ganglion. 'For a thousand pounds they must be quite revolting.'

'They are,' said Dundridge. Encouraged by Mr Ganglion's broad-mindedness, he opened his briefcase and took out the envelope. 'The thing is you've got to remember I was unconscious at the time.'

Mr Ganglion nodded understandingly. 'Of course, my dear fellow, of course.' He reached out and took the envelope and opened it. 'Good God,' he muttered as he looked at the first one. Dundridge squirmed in his chair and stared at the ceiling, and listened while Mr Ganglion thumbed through the photographs, grunting in an ecstasy of disgust and astonishment.

'Well?' he asked when Mr Ganglion sat back exhausted in his chair. The solicitor was staring at him incredulously.

'A thousand pounds? Is that really all they asked?' he said. Dundridge nodded. 'Well, all I can say is that you got off damned lightly.'

'But I didn't pay,' Dundridge reminded him. Mr Ganglion goggled at him.

'You didn't? You mean to tell me you baulked at a mere thousand pounds after having ...' he stopped at a loss for words while his finger wavered over a particularly revolting photograph.

'I couldn't,' said Dundridge feeling hard done by.

'Couldn't?'

'They never called me back. I had one phone call and I've been waiting for another.'

'I see,' said Mr Ganglion. He looked back at the photograph. 'And you've no idea who this remarkable woman is?'

'None at all. I only met her the once.'

'Once is enough by the look of things,' Mr Ganglion said. 'And no more phone calls? No letters?'

'Not until last night,' said Dundridge, 'and then I got a message from the girl at the desk at the Regional Planning Board.'

'The girl at the desk at the Regional Planning Board,' said Mr Ganglion, eagerly reaching for a pencil. 'And what's her name?'

'She's got nothing to do with it,' Dundridge said, 'she was simply phoning to give me the message. It said Lady Maud Lynchwood had called and wanted me to know that she had some photographs of particular interest to me ...' He stopped. Mr Ganglion had half-risen from his seat and was glaring at him furiously.

'Lady Maud?' he yelled. 'You come in here with this set of the most revolting photographs I've ever set eyes on and have the audacity to tell me that Lady Maud Lynchwood has something to do with them. My God, sir, I've half a mind to horse-whip you. Lady Maud Lynchwood is one of our most respected clients, a dear sweet lady, a woman of the highest virtues, a member of one of the best families . . .' He fell back into his chair, speechless.

'But—' Dundridge began.

'But me no buts,' said Mr Ganglion, trembling with rage. 'Get out of my office. If I have one more word out of you, sir, I shall institute proceedings for slander immediately. Do you hear me? One more word here or anywhere else. One breath of rumour from you and I won't hesitate, do you hear me?'

Dundridge could still hear him fulminating as he dashed downstairs and into the street clutching his briefcase. It was only when he got back to his apartment that he realized he had left his photographs on Mr Ganglion's desk. They could stay there for all he cared. He wasn't going back for the beastly things.

Behind him Mr Ganglion simmered down. On the desk in front of him Dundridge and the masked woman lay frozen in two-dimensional contortions. Mr Ganglion adjusted his bi-focals and studied them with interest. Then he put the photographs into the envelope and the envelope into his safe. The good name of the Handymans was safe with him. Mind you, come to think of it, he wouldn't put anything past her. Remarkable woman, Maud, quite remarkable.

*

By the time they reached London Lady Maud had explained Blott's new duties to him.

'You will hire a taxi and wait outside his flat until he comes out and then you will follow him wherever he goes. Particularly in the evening. I want to know where he spends his nights. If he goes into a block of flats, go in after him and make a note of the floor the lift stops at. Do you understand?'

Blott said he did.

'And on no account let him catch sight of you.' She studied him critically. In his dark grey suit Blott was practically unrec-ognizable anyway. Still, it was best to be careful. She would buy him a bowler at Harrods. 'If you see him with a woman follow them wherever they go and if they separate follow the woman. We have got to find out who she is and where she lives.'

'And then we break in and take the photographs of them?' said Blott eagerly.

'Certainly not,' said Lady Maud. 'When we find out who the woman is we'll decide what we're going to do.'

They took a taxi to an hotel in Kensington, stopping on the way to buy Blott's bowler, and at five o'clock Blott was sitting in a taxi outside Sir Giles' flat in Victoria.

'I suppose you know what you're doing,' said the driver when they had been sitting there for an hour with the meter running. 'This is costing you a packet.' Blott, with a hundred pounds in his pocket, said he knew what he was doing. He was enjoying himself watching the traffic go by and studying the pedestrians. He was in London, the capital of Great Britain, the heart of what had been the world's greatest Empire, the seat of those great Kings and Queens he had read so much about and all the romance in Blott's nature thrilled at the thought. What was even better he was tracking down him – Blott had never deigned to call him anything else – him and his mistress. He was doing Lady Maud a service after all.

At seven Sir Giles came out and drove to his Club for dinner. Behind him Blott's taxi followed relentlessly. At eight he came out and drove across to St John's Wood, Blott's taxi still behind. He parked in Elm Road and went into a house while Blott stared out of the taxi and noticed that he pressed the second bell. As soon as Sir Giles had gone inside, Blott got out and walked across the road and took a note of the name on the doorbell. It read Mrs Forthby. Blott went back to the taxi.

'Mrs Forthby, Mrs Forthby,' said Lady Maud when Blott reported to her. 'Elm Road.' She looked Mrs Forthby up in the telephone directory. 'That's very clever of you, Blott. Very clever indeed. And you say he didn't come out?'

'No. But the taxi-driver wouldn't wait any longer. He said it was time for his supper.'

'Never mind. You've done very well. Now the only thing to do is to find out what sort of woman she is. I would like to get to know Mrs Forthby a little better. I wonder how I can do that.'

'I can follow her,' said Blott.

'I don't see what good that would do,' said Lady Maud. 'And in any case how would you know her to follow?'

'She's the only woman living in the house,' Blott said. 'There's a Mr Sykes on the top floor and a Mr Billington on the ground floor.'

'Excellent,' said Lady Maud. 'You are an observant man. Now then how can I get to know her? There must be some way of arranging a meeting.'

'I could,' said Blott, adopting the voice of Sir Giles, 'ring her up and pretend I was him and ask her to meet me somewhere . . .' he said.

Lady Maud gazed at him. 'Of course. Oh Blott what would I do without you?' Blott blushed. 'But no, that wouldn't do,' Lady Maud continued. 'She would tell him. I'll have to think of something else.'

Blott went up to his room and went to bed. He was tired and very hungry but these little inconveniences counted for nothing beside the knowledge that Lady Maud was pleased with him. Blott fell asleep blissfully happy.

So did Lady Maud, though her happiness was more practical and centred on the solution to a problem that had been worrying her. Money. The fence for the Wildlife Park was going to cost at least thirty thousand pounds and the animals she had ordered came to another twenty. Fifty thousand pounds was a lot of money to pay to save the Hall and besides there was no guarantee that it would work. If anybody should be paying it was Giles, who was responsible for the whole wretched business. And she had found a way of making him pay. She would ruin him yet.

*

Next morning at eight o'clock she and Blott were sitting in a taxi at the end of Elm Road. At nine they saw Sir Giles leave.

Lady Maud paid the taxi-driver and with Blott at her heels strode down to number six.

'Now remember what to say,' Lady Maud told Blott as she pressed the bell. There was a buzz.

'Who is it?' Mrs Forthby asked.

'It's me. I've left my car keys,' said Blott in the accents of Sir Giles.

'And I thought I was the forgetful one,' said Mrs Forthby.

The door opened. Blott and Lady Maud went upstairs. Mrs Forthby opened the door of her flat. She was dressed in a housecoat and was holding a yellow duster.

'Good morning,' said Lady Maud and walked past her into the flat.

'But I thought . . .' Mrs Forthby began.

'Do let me introduce myself,' said Lady Maud. 'I am Lady Maud Lynchwood and you must be Mrs Forthby.' She took Mrs Forthby's hand. 'I've been looking forward to meeting you. Giles has told me so much about you.'

'Oh dear,' said Mrs Forthby. 'How frightfully embarrassing.' Behind her Blott closed the door. Lady Maud took stock of the furniture, including Mrs Forthby in the process, and then sat down in an armchair.

'Quite the little love nest,' she said finally. Mrs Forthby stood plumply in front of her wringing the duster.

'Oh this is awful,' she said, 'simply awful.'

'Nonsense. It's nothing of the sort. And do stop twisting that duster. You make me nervous.'

'I'm so sorry,' said Mrs Forthby. 'It's just that I feel . . . well . . . just that I owe you an apology.'

'An apology? What on earth for?' said Lady Maud.

'Well . . . you know . . .' Mrs Forthby shook her head helplessly.

'If you imagine for one moment that I have anything against you, you're mightily mistaken. As far as I am concerned you have been a positive godsend.'

'A godsend?' Mrs Forthby mumbled and sat down on the sofa.

'Of course,' said Lady Maud. 'I have always found my husband a positively disgusting man with the very vilest of personal habits. The fact that you appear to be prepared, presumably out of the goodness of your heart, to satisfy his obscene requirements leaves me very much in your debt.'

'It does?' said Mrs Forthby, her world being stood on its head by this extraordinary woman who sat in her armchair and addressed her in her own flat as if she were a servant.

'Very much so,' Lady Maud continued. 'And where do these absurdities take place? In the bedroom I suppose.' Mrs Forthby nodded. 'Blott, have a look in the bedroom.'

'Yes, ma'am,' said Blott and went through first one door and then another. Mrs Forthby sat and stared at Lady Maud, hypnotized.

'Now then, you and I are going to have a little chat,' Lady Maud continued. 'You seem to be a sensible sort of woman with a head on your shoulders. I'm sure we can come to some mutually advantageous arrangement.'

'Arrangement?'

'Yes,' said Lady Maud, 'arrangement. Tell me, have you ever been a co-respondent in a divorce case?'

'No, never,' said Mrs Forthby.

'Well my dear,' Lady Maud went on, 'unless you are prepared to do exactly what I tell you down to the finest detail I'm afraid you are going to find yourself involved in quite the most sordid divorce case this country has seen for a very long time.'

'Oh dear,' Mrs Forthby whimpered, 'how simply awful. What would Cedric think of me?'

'Cedric?'

'My first husband. My late husband I should say. The poor dear would be absolutely furious. He'd never speak to me again. He was very particular, you know. Doctors have to be.'

'Well, we wouldn't want to upset Cedric, would we?' said Lady Maud. 'And there will be absolutely no need to if you do what I say. First of all I want you to tell me what Giles likes you to do.'

'Well . . .' Mrs Forthby began only to be interrupted by Blott who emerged from the bedroom with the Miss Dracula, the Cruel Mistress, costume.

'I found this,' he announced.

'Oh dear, how frightfully embarrassing,' said Mrs Forthby.

'Not half as embarrassing, my dear, as it will be when we produce that in court as an exhibit. Now then, the details.'

Mrs Forthby got up. 'It's all written down,' she said. 'He writes it all down for me. You see I'm terribly forgetful and I do tend to get things wrong. I'll get you the game plan.' She went through to the bedroom and returned with a notebook. 'It's all there.'

Lady Maud took the book and studied a page. 'And what were you last night?' she asked finally. 'Miss Catheter, the Wicked Nurse, or Sister Florinda, the Nymphomaniac Nun?'

Mrs Forthby blushed. 'Doris, the Schoolgirl Sexpot,' she tittered.

Lady Maud looked at her doubtfully. 'My husband must have a truly remarkable imagination,' she said, 'but I find his literary style rather limited. And what are you going to be tonight?'

'Oh he doesn't come tonight. He's had to go to Plymouth for a business conference. He's coming again the day after tomorrow. That's Nanny Whip's night.'

Lady Maud put the book down. 'Now then, this is the arrangement,' she said. 'In return for your co-operation I will settle for a divorce on the grounds of incompatibility. There will be no mention of you at all and Sir Giles need know nothing about the help you have given me. All I want you to do is to go out for a little while on Thursday night so that I can have a little chat with him.'

Mrs Forthby hesitated. 'He'll be awfully cross,' she said.

'With me,' Lady Maud assured her. 'I don't think he'll worry about you by the time I've had my say. He'll have other things on his mind.'

'You won't do anything nasty to him, will you?' said Mrs Forthby. 'I wouldn't want him to be hurt or anything. I know he's not very nice but I'm really quite fond of him.'

'I won't touch him,' Lady Maud said. 'I give you my word of

honour I won't so much as lift a little finger to him. And let me say I think your feelings do you great credit.'

Mrs Forthby began to weep. 'You're very kind,' she said.

Lady Maud stood up. 'Not at all,' she said truthfully. 'And now if you'll be so good as to give me the key of the flat I'll send Blott to get a duplicate cut.'

By the time they left the flat Mrs Forthby was feeling better. 'It's been so nice meeting you and getting things straightened out,' she said. 'It's taken a great weight off my mind. I do hate deception so.'

'Quite,' said Lady Maud. 'Unfortunately men seem to live in a fantasy world and as the weaker sex we have to follow suit.'

'That's what I keep telling myself,' Mrs Forthby said. 'Felicia, I say, you may find it peculiar but if it makes him happy you can't afford to be choosey.'

'My sentiments exactly,' said Lady Maud. She and Blott went downstairs. They took a taxi across London to Sir Giles' flat in Victoria. On the way Lady Maud coached Blott in his new role.

19

In Worford Dundridge asserted himself. Now that he came to think about it, he could see that he had been wise to visit Mr Ganglion. The old man's reaction might have been violent but at least it had been genuine and served to indicate that the solicitor was far too respectable to be a party to a blackmail attempt by one of his clients no matter how influential she might be. And Mr Ganglion could do one of two things: he could let Lady Maud know that Dundridge had visited him and had accused her of blackmail, or, more likely, since it was unprofessional to disclose one client's business to another, he could keep silent. In either case Dundridge was in a fairly strong position. If Ganglion spoke to Lady Maud she would not dare to repeat her threat. If he kept silent . . . Dundridge considered the most likely consequence. There would be another message from her. Dundridge got up and went out and bought himself a tape recorder. The next time he visited Mr Ganglion he would tape evidence, solid evidence that Lady Maud was involved. That was the thing to do.

Having arrived at that conclusion he felt better. He had spiked the bitch's guns. Operation Overland could proceed. He went round to the Regional Planning Board and sent for Hoskins.

'We are going ahead,' he told him.

'Of course we are,' said Hoskins. 'Work has already started at Bunnington.'

'Never mind that,' said Dundridge, 'I want a task force to begin work in the Gorge.'

Hoskins consulted his schedule. 'We're not due there until October.'

'I know that but all the same I want work to begin there at once. Just a token force, you understand.'

'At Handyman Hall? A token force?'

'Not at the Hall. In the Gorge itself,' said Dundridge.

'But we haven't even served a compulsory purchase order on the Lynchwoods yet,' Hoskins protested.

'In that case it is about time we did. I want orders out to Miss Percival, General Burnett, and the Lynchwoods at once. We've got to bring pressure to bear on them as quickly as possible. Do you understand?'

'Well, I understand that,' said Hoskins who was beginning to resent Dundridge's authoritarian manner, 'but quite frankly I can't see what all the hurry is about.'

'You wouldn't,' said Dundridge, 'but I'm telling you to do it so get it done. In any case we don't need a compulsory purchase order for the entrance to the Gorge. It's common land. Move men in there tomorrow.'

'And what the hell do you expect them to do? Storm the bloody Hall under cover of darkness?'

'Hoskins,' said Dundridge, 'I'm getting a little tired of your sarcasm. You seem to forget that I am Controller Motorways Midlands and what I say goes.'

'Oh all right,' said Hoskins. 'Just remember that if anything goes wrong you'll have to take the can back. What do you want the task force to do?'

Dundridge looked at the plans for construction. 'It says here that the cliffs have to be cleared and the Gorge widened. They can start work on that.'

'That means dynamiting,' Hoskins pointed out.

'Excellent,' said Dundridge, 'that ought to serve notice on the old bag that we mean business.'

'It will do that all right,' said Hoskins. 'She'll probably be round here like a flash.'

'And I shall be only too glad to see her,' Dundridge said. Hoskins went back to his office puzzled. The more he saw of the Controller Motorways Midlands the odder he found him.

'I never thought he would stand up to Lady Maud like this,' he muttered. 'Well, better him than me.'

In his office Dundridge smiled to himself. Dynamite. That was just the thing to bring Lady Maud rushing into the trap he had set. He took the tape recorder out of his briefcase and tested it. The thing worked perfectly.

*

In Sir Giles' flat in Victoria, Lady Maud and Blott sat down by the desk. In front of her were the details of Sir Giles' shareholdings. In front of Blott the telephone and the script of his part.

'Ready?' said Lady Maud.

'Ready,' said Blott and dialled.

'Schaeffer, Blodger and Vaizey,' said the girl at the stockbrokers.

'Mr Blodger please,' said Blott.

'Sir Giles Lynchwood on the line for you, Mr Blodger,' he heard the girl say.

'Ah Lynchwood,' said Blodger, 'good morning.'

'Good morning Blodger,' said Blott. 'Now then, I want to sell the following at best. Four thousand President Rand. One thousand five hundred ICM. Ten thousand Rio Pinto. All my Zinc and Copper . . .'

At the other end of the line there was a choking sound. Mr Blodger was evidently having some difficulty coming to terms with Sir Giles' orders. 'I say, Lynchwood,' he muttered, 'are you all right?'

'All right? What the devil do you mean? Of course I'm all right,' snarled Blott.

'It's just that ... well ... I mean the market's rock bottom just at the moment. Wouldn't it be better to wait ...'

'Listen Blodger,' said Blott, 'I know what I'm doing and when I say sell I mean sell. And if you'll take my advice you'll get out now too.'

'You really think ...' Mr Blodger began.

'Think?' said Blott. 'I know. Now then see what you can get and call me back. I'll be here at the flat for the next twenty minutes.'

'Well if you say so,' said Mr Blodger.

Blott put the phone down.

'Brilliant, Blott, absolutely brilliant. For a moment even I thought it was Giles talking,' said Lady Maud. 'Well that should put the cat among the pigeons. Or the bulls among the bears. Now, when he calls back give him the second list.'

*

At the offices of Schaeffer, Blodger and Vaizey there was consternation. Blodger consulted Schaeffer and together they sent for Vaizey.

'Either he's gone out of his mind or he knows something,' shouted Blodger. 'He's dropping eighty thousand on the President Rand.'

'What about Rio Pinto?' Schaeffer yelled. 'He bought in at twenty-five and he's selling at ten.'

'He's usually right,' said Vaizey. 'In all the years we've handled his account he hasn't put a foot wrong.'

'A foot! He's putting his whole damned body wrong if you ask me.'

'Unless he knows something,' said Vaizey.

They looked at one another. 'He must know something,' said Schaeffer.

'Do you want to speak to him?' asked Blodger.

Schaeffer shook his head. 'My nerves couldn't stand it,' he muttered.

Blodger picked up the phone. 'Get me Sir Giles Lynchwood,' he told the girl on the switchboard. 'No, come to think of it, don't. I'll use the outside line.' He dialled Sir Giles' number.

Ten minutes later he staggered through to Schaeffer's office whitefaced.

'He wants out,' he said and slumped into a chair.

'Out?'

'Everything. The whole damned lot. And today. He knows something all right.'

*

'Well,' said Lady Maud, 'that's taken care of that. We had better spend another hour or two here in case they phone back. It's a great pity we can't do the same thing with some of his property. Still, there's no point in overdoing things.'

At two o'clock Blodger phoned again to say that Sir Giles' instructions had been carried out.

'Good,' said Blott. 'Send the transfers round tomorrow. I'm going to Paris overnight. And by the way, I want the money transferred to my current account at Westlands in Worford.'

*

Sir Giles returned from Plymouth the following afternoon by car. He was in a good humour. The conference had gone well and he was looking forward to an evening with Nanny Whip. He went to his flat, had a bath, dined in a restaurant and drove round to Elm Road to find Mrs Forthby already dressed for the part.

'Now then you naughty boy,' she said with just that touch of benign menace he found most affecting, 'off with your clothes.'

'No, no,' said Sir Giles.

'Yes, yes,' said Nanny Whip.

'No, no.'

'Yes, yes.'

Sir Giles succumbed to the allure of her apron. It smelt of

childhood. Nanny Whip's breath, on the other hand, suggested something more mature but Sir Giles was too intoxicated with her insistence that he behave himself while she fixed his nappy that he took no notice. It was only when he was finally strapped down and was having his bonnet adjusted that he caught a full whiff. It was brandy.

'You've been drinking,' he spluttered.

'Yes, yes,' said Mrs Forthby and stuffed a dummy into his mouth. Sir Giles stared up at her incredulously. Mrs Forthby never drank. The bloody woman was a teetotaller. It was one of the things he liked about her. She didn't cost much to entertain. She might be absent-minded but she was ... My God, if she was absent-minded sober what the hell was she going to be like drunk? Sir Giles writhed on the bed and realized that he was tied down rather more firmly than he had expected. Nanny Whip had excelled herself. He could hardly move.

'I'm just going to pop downstairs for some fish fingers,' she said, 'I won't be a moment.'

Sir Giles stared lividly at her while she took off her cap and put on a coat over her costume. What in God's name did the bloody woman want with fish fingers at this time of night? A moment? Sir Giles knew her moments. He was liable to be left strapped up in baby clothes and with a dummy in his mouth until the small hours while she went to some fucking concert. Sir Giles gnawed frantically at the dummy but the damned thing was tied on too tightly.

'Now you be a good boy while I'm away,' said Nanny Whip, 'and don't do anything I wouldn't do. Ta, ta.'

She went out and shut the door. Sir Giles subsided. There was no point in worrying now. He might as well enjoy his impotence while he could. There would probably be plenty of time later on for genuine concern. With the necessarily silent prayer that she hadn't been given tickets for the Ring Cycle he settled down to be Naughty Boy and he was just beginning to get into the role when the front doorbell rang. Sir Giles assumed an even greater rigidity. A moment later he was petrified.

'Is anyone at home?' a voice called. Sir Giles knew that voice. It was the voice of hell itself. It was Lady Maud.

'Oh well, the key's in the door,' he heard her say, 'so we might as well go in and wait.'

On the bed Sir Giles had palpitations. The thought of being discovered in this ghastly position by Lady Maud was bad enough but the fact that she had somebody with her was utterly appalling. He could hear them moving about the next room. If only they would stay there. And what the hell was Lady Maud doing there anyway? How on earth had she discovered about Mrs Forthby? And just at that moment the door opened and Lady Maud stood framed in it.

'Ah there you are,' she said cheerfully, 'I had an idea we'd find you here. How very convenient.'

From under his frilled bonnet Sir Giles peered up at her venomously, his face the colour of the sheet on which he was lying and his legs jerking convulsively in the air. Convenient! Convenient! The fucking woman was out of her mind. The next moment he was certain of it.

'You can come in, Blott,' she said, 'Giles won't mind.' Blott came into the room. He was carrying a camera and a flash gun.

'And now,' said Lady Maud, 'we're going to have a little chat.'

'What about the pictures?' said Blott. 'Shouldn't we take them first?'

'Do you think he would prefer the pictures first?' she asked. Blott nodded his head vigorously while Sir Giles shook his. For the next five minutes Blott went round the room taking photographs from every conceivable angle. Then he changed the film and took some close-ups. 'That will do for now,' he announced finally. 'We should have enough.'

'I'm sure we have,' said Lady Maud and drew up a chair beside the bed. 'Now then we are going to have our little chat about your future, my dear.' She bent over and took out the comforter.

'Don't touch me,' squealed Sir Giles.

'I have no intention of touching you,' said Lady Maud with evident disgust. 'It has been one of the few compensations for our wholly unsatisfactory marriage that I don't have to. I am simply here to arrange terms.'

'Terms? What terms?' squawked Sir Giles. Lady Maud rummaged in her handbag.

'The terms of our divorce,' she said and produced a document. 'You will simply append your signature here.'

Sir Giles stared up at it blankly. 'I need my reading-glasses,' he muttered.

Lady Maud perched them on his nose. Sir Giles read the document. 'You expect me to sign that?' he yelled. 'You really think I'm going to—'

Lady Maud replaced the dummy. 'You unspeakable creature,' she snarled, 'you'll sign this document if it's the last thing you do. And this.' She waved another piece of paper in front of him. 'And this.' Another. 'And this.'

On the bed Sir Giles struggled with the straps convulsively. Nothing on God's earth would make him sign a document that was an open confession that he had made a habit of deceiving his lawful wife, had denied her her conjugal rights, had committed adultery on countless occasions and had subjected her for six years to mental and physical cruelty. Lady Maud read his thoughts.

'In return for your signature I will not distribute copies of the photographs we have just taken to the Prime Minister, the Chief Whip, the members of your constituency party or the press. You will sign that document, Giles, and you will see that the motorway is stopped within a month. A month, do you hear me? Those are my terms. What do you say to that?' She removed the dummy.

'You filthy bitch.'

'Quite,' said Lady Maud, 'so you agree to sign?'

'I do not,' screamed Sir Giles and was promptly silenced.

'I don't know if you know your Shakespeare,' she said, 'but in *Edward the Second* . . .'

Sir Giles didn't know his Marlowe either but he did know about Edward the Second.

'Blott,' said Lady Maud, 'go into the kitchen and see if you can find—'

But already Sir Giles was nodding his head. He would sign anything now.

While Blott untied his right hand Lady Maud took a fountain pen out of her handbag. 'Here,' she said pointing to a dotted line. Sir Giles signed. 'Here,' and 'Here.' Sir Giles signed and signed. When he had finished Blott witnessed his signatures. Then he was tied down again.

'Good,' said Lady Maud, 'I will institute proceedings for divorce at once and you will stop the motorway or face the consequences. And don't you dare to set foot on my property again. I will have your things sent down to you.' She took out the dummy. 'Have you anything to say?'

'If I do manage to stop the motorway will you guarantee to let me have the photographs and negatives back?'

'Of course,' said Lady Maud, 'we Handymans may have our faults, but breaking our promises isn't one of them.' She stuffed the dummy back into his mouth and tied it behind his head. Then, having removed his glasses, she adjusted his bonnet and left the room.

On the staircase they met Mrs Forthby in a dither. 'You didn't do anything horrid, did you?' she asked.

'Of course not,' Lady Maud assured her, 'just got him to sign a document consenting to divorce.'

'Oh dear, I do hope he isn't too cross. He gets into such terrible tantrums.'

'Come, come, Nanny Whip, be your true self,' said Lady Maud. 'You must be firm.'

'Yes, you're quite right,' said Mrs Forthby. 'But it's very difficult. It's not in my nature to be unkind.'

'And before I forget, here's a little honorarium for your assistance.' Lady Maud produced a cheque from her bag but Mrs Forthby shook her head.

'I may be a silly woman and not very nice but I do have my

standards,' she said. 'And besides I'd probably forget to cash it.' She went upstairs a little wistfully.

*

'That woman,' said Lady Maud as they drove to Paddington to catch the train to Worford, 'is far too good for Giles. She deserves something better.' On the way they stopped to post the share transfers to Messrs Schaeffer, Blodger and Vaizey.

20

By the time they reached Handyman Hall it was two o'clock in the morning but the park was well lit. Under the floodlights men were busily engaged in erecting the fencing posts and already one side of the park was fenced in. Lady Maud drove round to have a look and congratulated Mr Firkin, the manager, on the progress.

'I'm afraid you're going to have to pay the bonus,' he told her. 'At this rate we'll be finished in ten days.'

'Make it a week,' said Lady Maud. 'Money's no problem.' She went into the house and up to bed well content. Money was no object now. In the morning she would withdraw every penny from their joint account at Westland Bank in Worford and deposit it in her own private account at the Northern. Sir Giles would scream blue murder but there was nothing he could do. He had signed the share transfer certificates if not of his own free will at least in circumstances which made it impossible for him to argue otherwise. And besides she still held one card up her sleeve, the photographs of Dundridge. She would call on the little goose and force him to admit that he had been blackmailed by Giles. Once she had proof of that there would be no question of the motorway continuing. She wouldn't even have to bother with her own awful photographs. Giles would be in jail, his seat in Parliament empty, a bye-election, and the whole wretched business finished.

Whatever happened now she was safe and so was the Hall. 'Fight fire with fire,' she thought and lay in bed considering the strange set of circumstances that had turned her from a plain, simple home-loving woman, a Justice of the Peace and a respectable member of the community, into a blackmailer dealing in obscene photographs and extorting signatures under threat of torture. Evidently the blood of her ancestors who had held the Gorge (by fair means and foul) against all comers still ran in her veins.

'You can't make omelettes without breaking eggs,' she murmured, and fell asleep.

*

In Mrs Forthby's flat one of the eggs in question lay in his frilly bonnet desperately trying to think of some way out of both his predicaments and promising himself that he would murder Nanny Fucking Whip as soon as he got free. Not that there seemed much chance of that before morning. Nanny Whip was snoring loudly on the sofa in the sitting-room. One look at Sir Giles' suffused face had been enough to persuade her that Naughty Boy's naughtiness had not diminished during her absence. A policy of continued restraint seemed called for. Nanny Whip went into the kitchen and hit the bottle of cooking brandy. 'A drop will give me some Dutch courage,' she thought and poured herself a large glass. By the time she had finished it she had forgotten what she had been taking it for. 'A little of what you fancy does you good,' she murmured, and collapsed on to the sofa.

A little of what Sir Giles fancied wasn't doing him any good at all. Besides, eight hours wasn't a little. As the clock on the mantelpiece chimed the hours Sir Giles' thoughts turned from murder to the more lurid forms of slow torture and in between he tried to think what the hell to do about Maud. There didn't seem anything he could do short of applying for the Chiltern Hundreds, resigning from all his clubs, realizing his assets and taking a quick trip to Brazil where the extradition laws didn't apply. And even then he wasn't sure he had any assets to realize. At about four in the morning it dawned on him that some of those pieces of paper he had signed had looked remarkably like share transfer certificates. At the time he hadn't been in any shape to consider them at all carefully. Not that he was in any better shape now but at least the threat of following Edward the Second to an agonizing death had been removed. Finally exhausted by his ordeal he fell into a semi-coma, waking every now and then to consider new and more awful fates for that absent-minded old sot in the next room.

Mrs Forthby woke with a hangover. She staggered off the sofa and ran a bath and it was only when she was drying herself that she remembered Sir Giles.

'Oh dear, he will be cross,' she thought, and went through to the kitchen to make a pot of tea. She carried the tray through to the bedroom and put it down on the bedside table. 'Wakey, wakey, rise and shine,' she said cheerfully and untied the straps. Sir Giles spat the dummy out of his mouth. This was the moment he had been waiting twelve hours for but there was no rising and shining for Sir Giles. He slithered sideways off the bed and crawled towards Mrs Forthby like a crab with rheumatoid arthritis.

'No, no, you naughty boy,' said Mrs Forthby horrified at his colour. She rushed out of the room and locked herself in the bathroom. There was no need to hurry. Behind her Sir Giles was stuck in the bedroom door and one of his legs had attached itself inextricably to a standard lamp.

*

In his office at the Regional Planning Board the Controller Motorways Midlands was having second thoughts about his plan for proving that Lady Maud was a blackmailer. The wretched woman had phoned the switchboard to say that she was coming in to Worford and wanted a word in private with him. Dundridge could well understand her desire for privacy but he did not share it. He had seen more than enough of Lady Maud in private and he had no intention of seeing any more. On the other hand she was hardly likely to threaten him with blackmail in front of a large audience. Dundridge paced up and down his office trying to find some way out of the quandary. In the end he decided to use Hoskins as a bodyguard. He sent for him.

'We've flushed the old cow out with that dynamiting,' he said.

'We've done what?' said Hoskins.

'She's coming to see me this morning. I want you to be present.'

Hoskins had his doubts. 'I don't know about that,' he muttered. 'And anyway, we haven't started dynamiting yet.'

'But the task force has moved in, hasn't it?'

'Yes, though I do wish you wouldn't call it a task force. All this military jargon is getting on my nerves.'

'Never mind that,' said Dundridge. 'The point is that she's coming. I want you to conceal yourself somewhere where you can hear what she has to say and make an appearance if she turns nasty.'

'*Turns* nasty?' said Hoskins. 'The bloody woman *is* nasty. She doesn't have to turn it.'

'I mean if she becomes violent,' Dundridge explained. 'Now then, we've got to find somewhere for you to hide.' He looked hopefully at a filing cabinet but Hoskins was adamant.

'Why can't I just sit in the corner?' he asked.

'Because she wants to see me in private.'

'Well then see her in private for God's sake,' said Hoskins. 'She isn't likely to assault you.'

'That's what you think,' said Dundridge. 'And in any case I want you as a witness. I have reason to believe that she is going to make an attempt to blackmail me.'

'Blackmail you?' said Hoskins turning pale. He didn't like that 'reason to believe'. It smacked of a policeman giving evidence.

'With photographs,' said Dundridge.

'With photographs?' echoed Hoskins, now thoroughly alarmed.

'Obscene photographs,' said Dundridge, with a deal more confidence than Hoskins happened to know was called for.

'What are you going to do?' he asked.

'I'm going to tell her to go jump in a lake,' said Dundridge.

Hoskins looked at him incredulously. To think that he had once described this extraordinary man as a nincompoop. The bastard was as tough as nails.

'I'll tell you what I'll do,' he said finally, 'I'll stand outside the door and listen to what she says. Will that do?'

Dundridge said it would have to and Hoskins hurried back to his office and phoned Mrs Williams.

'Sally,' he said, 'this is you-know-who.'

'I don't, you know,' said Mrs Williams, who had had a hard night.

'It's me. Horsey, horsey catkins,' snarled Hoskins desperately searching for a pseudonym that would deceive anyone listening in on the switchboard.

'Horsey horsey catkins?'

'Hoskins, for God's sake,' whispered Hoskins.

'Oh, Hoskins, why didn't you say so in the first place?'

Hoskins controlled his frayed temper. 'Listen carefully,' he said, 'the gaff's blown. The gaff. Gee for Gifuckingraffe. A for Animal. F for Freddie.'

'What's it mean?' interrupted Mrs Williams.

'The fuzz,' said Hoskins. 'It means the balloon's going to go up. Burn the lot, you understand. Negatives, prints, the tootee. You've never heard of me and I've never heard of you. Get it. No names, no pack drill. And you've never been near the Golf Club.'

By the time he had put the phone down Mrs Williams had got the message. So had Hoskins. If Mrs Williams was going to be nabbed, he could be sure that he would be standing in the dock beside her. She had left him in no doubt about that.

He went back to Dundridge's office and was there to open the door for Lady Maud when she arrived. Then he stationed himself outside and listened.

Inside Dundridge nerved himself for the ordeal. At least with Hoskins outside the door he could always call for help and in any case Lady Maud seemed to be rather better disposed towards him than he had expected.

'Mr Dundridge,' she said, taking a seat in front of his desk, 'I would like to make it quite clear that I have come here this morning in no spirit of animosity. I know we've had our little contretemps in the past but as far as I am concerned all is forgiven and forgotten.'

Dundridge looked at her balefully and said nothing. As far as he was concerned nothing was ever likely to be forgotten and certainly he wasn't in a forgiving mood.

'No, I have come here to ask for your co-operation,' she went on, 'and I want to assure you that what I am about to say will go no further.'

Dundridge glanced at the door and said he was glad to hear it.

'Yes, I rather thought you might,' said Lady Maud. 'You see I have reason to believe that you have been the subject of a blackmail attempt.'

Dundridge stared at her. She knew damned well he had been subject to blackmail.

'What makes you think that?'

'These photographs,' said Lady Maud and, producing an envelope from her handbag, she spread the torn and charred fragments of the photographs out on the desk. Dundridge studied them carefully. Why the hell were they torn and charred? He sorted through them looking for his face. It wasn't there. If she thought she was going to blackmail him with this lot she was very much mistaken.

'What about them?' he asked.

'You know nothing about them?'

'Certainly not,' said Dundridge, thoroughly confident now. He knew what had happened. He had left these photographs on Mr Ganglion's desk. Ganglion had torn them up and thrown them in the fire and had then changed his mind. He had taken them out and had visited Lady Maud and explained that he, Dundridge, had accused her of blackmail. And here she was trying to wriggle out of it. Her next remark confirmed this theory.

'Then my husband has never tried to influence you in any of your decisions by using these photographs,' she said.

'Your husband? Your husband?' said Dundridge indignantly. 'Are you suggesting that your husband has attempted to blackmail me with these ... obscene photographs?'

'Yes,' said Lady Maud, 'that is exactly what I am suggesting.'

'Then all I can say is that you are mistaken. Sir Giles has always treated me with the greatest consideration and courtesy, which is,' he glanced at the door before continuing courageously, 'more than I can say for you.'

Lady Maud looked at him, mystified. 'Is that all you have to say?'

'Yes,' said Dundridge, 'except this. Why don't you take those photographs to the police?'

Lady Maud hesitated. She hadn't bargained on this attitude from Dundridge. 'I don't think that would be very sensible, do you?'

'Yes,' said Dundridge, 'as a matter of fact I do. Now then I am a busy man and you are wasting my time. You know your way out.'

Lady Maud rose from her chair wrathfully. 'How dare you speak to me like that?' she shouted.

Dundridge leapt out of his chair and opened the door. 'Hoskins,' he said, 'show Lady Maud Lynchwood out.'

'I will find my own way,' said Lady Maud, and stormed past them and down the corridor. Dundridge went back into his office and collapsed into his chair. He had called her bluff. He had shown her the door. Nobody could say the Controller Motorways Midlands wasn't master in his own house. He was astonished at his own performance.

So was Hoskins. He stared at Dundridge for a moment and staggered back to his own office shaken by what he had just heard. She had confronted Dundridge with those awful photographs and he had had the nerve to tell her to take them to the police. My God, a man who could do that was capable of doing anything. The fat was really in the fire now. On the other hand she had said it wouldn't be sensible. Hoskins agreed with her wholeheartedly. 'She must be protecting Sir Giles,' he thought and wondered how the hell she had got hold of the photographs in the first place. For a moment he thought of phoning Sir Giles but decided against it. The best thing to do was to sit tight and keep his mouth shut and hope that things would blow over.

He had just reached this comforting conclusion when the bell rang. It was Dundridge again. Hoskins went back down the corridor and found the Controller in a jubilant mood.

'Well that's put paid to that little scheme,' he said. 'You heard her threatening me with filthy photographs. She thought she was going to get me to use my influence to change the route of the motorway. I told her.'

'You most certainly did,' said Hoskins deferentially.

'Right,' said Dundridge turning to a map he had pinned on the wall, 'we must strike while the iron is hot. Operation Overland will proceed immediately. Have the compulsory purchase orders been served?'

'Yes,' said Hoskins.

'And the task force has begun demolition work in the Gorge?'

'Demolition work?'

'Dynamiting.'

'Not yet. They've only just moved in.'

'They must start at once,' said Dundridge. 'We must keep the initiative and maintain the pressure. I intend to establish a mobile HQ here.' He pointed to a spot on the map two miles east of Guildstead Carbonell.

'A mobile HQ?' said Hoskins.

'Arrange for a caravan to be set up there. I intend to supervise this operation personally. You and I will move our offices out there.'

'That's going to be frightfully inconvenient,' Hoskins pointed out.

'Damn the inconvenience,' said Dundridge, 'I mean to have that bitch out of Handyman Hall before Christmas come hell or high water. She's on the run now and by God I mean to see she stays there.'

'Oh all right,' said Hoskins gloomily. He knew better than to argue with Dundridge now.

*

Lady Maud drove back to the Hall pensively. She could have sworn that the thin legs in the photographs were the legs she had seen twinkling across the marble floor but evidently she had been wrong. Dundridge's self-righteous indignation had been wholly convincing. She had expected the wretched little man to blush and stammer and make excuses but instead he had stood up to her and ordered her out of his office. He had even suggested she should take the photographs to the police and, considering his pusillanimity in other less threatening circumstances, it was impossible to suppose he had been bluffing. No, she had been wrong. It was a pity. She would have liked to have seen Sir Giles in court, but it hardly mattered. She had enough to be going on with. Sir Giles would move heaven and earth to see that the motorway was stopped now and if he failed she would force him to resign his seat. There would have to be another bye-election and what had worked in the case of Ottertown would work again in the case of the Gorge. The Government would cancel the motorway. And finally if that too failed there was always the Wildlife Park. It was one thing to demolish half a dozen houses and evict the families that lived there, but it was quite a different kettle of fish to deprive ten lions, four giraffes, a rhinoceros and a dozen ostriches of their livelihood. The British public would never stand for cruelty to animals. She arrived at the Hall to find Blott busy washing his films in the kitchen.

'I've turned the boiler-room into a darkroom,' he explained, and held up a film for her to look at. Lady Maud studied it inexpertly.

'Have they come out all right?' she asked.

'Very nicely,' said Blott. 'Quite lovely.'

'I doubt if Giles would share your opinion,' said Lady Maud and went out into the garden to pick a lettuce for lunch. Blott finished washing his films in the sink and took them down to the boiler-room and hung them up to dry. When he came back lunch was ready on the kitchen table.

'You'll eat in here with me,' said Lady Maud. 'I'm very pleased with you, Blott, and besides, it's nice to have a man about the house.'

Blott hesitated. It seemed an illogical remark. There appeared to be a great many men about the house, tramping up and down the servants' stairs to their bedrooms and working day and night on the fencing. Still, if Lady Maud wanted him to eat with her, he was not going to argue. Things were looking up. She was going to get a divorce from her husband. He was in love and while he had no hope of ever being able to do anything about it, he was happy just to sit and eat with her. And then there was the fence. Blott was delighted by the fence. It brought back memories of the war and his happiness as a prisoner. It would shut out the world and he and Maud would live singly but happily ever after.

They had just finished lunch and were washing-up when there was a dull boom in the distance and the windows rattled.

'I wonder what that was,' said Lady Maud.

'Sounds like blasting,' said Blott.

'Blasting?'

'In a quarry.'

'But there aren't any quarries round here,' said Lady Maud. They went out on to the lawn and stood looking at a cloud of dust rising slowly into the sky a mile or two to the east.

Operation Overland had begun.

21

And Operation Overland continued. Day after day the silence of the Gorge was broken by the rumbling of bulldozers and the dull thump of explosions as the cliffs were blasted and the rocks cleared. Day after day the contractors complained to Hoskins that the way to build a motorway was to start at the beginning and go on to the end, or at least to stick to some sort of predetermined schedule and not go jumping all over the place digging up a field here and rooting out a wood there, starting a bridge and then abandoning construction to begin a flyover. And day after day Hoskins took their complaints and some of his own to Dundridge, and was overruled.

'The essential feature of Operation Overland lies in the random nature of our movements,' Dundridge explained. 'The enemy never knows where we are going to be next.'

'Nor do I, come to that,' said Hoskins bitterly. 'I had a job finding this place this morning. You might have warned me you were going to move it before I went home last night.'

Dundridge looked round the Mobile Headquarters. 'That's odd,' he said, 'I thought *you* had it moved.'

'Me? Why should I do that?'

'I don't know. To be nearer the front line I suppose.'

'Nearer the front line?' said Hoskins. 'All I want is to be back in my bloody office, not traipsing round the countryside in a fucking caravan.'

'Well anyway, whoever had it moved had a good idea,' said Dundridge. 'We are nearer the scene of action.'

Hoskins looked out of the window as a giant dumper rumbled past.

'Nearer?' he shouted above the din. 'We're bloody well in it if you ask me.' As if to confirm his words there was a deafening roar and two hundred yards away a portion of cliff collapsed. As the dust settled Dundridge surveyed the scene with satisfaction. This was nature as man, and in particular Dundridge, intended. Nature conquered, nature subdued, nature disciplined. This was progress, slow progress but inexorable. Behind them cuttings and embankments, concrete and steel, ahead the Gorge and Handyman Hall.

'By the way,' said Hoskins when he could hear himself speak, 'we've had a complaint from General Burnett. He says one of our trucks damaged his garden wall.'

'So what?' said Dundridge. 'He won't have a garden or a wall in two months' time. What's he complaining about?'

'And Mr Bullett-Finch phoned to say—'

But Dundridge wasn't interested. 'File all complaints,' he said dismissively, 'I haven't got time for details.'

*

In London Sir Giles didn't share his opinion. He was obsessed with details, particularly those concerned with the sale of his shares and what Lady Maud was going to do with those damned photographs.

'I lost half a million on those shares,' he yelled at Blodger. 'Half a bleeding million.'

Blodger commiserated. 'I said at the time I thought you were being a little hasty,' he said.

'You thought? You didn't think at all,' Sir Giles screamed. 'If you'd thought you would have known that wasn't me on the phone.'

'But it sounded like you. And you asked me to call you back at your flat.'

'I did nothing of the sort. You don't seriously imagine I would sell four thousand President Rand when the market was at rock bottom. I'm not fucking insane you know.'

Blodger looked at him appraisingly. The thought had crossed his mind. It was Schaeffer who brought the altercation to an end.

'If you must swear,' he said, 'I can only suggest that you would do so more profitably before a Commissioner of Oaths.'

'And what would I want with a Commissioner of Fucking Oaths?'

'A sworn statement that the signatures on the share transfer certificates were forgeries,' said Schaeffer coldly.

Sir Giles picked up his hat. 'Don't think this is the end of the fucking matter,' he snarled. 'You'll be hearing from me again.'

Schaeffer opened the door for him. 'I can only hope fucking not,' he said.

*

But if his stockbrokers were not sympathetic, Mrs Forthby was.

'It's all my fault,' she wailed squinting at him through the two black eyes he had given her for her pains. 'If only I hadn't gone out for those fish fingers this would never have happened.'

'Fish fucking . . .' he began and pulled himself up. He had to keep a grip on his sanity and Mrs Forthby's self-denunciations didn't help. 'Never mind about that. I've got to think what to do. That bloody wife of mine isn't going to get away with this if I can help it.'

'Well, if all she wants is a divorce . . .'

'A divorce? A divorce? If you think that's all she wants . . .' He stopped again. Mrs Forthby mustn't hear anything about those photographs. Nobody must hear about them. The moment that information got out he would be a ruined man and he had just three weeks to do something about them. He went back to his flat and sat there trying to think of some way of stopping the motorway. There wasn't much he could do in London. His request to discuss the matter with the Minister of the Environment had been turned down, his demand for a further Enquiry denied. And his private source in the Ministry had been adamant that it was too late to do anything now.

'The thing is under construction already. Barring accidents nothing can stop it.'

Sir Giles put down the phone and thought about accidents, nasty accidents, like Maud falling downstairs and breaking her neck or having a fatal car crash. It didn't seem very likely somehow. Finally he thought about Dundridge. If Maud had something on him, he had something on the Controller Motorways Midlands. He telephoned Hoskins at the Regional Planning Board.

'He's out at SHMOCON,' said the girl on the switchboard.

'Shmocon?' said Sir Giles desperately trying to think of a village by that name in South Worfordshire.

'Supreme Headquarters Motorway Construction,' said the girl. 'He's Deputy Field Commander.'

'What?' said Sir Giles. 'What the hell's going on up there?'

'Don't ask me,' said the girl, 'I'm only a field telegraphist. Shall I put you through?'

'Yes,' said Sir Giles. 'It sounds batty to me.'

'It is,' said the girl. 'It's a wonder I don't have to use morse code.'

Certainly Hoskins sounded peculiar when Sir Giles finally got through to him. 'Deputy Field—' he began but Sir Giles interrupted.

'Don't give me that crap, Hoskins,' he shouted. 'What the hell do you think you're playing at? Some sort of war game?'

'Yes,' said Hoskins looking nervously out of the window. There was a deafening roar as a charge of dynamite went off.

'What the hell was that?' yelled Sir Giles.

'Just a near miss,' said Hoskins as small fragments of rock rattled on the roof of the caravan.

'You can cut the wisecracks,' said Sir Giles, 'I didn't call you to talk nonsense. There's been a change of plan. The motorway has got to be stopped. I've decided . . .'

'Stopped?' Hoskins interrupted him. 'You haven't a celluloid rat's hope in hell of stopping this little lot now. We're advancing into the Gorge at the rate of a hundred yards a day.'

'Into the Gorge?'

'You heard me,' said Hoskins.

'Good God,' said Sir Giles. 'What the hell's been going on? Has Dundridge gone off his head or something?'

'You could put it like that,' said Hoskins hesitantly. The Controller Motorways Midlands had just come into the caravan covered in dust and was taking off his helmet.

'Well, stop him,' shouted Sir Giles.

'I'm afraid that is impossible, sir,' said Hoskins modulating his tone to indicate that he was no longer alone. 'I will make a note of your complaint, and forward it to the appropriate authorities.'

'You'll do more than that,' bawled Sir Giles, 'you'll use those photographs. You will—'

'I understand the police deal with these matters, sir,' said Hoskins. 'As far as we are concerned I can only suggest that you use an incinerator.'

166

'An *incinerator*? What the hell do I want with an incinerator?'

'I have found that the best method is to burn that sort of rubbish. The answer is in the negative.'

'In the negative?'

'Quite, sir,' said Hoskins. 'I have found that it avoids the health risk to incinerate inflammable material. And now if you'll excuse me, I have someone with me.' Hoskins rang off and Sir Giles sat back and deciphered his message.

'Incinerators. Police. Negative. Health risks.' These were the words Hoskins had emphasized and it dawned on Sir Giles that all hope of influencing Dundridge had gone up in flames. He was particularly alarmed by the mention of the police. 'Good God, that little bastard Dundridge has been to the cops,' he muttered, and suddenly recalled that his safe at Handyman Hall contained evidence that hadn't been incinerated. Maud was sitting on a safe containing photographs that could send him to prison. 'Inflammable material. That bitch can get me five years,' he thought. 'I'd like to incinerate her.' Incinerate her? Sir Giles stared into space. He had suddenly seen a way out of all his problems.

He picked up a pencil and detailed the advantages. Number One, he would destroy the evidence of his attempt to blackmail Dundridge. Number Two, he would get rid of those photographs Blott had taken of him in Mrs Forthby's flat. Number Three, by acting before Maud could divorce him he would still be the owner of the ashes of Handyman Hall and liable for the insurance money and possibly the compensation from the motorway. Number Four, if Maud were to die ... Number Four was a particularly attractive prospect and just the sort of accident he had been hoping for.

He picked up the sheet of paper and carried it across to the fireplace and lit a match. As the paper flared up Sir Giles watched it with immense satisfaction. There was nothing like a good fire for cleansing the past. All he needed now was a perfect alibi.

At Handyman Hall Lady Maud surveyed her handiwork with equal satisfaction. The fence had been finished in ten days, the lions, giraffes, and the rhinoceros had been installed and the ostriches were accommodated in the old tennis court. It was really very pleasant to wander round the house and watch the lions padding across the park or lying under the trees.

'It gives one a certain sense of security,' she told Blott, whose movements had been restricted to the kitchen garden and who complained that the rhinoceros was mucking up the lawn.

'It may give you a sense of security,' said Blott, 'but the postman has other ideas. He won't come further than the Lodge and the milkman won't either.'

'What nonsense,' said Lady Maud. 'The way to deal with lions is to put a bold front on and look them squarely in the eyes.'

'That's as maybe,' said Blott, 'but that rhino needs spectacles.'

'The thing with rhinos,' said Lady Maud, 'is to move at right angles to their line of approach.'

'That didn't work with the butcher's van. You've no idea what it did to his back mudguard.'

'I have a very precise idea. Sixty pounds worth of damage but it didn't charge the van.'

'No,' said Blott, 'it just leant up again it and scratched its backside.'

'Well at least the giraffes are behaving themselves,' said Lady Maud.

'What's left of them,' said Blott.

'What do you mean "What's left of them"?'

'Well, there's only two left.'

'Two? But there were four. Where have the other two got to?'

'You had better ask the lions about that,' Blott told her. 'I have an idea they rather like giraffes for dinner.'

'In that case we had better order another hundredweight of meat from the butchers. We can't have them eating one another.'

She strode off across the lawn imperiously, stopping to prod the rhinoceros with her shooting stick. 'I won't have you in the rockery,' she told it. Outside the kitchen door a lion was snoozing in the sun. 'Be off with you, you lazy beast.' The lion got up and slunk away.

Blott watched with admiration and then shut the door of the kitchen garden. 'What a woman,' he murmured and went back to the tomatoes. He was interrupted five minutes later by a dull thump from the Gorge. Blott looked up. They were getting nearer. It was about time he did something about that business. So far his efforts had been confined to moving Dundridge's mobile headquarters about the countryside at night and altering the position of the pegs that marked the route so that had the motorway proceeded as the contractors desired it would have been several degrees off course. Unfortunately Dundridge's insistence on random construction had defeated Blott's efforts. His only success had been the felling of all the trees in Colonel Chapman's orchard which was a quarter of a mile away from the supposed route of the motorway. Blott was rather proud of that. The Colonel had raised Cain with the authorities and had been promised additional compensation. A few more miscalculations like that and there would be a public outcry. Blott applied his mind to the problem.

*

That night Blott visited the Royal George at Guildstead Carbonell for the first time in several weeks.

Mrs Wynn greeted him enthusiastically. 'I'm so glad you've come,' she said, 'I thought you'd given me up for good.'

Blott said he had been busy. 'Busy?' said Mrs Wynn. 'You're one to talk. I've been rushed off my feet with all the men from the motorway. They come in here at lunch and they're back at night. I tell you, I can't remember anything like it.'

Blott looked round the bar and could see what she meant. The pub was filled with construction workers. He helped himself to a pint of Handyman Brown and went to a table in the corner. An hour later he was deep in conversation with the driver of a bulldozer.

'Must be interesting work knocking things down,' said Blott.

'The pay's good,' said the driver.

'I imagine you've got to be a real expert to demolish a big building like Handyman Hall.'

'I don't know. The bigger they is the harder they falls is what I say,' said the driver, flattered by Blott's interest.

'Let me get you another pint,' said Blott.

Three pints later the driver was explaining the niceties of demolition to a fascinated Blott.

'It's a question of hitting the corner stone,' he said. 'Find that, swing the ball back and let it go and Bob's your uncle, the whole house is down like a pack of cards. I tell you I've done that more times than you've had hot dinners.'

Blott said he could well believe it. By closing time he knew a great deal about demolition work and the driver said he looked forward to meeting him again. Blott helped Mrs Wynn with washing the glasses and then did his duty by her but his heart wasn't in it. Mrs Wynn noticed it.

'You're not your usual self tonight,' she said when they had finished. Blott grunted. 'Mind you I can't say I'm any great shakes myself. My legs are killing me. What I need is a holiday.'

'Why don't you take a day off?' said Blott.

'How can I? Who would look after the customers?'

'I would,' said Blott.

*

At five he was up and cycling down the main street of Guild-stead Carbonell towards Handyman Hall. At seven he had fed the lions and when Lady Maud came down to breakfast Blott was waiting for her.

'I'm taking the day off,' he announced.

'You're what?' said Lady Maud. Blott didn't take days off.

'Taking the day off. And I'll need the Land-Rover.'

'What for?' said Lady Maud who wasn't used to being told by her gardener that he needed her Land-Rover.

'Never you mind,' said Blott. 'No names, no pack drill.'

'No names, no pack drill? Are you feeling all right?'

'And a note for Mr Wilkes at the Brewery to say he's to give me Very Special Brew.'

Lady Maud sat down at the kitchen table and looked at him doubtfully. 'I don't like the sound of this, Blott. You're up to something.'

'And I don't like the sound of that,' said Blott as a dull thump came from the Gorge. Lady Maud nodded. She didn't like the sound of it either.

'Has it got anything to do with that?' she asked. Blott nodded. 'In that case you can have what you want but I don't want you getting into any trouble on my account, you understand.'

She went through to the study and wrote a note to Mr Wilkes, the manager of the Handyman Brewery in Worford, telling him to give Blott whatever he asked for.

At ten Blott was in the manager's office.

'Very Special?' said Mr Wilkes. 'But Very Special is for special occasions. Coronations and suchlike.'

'This is a special occasion,' said Blott.

Mr Wilkes looked at the letter again. 'If Lady Maud says so, I suppose I must, but it's strictly against the law to sell Very Special. It's twenty per cent proof.'

'And ten bottles of vodka,' said Blott. They went down to the cellar and loaded the Land-Rover.

'Forget you've seen me,' Blott said when they had finished.

'I'll do my best,' said the manager, 'this is all bloody irregular.'

*

Blott drove to the Royal George and saw Mrs Wynn on to the bus. Then he went back into the pub and set to work. By lunchtime he had emptied one barrel of Handyman Bitter down the drain and had refilled it with bottles of Very Special and five bottles of vodka. He tried it out on a couple of customers and was delighted with the result. During the afternoon he had a nap and then took a stroll through the village and up past the Bullett-Finches' house. It was a large house in mock Tudor set back from the road and with a very fine garden. Outside the gates a sign announced that Finch Grove was For Sale. The Bullett-Finches didn't fancy living within a hundred yards of a motorway. Blott didn't blame them. Then he walked back through the village and looked at Miss Percival's cottage. That wasn't for sale. It was due for demolition and Miss Percival had already vacated it. A large crane with a steel ball on the end of its arm stood nearby. Blott climbed into the driver's seat and played with the controls. Then he walked back to the pub and sat behind the bar, waiting for opening time.

22

Sir Giles busied himself in Mrs Forthby's flat. He altered the date on the clock on the mantelpiece. He turned the pages of the *Radio Times* to the following day and hid the newspaper. Several times he asserted that today was Wednesday.

'That just goes to show what a muddlehead I am,' said Mrs Forthby, who was busy making supper in the kitchen, 'I could have sworn it was Tuesday.'

'Tomorrow's Thursday,' said Sir Giles.

'If you say so, dear,' said Mrs Forthby. 'I'm sure I don't know what day of the week it is. My memory is simply shocking.'

Sir Giles nodded approvingly. It was on Mrs Forthby's appalling memory that his alibi depended, that and sleeping pills. 'Silly old bitch won't miss a day in her life,' he thought as he crunched six tablets up in the bottom of a glass with the handle of a toothbrush before adding a large tot of whisky. According to his doctor the lethal dose was twelve. 'Six would probably put you out for twenty-four hours,' the doctor had told him and twenty-four hours was all Sir Giles needed. He went through to the kitchen and had supper.

'What about a nightcap?' he said when they had finished.

'You know I never drink,' said Mrs Forthby.

'You did the other night. You finished half a bottle of cooking brandy.'

'That was different. I wasn't feeling myself.'

It was on the tip of Sir Giles' tongue to tell her that she wouldn't feel anything let alone herself by the time she had finished that little lot but he restrained himself. 'Cheers,' he said, and finished his glass.

'Cheers,' said Mrs Forthby doubtfully and sipped her whisky.

Sir Giles poured himself another glass. 'Down the hatch,' he said.

Mrs Forthby took another sip. 'You know I could have sworn today was Tuesday,' she said.

Sir Giles could have sworn, period. 'Today is Wednesday.'

'But I've got a hair appointment on Wednesday. If today is Wednesday I must have missed it.'

'You have,' said Sir Giles truthfully. Whatever happened, Mrs Forthby had missed her hair appointment. He raised his glass. 'Mud in your eye.'

'Mud in your eye,' said Mrs Forthby and sipped again. 'If today is Wednesday, tomorrow must be Thursday in which case I've got a pottery class in the afternoon.'

Sir Giles poured himself another whisky hurriedly. It was on just such insignificant details that the best plans foundered. 'I was thinking of going down to Brighton for the weekend,' he improvised. 'I thought you would like that.'

'With me?' said Mrs Forthby, her eyes shining.

'Just us two together,' said Sir Giles.

'Oh, you are thoughtful.'

'A votre santé,' said Sir Giles.

Mrs Forthby finished her drink and got to her feet. 'It's Nurse Catheter tonight, isn't it?' she said moving unsteadily towards him.

'Forget it,' said Sir Giles, 'I'm not in the mood.' Nor was Mrs Forthby. He carried her through to the bedroom and put her to bed. When he left the flat five minutes later she was snoring soundly. By the time she woke up he would be back and in bed beside her. He got into his car and began the drive north.

*

At the Royal George in Guildstead Carbonell Blott's experiment in induced narcosis proceeded more slowly but with gayer results. By nine o'clock the pub was filled with singing dumper drivers, two fights had erupted and died down before they could get well under way, a darts match had had to be cancelled when a non-participant had been pinned by his ear to last year's calendar, and two consenting adults had been ejected from the Gents by Blott and Mrs Wynn's Alsatian. By ten o'clock Blott's promise that the Very Special was needed for a special occasion had been fulfilled to the letter. Two more fights, this time between locals and the men from the motorway, had started and had not died down but had spread to the Saloon Bar where the operator of a piledriver was attempting to demonstrate his craft to the fiancée of the secretary of the Young Conservatives, the darts match had been resumed using a portrait of Sir Winston Churchill as a dartboard, and half a dozen bulldozer drivers were giving an exhibition of clog dancing on the bar-billiards table. In between whiles Blott had coaxed Mr Edwards, who claimed to have knocked down more houses than Blott had had hot dinners, into a nicely belligerent mood.

'I can knock any damned house you like to show me down with one bloody blow,' he shouted.

Blott raised an eyebrow. 'Tell me another one.'

'I tell you I can,' Mr Edwards asserted. 'One knock in the right place and Bob's your uncle.'

'I'll believe it when I see it,' said Blott and poured him another pint of Very Special.

'I'll show you. I'll bloody show you,' said Mr Edwards and took a swig.

By closing time Very Special had cast if not a healing balm at least a soporific one on the whole proceedings. As the motorway men stumbled off to their cars and the Young Conservatives drove off nursing their wounds, Blott shut up shop and helped Mr Edwards to his feet.

'I tell you I can,' he mumbled.

'Never,' said Blott.

Together they staggered off down the street towards Miss Percival's cottage, Blott clutching a bottle of vodka and Mr Edwards' arm.

'I'll show you,' said Mr Edwards as they crossed the field to the cottage. 'I'll fucking show you.'

He climbed into the crane and started it up. Blott stood behind him and watched.

'Oh what a pity she's only one titty to bang against the wall,' Mr Edwards sang as the crane jerked forward through the hedge and into the garden. Behind them the iron ball wobbled and swung. Mr Edwards stopped the crane and adjusted the controls. The arm of the crane swung round and the ball followed. It went wide.

'I thought you said you could do it in one,' said Blott.

'That,' said Mr Edwards, 'was just a practice swing.' He lowered the crane and a sundial disintegrated. Mr Edwards raised it again.

'Never been laid, never been made, Queen of all the Fairies,' he bawled. The crane swung round and Blott darted out of the way as the iron ball lolloped past him. The next moment it hurtled into the side of the cottage. There was a roar of falling bricks, tiles, breaking glass and a great cloud of dust momentarily obscured what had once been Miss Percival's attractive home. When the dust finally cleared what remained of the cottage held few attractions. On the other hand it was not entirely demolished. A chimney still stood and the roof while hanging at a disreputable angle was still recognizably the roof. Blott regarded the result sceptically.

'I don't think much of that,' he said superciliously. 'Still I suppose there's always a first time.'

'Whadja mean always a first time?' said Mr Edwards. 'I knocked it down, didn't I?'

'No,' said Blott, 'not with one blow.'

Mr Edwards consoled himself with vodka. ' 'sonly a fucking cottage. Can't expect much with a cottage. Got no bulk to it.

Gotta have bulk, got to have weight. Show me a house, a proper house, a big bulky house and I'll . . .' He slumped over the controls. Blott climbed up into the cab and shook him.

'Wake up,' he shouted. Mr Edwards woke up.

'Show me a proper house . . .'

'All right, I will,' said Blott. 'Show me how to drive this thing and I'll show you a proper house.'

Mr Edwards did his best to show him. 'You pull that lever and you press that 'celerator.' Five minutes later Guildstead Carbonell, already disturbed by the eruption of violence at the Royal George, was convulsed a second time as Blott with Mr Edwards' assistance attempted to negotiate the High Street at something over the statutory speed limit. As the mobile crane hurtled into the first of several corners at forty miles per hour Blott struggled to keep it on the road. He wasn't helped by Mr Edwards' inertia nor by that of the iron ball which, swinging behind, tended to demonstrate the attractions of centrifugal force. On the first corner it gave a glancing blow to the plate-glass window of a newly opened mini-market, bounced off the roof of a parked car, entered the front parlour of Mrs Tate's house and came out through Mr and Mrs Williams' sitting-room, decapitated the War Memorial and took a telegraph pole and fifty yards of wire in tow. On the second it took a short cut through the forecourt of Mr Dugdale's garage neatly severing the stanchions that had formerly supported the roof and de-molishing four petrol pumps and a sign advertising free tumblers. By the time they had traversed the rest of the High Street, the ball had left its imprint on seven more cars and the façades of twelve splendid examples of eighteenth-century domestic architecture while the telegraph pole, not to be left out of things, had vaulted through every third window before disentangling itself from the crane and coming to rest in the vestry of the Primitive Methodist Chapel taking with it a large sign announcing the Coming of the Lord. As they left the vil-lage, the iron ball made its last contribution to the peace and tranquillity of the place by nudging an electricity transformer which exploded with a galaxy of blue sparks and plunged the entire district into darkness. At this point Mr Edwards woke up.

'Where are we?' he mumbled.

'Almost there,' said Blott, managing to slow the crane down. Mr Edwards took another swig of vodka.

'Show me the way to go home,' he sang, 'I'm tired and I want to go to bed.'

'Not yet,' said Blott and turned the crane up the drive towards the Bullett-Finches' house.

*

It was one of Mrs Bullett-Finch's pleasanter qualities from her husband's point of view that she went to bed early. 'It's the early bird that catches the worm,' she would say at nine o'clock every night and take herself upstairs, leaving Mr Bullett-Finch to sit up by himself and read about lawns in peace and quiet. And lawns interested him. They held a charm for him that Ivy Bullett-Finch had long since relinquished. Lawns improved with age, which was more than could be said for wives and what Mr Bullett-Finch didn't know about browntop and chewing fescue and velvet bent was not worth knowing. And the lawns around Finch Grove were in his opinion among the finest in the country. They stretched immaculately in front of the house down to the stream at the bottom of the garden. Not a dandelion scarred their surface, not a plantain, not a daisy. For six years Mr Bullett-Finch had nurtured his lawns, sanding, mowing, spiking, fertilizing, weedkilling, even going so far as to prohibit visitors with high heels from walking on them. And when Ivy wanted to go down to the orchard she had to wear her bedroom slippers. It may have been this insistence on his part that the front garden was sacrosanct that had contributed to her nervous disposition and sense of guilt. What the garden was to her husband, the house was to Ivy, a source of obsessive concern in which everything had its place, was dusted twice a day and polished three times a week so that she went to bed early less out of indolence than from sheer exhaustion and lay there wondering if she had turned everything off.

On this particular night Mr Bullett-Finch was deep in a chapter on hormone weedkillers when the lights went out. He got up and stumbled through to the fusebox only to find that the fuses were intact.

'Must be a power failure,' he thought and went up to bed in the dark. He had just undressed and was putting on his pyjamas when he became aware that something extremely large and powered by an enormous diesel engine appeared to be making its way up his drive. He rushed to the window and peered out into two powerful headlights. Temporarily blinded, he groped for his dressing-gown and slippers, found them and put them on and looked out of the window again. What looked like a gigantic crane had stopped on the gravel forecourt and was backing on to his lawn. With a scream of rage Mr Bullett-Finch told it to stop but it was too late. A moment later there was a winching noise and the crane began to swing. Mr Bullett-Finch pulled his head in the window and raced for the stairs. He was halfway down them when all concern for his precious lawn disappeared, to be replaced by the absolute conviction that Finch Grove was at the very centre of some gigantic earthquake. As the house disintegrated around him – Mr Edwards' claim to be a demolition expert entirely vindicated – Mr Bullett-Finch clung to the banisters and peered through a dust-storm of plaster and powdered brick while the furnishings of which his wife had been so rightly proud hurtled past him from the upstairs rooms. Among them came Mrs Bullett-Finch herself, screaming and hysterically proclaiming her innocence, which had until then never been in doubt, and he was just debating why she should assume responsibility for what was obviously a natural cataclysm when he was saved the trouble by the roof collapsing on top of him and the staircase collapsing underneath. Mr Bullett-Finch descended into the cellar and lay unconscious, surrounded by his small stock of claret. Mrs Bullett-Finch, still clinging to her mattress and the conviction that she had left the gas on, had meanwhile been catapulted into the herb-garden where she sobbed convulsively among the thyme.

From the cab of his crane Mr Edwards regarded his handiwork with pride.

'Told you I could do it,' he said and seized the bottle of vodka from Blott who had been steadying his nerves with it. Blott let him finish it. Then dragged him down from the cab and climbed back to wipe any fingerprints from the controls. Finally, hoisting Mr Edwards over his shoulder, he set off down the drive.

By the time he reached the Royal George Mrs Wynn was back from Worford, and washing glasses by candlelight.

'Look at all this mess,' she said irately, 'I leave you to look after the place for one day and what do I find when I get back. Anyone would think there had been an orgy here. And what's been going on in the village, I'd like to know? The place looks like it's been bombed.'

Blott helped with the glasses and then went out to the Land-Rover. Mr Edwards was still sleeping soundly in the back. He drove slowly out of the yard and turned towards Ottertown. It was a longer way round but Blott didn't want to be seen in the High Street. He stopped at the caravan site where the motorway workers lived and deposited Mr Edwards on the grass. Then he drove on towards the Gorge and Handyman Hall. At two o'clock he was in bed in the Lodge. All in all it had been a good day's work.

*

In Dundridge's flat the phone rang. He groped for it sleepily and switched on the light. It was Hoskins. 'What the hell do you want? Do you realize what time it is?'

'Yes,' said Hoskins, 'as a matter of fact I do. I just wanted to tell you that you've gone too far this time.'

'Gone too far?' said Dundridge. 'I haven't gone anywhere.'

'Don't give me that,' said Hoskins. 'You and your random sorties and your task forces and assault groups. Well you've certainly landed us in it this time. There were people living in that fucking house, you know, and it wasn't even scheduled for demolition in the first place and as for what you've done to Guildstead Carbonell . . . I hope you realize that the motorway wasn't supposed to go within a mile of that village. It's a historical monument, Guildstead Carbonell is ... was. It's a fucking ruin now, a disaster area.'

'A disaster area?' said Dundridge. 'What do you mean a disaster area?'

'You know very well what I mean,' shouted Hoskins hysterically. 'I always thought you were mad but now I know it.' He slammed the phone down, leaving Dundridge mystified. He sat on the edge of his bed and wondered what to do. Clearly something had gone wrong with Operation Overland. He was just about to call Hoskins back when the phone rang again. This time it was the police.

'Is that Mr Dundridge?'

'Yes, speaking.'

'This is the Chief Constable. I wonder if I could have a word with you. It's about this business at Guildstead Carbonell ...'

Dundridge got dressed.

*

Sir Giles parked his car outside Wilfrid's Castle Church. It was an unfrequented spot and nobody was likely to be out and about at two o'clock in the morning. It was one of the great advantages of a Bentley that it was not a noisy car. For the last five miles Sir Giles had driven without lights, coasting past farmhouses and keeping to back roads. He had seen no other vehicles and, so far as he could tell, had been seen by nobody. So far so good. Leaving the car he made his way down the footpath to the bridge. It was dark down there under the trees and he had some difficulty in finding his way. On the far side of the bridge he came to a wire-mesh gate. Using his torch briefly he unlatched it and went through into the pinetum. The gate puzzled Sir Giles. It was a long time since he had been over the bridge, not since the day of his wedding in fact, but he felt sure there had been no gate there then. Still he hadn't time to worry about little things like that. He had to move quickly. It wasn't easy. The pinetum was dark enough by daylight. At night it was pitch black. Sir Giles shone his torch on the ground and moved forward cautiously grateful to the carpet of pine needles that deadened his footsteps. He was halfway through the wood when he became conscious that he was not alone. Something was breathing nearby.

He switched off his torch and listened. Above him the pine trees sighed in a light breeze and for a moment Sir Giles hoped he had been mistaken. The next moment he knew he hadn't. An extraordinary whistling, wheezing noise issued from the wood. 'Must be a cow with asthma,' he thought though how an asthmatic cow had got into the pinetum he couldn't imagine. A moment later he was disabused of the notion of a cow. With a horrible snort whatever it was got to its feet, a process that involved breaking a number of branches, large branches by the sound of things, and lumbered off with a singlemindedness of purpose that seemed to bring it into contact with a great many trees. Sir Giles stood and quaked, partly from fear and partly because the ground beneath his feet was also quaking, and when finally the creature smashed through the iron fence at the edge of the wood with as little regard for property as for its own health and welfare he was in two minds about going on. In the end he forced himself to continue, though more cautiously. After all, whatever he had disturbed, it *had* run away.

Sir Giles came to the gate and stared at the house. The place was in darkness. He walked quickly across the lawn and round to the front door. Then taking off his shoes he unlocked the door and stepped inside. Silence. He went down the corridor to his study and shut the door. Then he switched on his torch and shone it on the safe – or rather on the hole in the wall where the safe had been. Sir Giles stared at it in horror. No wonder Hoskins had talked so insistently about incinerators and inflammable material and health risks. It hadn't been Dundridge who had been threatening to go to the police. It was Maud. But had she been already? There was no way of telling. He switched off the torch and stood in the darkness thinking. There was certainly one way of ensuring that if she hadn't been already she wasn't going to in future. Any doubts he had had, and they were few, about the wisdom of disposing of Handyman Hall and Maud disappeared. He would make certain of the bitch. He opened the door of the study and listened for a moment before tiptoeing down the passage towards the kitchen. Kitchens were the logical place for fires to start of their own accord and besides there were the oil tanks that fed the Aga cooker. On the way he stopped to put on his Wellington boots in the cloakroom under the stairs.

*

The twang of the iron fence woke Lady Maud. She sat up in bed and wondered what it portended. Iron fences didn't twang of their own accord and rhinoceroses didn't go charging across rockeries in the small hours of the morning without good reason. She switched on the bedside lamp to see what time it was but thanks to the power failure at Guildstead Carbonell the light didn't come on. Peculiar. She got out of bed and went to the window and was just in time to see a shadow slip across the lawn and disappear round the side of the house. It was a distinctly furtive shadow and it came from the pinetum. For a moment she supposed it to be Blott, but there was no reason for Blott to be running furtively about the park at ... she looked at her watch ... half past two in the morning. Anyway she could always check. She picked up the phone and dialled the Lodge.

'Blott,' she whispered, 'are you there?'
'Yes,' said Blott.
'Are the gates locked?'
'Yes,' said Blott, 'why?'
'I just wanted to make sure.' She put the phone down gently and got dressed. Then she went downstairs quietly and tried the front door. It was unlocked. Lady Maud looked around. A pair of shoes on the doorstep. She picked them up and sniffed. Giles. Unmistakably Giles. Then she put the shoes down again and shutting the front door behind her went round to the workshop. So the little beast had come back. She could imagine what for. Well, come back he might but he wouldn't get away so easily. A moment later she was running, remarkably swiftly for so large a woman and so dark a night, across the lawn towards the pinetum. Even there in the pitch darkness

her pace did not slacken. A life-time's familiarity with the path gave her an unerring sense of when to twist or turn through the trees. Five minutes later she was at the gate to the footbridge. She reached into her pocket and took out a large lock, fitted it to the bolt and closed the hasp. Then, having tested it to see that it was firmly fastened, she turned and made her way back towards the Hall.

*

In the kitchen Sir Giles took his time. The essence of successful arson lay in simplicity, and murder was best when it looked like natural death. The Aga cooker was self-igniting. It came on automatically at intervals during the night. Sir Giles shone his torch on the time switch and saw that it was set for four o'clock. Plenty of time. He took an adjustable spanner out of his pocket and undid the nut that secured the feedpipe from the oil tanks to the stove. Oil began to pour out over the floor. Sir Giles sat down on a chair and listened to it. It slurped out steadily and spread under the table. Presently it would begin to run down the passage into the hall. There were a thousand gallons of heating oil in those tanks and as Sir Giles knew they had recently been filled. He would wait until they were empty and then replace the feedpipe but not tightly. To the police and the insurance investigators it would look as though there had been a simple leak. Yes, a thousand gallons of heating oil would certainly do the trick. Handyman Hall would turn into a raging furnace in seconds. The fire brigade would take at least half an hour to come from Worford and by that time the place would be in ashes. So would Maud. Sir Giles knew her too well to suppose that she would be sensible enough to jump from her bedroom window even if she had time. She might not even wake before the flames reached the first floor and if she did her first thought would be to rush out on to the landing and try to save her precious family home. It would be Blott in the Lodge who would raise the alarm. It was a pity about Blott. Sir Giles would have liked him to be cremated too.

*

Outside in the garden Lady Maud stood looking at the house.

Giles had come back to look for the negatives of the pictures they had taken of him. Well, he was hardly likely to find them. Blott had cut them into strips of six and had taken them back to the Lodge with him. Or perhaps he had come to get those photographs from his safe. He was going to be disappointed there too. Whichever way she looked at it he was going to be in for a nasty surprise. She went round to the front door and picked up his shoes. It might not be a bad idea to remove those while she was about it. She took them round to the garage and put them in an empty bucket and she was just coming out again when it struck her that there might be a more sinister purpose in Giles' visit. Six years of cohabitation with the brute had taught her that he was as ruthless as he was devious. It would pay her to be careful.

'I had better watch my step,' she thought, and went round to the kitchen door. She was just about to unlock it when she stepped in something slippery. She steadied herself and reached down. Oil. It was seeping out from under the kitchen door and down the steps into the yard. A moment later she understood the purpose of his visit. He was going to burn the Hall. By God, he wasn't. With a howl of rage Lady Maud hurled herself at the door, unlocked it and charged into the kitchen. For a moment she remained upright, the next she was flat on her back and sliding across the floor. So was Sir Giles though in a different direction. As Lady Maud's great bulk swept under him carrying his chair with her, Sir Giles catapulted through the air, landed on his face and slid irresistibly down the corridor and across the marble floor of the great hall. As he floundered about trying to get to his feet in a sea of oil he could hear Maud ricocheting about the kitchen. By the sound of things she had been joined by the entire complement of pots, pans, and kitchen utensils. Sir Giles slithered to the front door and managed to get to his feet on the mat. He grasped the handle and tried to turn it. The fucking thing wouldn't turn. He groped in his pocket for a handkerchief and wiped his hands and the doorknob and an instant later he was outside and reaching for his shoes. The bloody things weren't there.

There wasn't time to look for them. Behind him Maud had finally overcome the combined forces of grease and gravity and was coming down the passage promising to strangle him with her own bare hands. Sir Giles waited no longer. He galumphed off in his gumboots down the drive and across the lawn towards the pinetum. Behind him Lady Maud slithered into the downstairs lavatory and emerged with a shotgun. She went to the front door and opened it. Sir Giles was still visible across the lawn. Lady Maud raised the gun and fired. He was out of range but at least she had the satisfaction of knowing that he wouldn't come near the house again in a hurry. She put the gun back and began to clean up the mess.

23

In the Lodge Blott heard the shot and leapt out of bed. Lady Maud's telephone call had disturbed him. Why should she want to know if the gates were locked? And why had she whispered? Something was up. And with the sound of the shotgun Blott was certain. He dressed and went downstairs with his twelve-bore to the Land-Rover which he had parked just inside the archway. Before getting in he checked the lock on the gate. It was quite secure. Then he drove off up to the Hall and parked outside the front door and went inside.

'It's me, Blott,' he called into the darkness. 'Are you all right?'

From the kitchen there came the sound of someone sliding about and a muffled curse.

'Don't move,' Lady Maud shouted. 'There's oil everywhere.'

'Oil?' said Blott. Now that he came to think of it there was a stench of oil in the house.

'He's tried to burn the house down.'

Blott stared into the darkness and promised that if he got the chance he would kill him. 'The bastard,' he muttered. Lady Maud slithered down the passage with a squeegee.

'Now listen carefully, Blott,' she said. 'I want you to do something for me.'

'Anything,' said Blott gallantly.

'He came in through the pinetum. I've locked the gate there so he can't get out but his car must be up at Wilfrid's Castle. I want you to drive round there and remove the dis . . . the thing that goes round.'

'The rotor arm,' said Blott.

'Right,' said Lady Maud. 'And while you are about it you might as well put extra locks on both the gates. We must make quite sure that innocent people don't get into the park. Do you understand?'

Blott smiled in the darkness. He understood.

'I'll take the rotor arm off the Land-Rover too,' he said.

'A wise precaution,' Lady Maud agreed. 'And when you have finished come back here. I don't think he'll return tonight but it might be as well to take precautions.'

Blott turned to the door.

'There's just one other thing,' said Lady Maud. 'I don't think we'll feed the lions in the morning. They'll just have to fend for themselves for a day or two.'

'I didn't intend to,' said Blott and went outside.

Lady Maud sighed happily. It was so nice to have a real man about the house.

* * *

At Finch Grove Ivy Bullett-Finch's feelings were quite the reverse. What was left of the house seemed to be about the man and in any case what was left of Mr Bullett-Finch was real only in a material sense. He had died, as he had lived, concerned for the welfare of his lawn. Dundridge arrived with the Chief Constable in time to pay his last respects. As firemen carried her husband's remains out of the cellar, Mrs Bullett-Finch, relieved of the burden of guilt about the oven, vented her feelings on the Controller Motorways Midlands.

'You murderer,' she screamed, 'you killed him. You killed him with your awful ball.' She was led away by a policewoman. Dundridge looked balefully at the ball and crane.

'Nonsense,' he said, 'I had nothing to do with it.'

'We have been led to understand by your deputy, Mr Hoskins, that you gave orders for random sorties to be made by task forces of demolition experts,' said the Chief Constable. 'It would rather appear that they've carried out your instructions to the letter.'

'My instructions?' said Dundridge. 'I gave no instructions for this house to be demolished. Why should I?'

'We were rather hoping you would be able to tell us,' said the Chief Constable.

'But it's not even scheduled for demolition.'

'Quite. Nor to the best of my knowledge was the High Street. But since your equipment was used in both cases—'

'It's not my equipment,' shouted Dundridge, 'it belongs to the contractors. If anyone is fucking responsible—'

'I'd be glad if you didn't use offensive language,' said the Chief Constable. 'The situation is unpleasant enough as it is. Local feeling is running high. I think it would be best if you accompanied us to the station.'

'The station? Do you mean the police station?' said Dundridge.

'It's just for your own protection,' said the Chief Constable. 'We don't want any more accidents tonight, now do we?'

'This is monstrous,' said Dundridge.

'Quite so,' said the Chief Constable. 'And now if you'll just step this way.'

*

As the police car wound its way slowly through the rubble that littered the High Street, Dundridge could see that Hoskins had been telling the truth when he called Guildstead Carbonell a disaster area. The transformer still smouldered in the grey dawn, the Primitive Methodist Chapel lived up to at least part of its name, while the horribly mis-shapen relics of a dozen cars crouched beside the glass-strewn pavement. What the iron ball hadn't done with the aid of the telegraph pole to end Guild-stead Carbonell's reputation for old-world charm, the conflagration at Mr Dugdale's garage had. Ignited by some un-identifiable public-spirited person who had brought out a paraffin lamp to warn passers-by to watch out for the debris, the blast from the petrol storage tanks had blown in what few windows remained unbroken after Blott's passing and had set fire to the thatched roofs of several delightful cottages. The fire had spread to a row of almshouses. The simultaneous arrival of fire engines from Worford and Ottertown had added to the chaos. Working with high-pressure hoses in total darkness they had swept a number of inadequately clothed old-age pensioners who had escaped from the almshouses down the street before turning their attention to the Public Library which they had filled with foam. To Dundridge, staring miserably out of the window of the police car, the knowledge that he was held responsible for the catastrophe was intolerable. He wished now that he had never set eyes on South Worfordshire.

'I must have been mad to have come up here,' he thought.

The same thought had already occurred to Sir Giles though in his case the madness he had in mind was in no way meta-phorical. As dawn broke over the Park, Sir Giles wrestled with the lock on the gate to the footbridge and tried to imagine how it had got there. It had not been on the gate when he arrived. He wouldn't have been able to enter if it had. But if the exist-ence of the lock was bad enough, that of the fence was worse and it certainly hadn't been there when he had last been at the Hall. It was an extremely high fence with large metal brackets at the top and four strands of heavy barbed-wire overhanging the Park so that it was evidently designed to stop people get-ting out rather than trespassers getting in.

It was at this point that Sir Giles gave up the struggle with the lock and decided to look for some other way out. He fol-lowed the fence along the edge of the pinetum and was about to clamber over the iron railings when the sense of unreality that had come over him with the sudden appearance of a large lock where no lock had previously been took a decided turn for the worse. Against the grey dawn sky he saw a head, a small head with a long nose and knobs on it. Below the head there was a neck, a long neck, a very long neck indeed. Sir Giles shut his eyes and hoped to hell that when he opened them he wouldn't see what he thought he had seen. He opened them but the giraffe was still there. 'Oh my God,' he murmured and was about to move away when his eye caught sight of something even more terrifying. In the long grass fifty yards behind the giraffe there was another face, a large face with a mane and whiskers.

Sir Giles gave up all thought of looking for a way out in that direction. He turned and stumbled back into the pinetum. Either he had gone mad or he was in the middle of some fucking zoo. Giraffes? Lions? And what the hell was it that he had almost stumbled across during the night? An elephant? He got back to the gate and looked at the lock hopefully. But instead of one lock there were now two and the second was even larger than the first. He was just trying to think what this meant when he heard a noise on the path across the river. Sir Giles looked up. Blott was standing there with a shotgun, smiling down at him. It was a horrible smile, a smile of quiet satisfaction. Sir Giles turned and ran into the pinetum. He knew death when he saw it.

*

By the time Blott got back to the Hall Lady Maud was down and making breakfast in the kitchen.

'What took you so long?' she asked.

'I moved the Bentley,' Blott told her. 'I brought it round and put it in the garage. I thought it would look more natural.'

Lady Maud nodded. 'You are probably right,' she said. 'People might have started asking questions if they found it left up by the church. Besides if he did get out he might have telephoned the AA for assistance.'

'He isn't going to get out,' said Blott, 'I saw him. He's in the pinetum.'

'Well it's his own fault. He came up here to burn the house down and whatever happens now he has only himself to blame.' She handed Blott a plate of cereal. 'I'm afraid I can't give you a cooked breakfast. The electricity has been cut off. I telephoned the electricity office in Worford but they say there has been a power failure.'

Blott ate his cereal in silence. There didn't seem much point in telling her about his part in the power failure and besides she seemed in a talkative mood herself.

'The trouble with Giles was,' she said using the past tense in a way that Blott found most agreeable, 'that he liked to think of himself as a self-made man. I have always thought it an extremely presumptuous phrase and in his case particularly inappropriate. I suppose he had some right to call himself a man, though from my experience of him I wouldn't have said virility was his strong point, but as for being self-made, he was nothing of the kind. He made his money, and of course that's what he meant by self, by speculating in property, by evicting people from their homes and by obtaining planning permission to put up office blocks. At least my family made its money selling beer, and very good beer at that. And it took them generations to do it. There's nothing so splendid about that but at least they were honest men.' She was still talking and doing the washing-up when Blott left to go out to the kitchen garden.

'Is there anything else you want done about him?' he asked as he left.

Lady Maud shook her head. 'I think we can just leave nature to take its course,' she told him. 'He was a great believer in the law of the jungle.'

*

In Worford Police Station Dundridge was having difficulty with the law of the land. Hoskins had been no great help.

'According to him,' said the Superintendent in charge of the case, 'you gave specific orders for random sorties to be made by bulldozers on various properties. Now you say you didn't.'

'I was speaking figuratively,' Dundridge explained. 'I certainly didn't give any instructions that could lead anyone but a complete idiot to suppose that I wanted the late Mr Bullett-Finch's house demolished.'

190

'Nevertheless it was demolished.'

'By some lunatic. You don't seriously imagine I went out there and smashed the house up myself?'

'If you'll just keep calm, sir,' said the Superintendent, 'all I am trying to do is to establish the chain of circumstances that led up to this murder.'

'Murder?' mumbled Dundridge.

'You're not claiming it was an accident, are you? A person or persons unknown deliberately take a large crane and use it to pulverize a house in which two innocent people are sleeping. You can call that all sorts of things but not an accident. No sir, we are treating this as a case of murder.'

Dundridge thought for a moment. 'If that's the case there must have been a motive. Have you given any thought to that?'

'I'm glad you mentioned motive, sir,' said the Superintendent. 'Now I understand that Mr Bullett-Finch was an active member of the Save the Gorge Committee. Would you say that your relations with him were marked by an unusual degree of animosity?'

'Relations?' shouted Dundridge. 'I didn't have any relations with him. I never met the man in my life.'

'But you did speak to him over the telephone on a number of occasions.'

'I may have done,' said Dundridge. 'I seem to remember his phoning once to complain about something or other.'

'Would that have been the occasion on which you told him that quote "If you don't stop pestering me I'll see to it that you'll lose a bloody sight more than a quarter of an acre of your bleeding garden" unquote?'

'Who told you that?' snarled Dundridge.

'The identity of our informant is irrelevant, sir. The question is did you or did you not say that.'

'I may have done,' Dundridge admitted, promising himself that he would make Hoskins' life difficult for him in future.

'And wouldn't you agree that the late Mr Bullett-Finch has in fact lost more than a quarter of an acre of his bleeding garden?'

Dundridge had to admit that he had.

As the morning wore on the Controller Motorways Midlands had the definite impression that a trap was closing in around him.

*

In Sir Giles' case there was the absolute conviction. His attempts to scale the wire fence had failed miserably. Oily gumboots were not ideal for the purpose and Sir Giles' physical activities had been of too passive a nature to prepare him at all adequately for scrambling up wire mesh or coping with barbed-wire overhangs. What he needed was a ladder, but his only attempt to leave the pinetum to look for one had been foiled by the sight of a rhinoceros browsing in the rockery and of a lion sunning itself outside the kitchen door. Sir Giles stuck to the pinetum and waited for an opportunity. He waited a long time.

By three o'clock in the afternoon he was exceedingly hungry. So were the lions. From the lower branches of a tree overlooking the park Sir Giles watched as four lionesses stalked a giraffe, one moving upwind while the other three lay in the grass downwind. The giraffe moved off and a moment later was thrashing around in its death throes. From his eyrie Sir Giles watched in horror as the lionesses finished it off and were presently joined by the lions. Stifling his disgust and fear Sir Giles climbed down from the branch. This was his opportunity. Ignoring the rhinoceros which had its back to him he raced across the lawn towards the house as fast as his gumboots would allow. He reached the terrace and hurried round past the conservatory where Lady Maud was watering a castor-oil plant. As he ran past she looked up and for a moment he had an impulse to stop and beg her to let him in but the look on her face was enough to tell him he would be wasting his time. It expressed an indifference to his fate, almost an ignorance of his existence, which was in its way even more frightening than Blott's terrible smile. As far as Maud was concerned he simply wasn't there. She had married him to save the Hall and preserve the family. And now she was prepared to murder him by proxy for the same purpose. Sir Giles had no doubt about that.

He ran on into the yard and opened the garage door. Inside stood the Bentley. He could get away at last. He pushed the doors back and got into the car. The keys were still in the ignition. He turned them and the starter whirred. He tried again but the car wouldn't start.

* * *

In the kitchen garden Blott listened to the engine turning over. He was wasting his time. He could go on till Doomsday and the car wouldn't start. Blott had no sympathy for him. 'Nature must take its course,' Lady Maud had said and Blott agreed. Sir Giles meant nothing to him. He was like the pests in the garden, the slugs or the greenfly. No that wasn't true. He was worse. He was a traitor to the England that Blott revered, the old England, the upstanding England, the England that had carved an Empire by foolhardiness and accident, the England that had built this garden and planted the great oaks and elms not for its own immediate satisfaction but for the future. What had Sir Giles done for the future? Nothing. He had desecrated the past and betrayed the future. He deserved to die. Blott took his shotgun and went round to the garage.

* * *

Lady Maud in the conservatory was having second thoughts. The look on Sir Giles' face as he hesitated outside had awakened a slight feeling of pity in her. The man was afraid, desperately afraid, and Lady Maud had no time for cruelty. It was one thing to talk in the abstract about the law of the jungle, but it was another to participate in it.

'He's learnt his lesson by now,' she thought, 'I had better let him go.' And she was about to go out and look for him when the phone rang. It was General Burnett.

'It's about this business of poor old Bertie,' said the General. 'The committee would like to come over and have a chat with you.'

'Bertie?' said Lady Maud. 'Bertie Bullett-Finch?'

'You know he's dead, of course,' said the General.

'Dead?' said Lady Maud. 'I had no idea. When did this happen?'

'Last night. House was knocked down by the motorway swine. Bertie was inside at the time.'

Lady Maud sat down, stunned by the news. 'How absolutely dreadful. Do they know who did it?'

'They've taken that fellow Dundridge in for questioning,' said the General. Lady Maud could think of nothing to say. 'Knocked half Guildstead down too. The Colonel and I thought we ought to come over and have a talk to you about it. Puts a very different complexion on the whole business of the motorway, don't you know.'

'Of course,' said Lady Maud. 'Come over at once.' She put the phone down and tried to imagine what had happened. Dundridge taken in for questioning. Mr Bullett-Finch dead. Finch Grove demolished. Guildstead Carbonell . . . It was such astonishing news that it drove all thoughts of Giles from her mind.

'I must phone poor dear Ivy,' she muttered and dialled Finch Grove. Not surprisingly, she got no reply.

*

In the garage Sir Giles was doing his best to persuade Blott to stop pointing the twelve-bore at his chest.

'Five thousand pounds,' he said. 'Five thousand pounds. All you've got to do is open the gates.'

'You get out of here,' said Blott.

'What do you think I want to do? Stay here?'

'Out of the garage,' said Blott.

'Ten thousand. Twenty thousand. Anything you ask . . .'

'I'll count to ten,' said Blott. 'One.'

'Fifty thousand pounds.'

'Two,' said Blott.

'A hundred thousand. You can't ask better than that.'

'Three,' said Blott.

'I'll make it—'

'Four,' said Blott.

Sir Giles turned and ran. There was no mistaking the look on Blott's face. Sir Giles stumbled round the house and across the lawn to the pinetum. He scrambled over the iron railings and climbed back into his tree. The lions had finished the giraffe and were licking their paws and wiping their whiskers. Sir Giles wiped the sweat off his face with an oily handkerchief and tried to think what to do next.

*

Dundridge was saved that trouble by the discovery of an empty vodka bottle in the cab of the crane and by eye-witnesses who testified that one of the two men seen driving the crane up the High Street had been singing bawdy songs and was very clearly intoxicated.

'There seems to have been some mistake,' the Super-intendent told him apologetically. 'You're free to go.'

'But you told me you were treating the case as one of murder,' shouted Dundridge indignantly. 'Now you turn round and say it was simply drunken driving.'

'Murder in my view implies premeditation,' explained the Superintendent. 'Now, two blokes go out and have one too many. They get a bit merry and pinch a crane and knock a few houses down, well you can't feel the same about it, can you? There's no premeditation there. Just a bit of fun, that's all. Now I'm not saying I approve. Don't get me wrong. I'm as hard on vandalism and drunkenness as the next man, but there are mitigating circumstances to be taken into account.'

Dundridge left the police station unconvinced, and as far as Hoskins' behaviour was concerned he could find no mitigating circumstances whatsoever.

'You deliberately led the police to believe that I had given orders for the Bullett-Finches' house to be demolished,' he shouted at him in the Mobile HQ. 'You gave them to under-stand that I set out to murder Mr Bullett-Finch.'

'I only told them that you had had a row with him on the phone. I'd have said the same thing about Lady Maud if they had asked me,' Hoskins protested.

'Lady Maud doesn't happen to have been murdered,' yelled Dundridge. 'Nor does General Burnett or the Colonel and I've had rows with them too. I suppose if any of them get run over by a bus or die of food poisoning you'll tell the police I'm responsible.'

Hoskins said he didn't think that was being fair.

'Fair,' yelled Dundridge, 'fair? Now you just listen to what I've had to put up with since I've been up here. I've been threatened. I've been given doctored drinks. I've been . . . Well never mind about that. I've been shot at. I've been subject to abuse. I've had my car tyres slashed. I've been accused of murder and you have the fucking gall to stand there and talk to me about fairness. My God, I've fought clean up to now but not any longer. From now on anything goes and the first thing to go is you. Get out of here and don't come back.'

'There's just one thing I think you ought to know,' said Hoskins edging towards the door. 'You've got a new problem on your hands. Lady Maud Lynchwood is opening a Wildlife Park at Handyman Hall on Sunday.'

Dundridge sat down slowly and stared at him.

'She is what?'

Hoskins edged back into the office. 'Opening a Wildlife Park. She's had the whole place wired in and she's got lions and rhinoceroses and . . .'

'But she can't do that. She's had a compulsory purchase order served on her,' said Dundridge stunned by this latest example of opposition.

'She's done it all the same,' said Hoskins. 'There are signs up along the Ottertown Road and there was an advertisement in last night's *Worford Advertiser*. I've got a copy here.' He went through to his office and returned with a full-page advertisement announcing Open Day at Handyman Hall Wildlife Park. 'What are you going to do about that?'

Dundridge reached for the phone. 'I'm going to get on to the legal department and tell them to apply for an injunction to stop her,' he said. 'In the meantime you can see that work resumes in the Gorge immediately.'

'Don't you think we should hold off for a day or two,' said Hoskins, 'and wait for this fuss over the Bullett-Finches' house and Guildstead Carbonell to die down a bit.'

'Certainly not,' said Dundridge. 'If the police choose to

regard the whole thing as a trivial matter, I see no reason why we shouldn't. Work will proceed as before. If anything, faster.'

24

At Handyman Hall what was left of the Save the Gorge Committee met in the sitting-room lamenting the passing of Mr Bullett-Finch and seeking to take advantage from his sacrifice.

'The whole thing is an outrage against humanity,' said Colonel Chapman. 'A more inoffensive fellow than poor old Bertie you couldn't imagine. Never a harsh word from him.'

Lady Maud could remember several harsh words from Mr Bullett-Finch when she had taken the liberty of walking across his lawn, but she kept her thoughts to herself. Whatever his faults in life, Mr Bullett-Finch dead had been canonized. General Burnett put her thoughts into words.

'Terrible way to go,' he said, 'having a dashed great iron ball smash you to smithereens like that. Rather like a gigantic cannonball.'

'He probably didn't feel a thing,' said Colonel Chapman. 'It was late at night and he was in bed . . .'

'He wasn't you know. They found him in his dressing-gown. Must have heard it coming.'

'In the midst of life we are . . .' Miss Percival began but Lady Maud interrupted her.

'There is no point in dwelling on the past,' she said. 'We must concentrate our mind on the future. I have invited Ivy to come and stay here.'

'I rather doubt if she will accept,' said Colonel Chapman looking nervously out of the window. 'Her nerves were never up to much and this latest shock hasn't done them any good and those lions . . .'

'Nonsense,' said Lady Maud briskly. 'Perfectly harmless

creatures provided you know how to handle them. The main thing is to show you're not afraid of them. The moment they smell fear they become dangerous.'

'I'm sure I'd be no good at all,' said Miss Percival. General Burnett nodded.

'I remember once in the Punjab . . .' he began.

'I think we should keep to the matter in hand,' said Lady Maud. 'Much as I regret what has happened to poor Mr Bullett-Finch and indeed to Guildstead Carbonell, there is this to be said for it, it does put us all in a much stronger position vis-à-vis the Ministry of the Environment and this infernal motorway. I think you said, General, that the police were questioning that man Dundridge.'

General Burnett shook his head. 'The Chief Constable has been keeping me abreast of events,' he said. 'I'm afraid they've dropped that line of enquiry. It appears that there was some sort of shindig at the Royal George last night. Seems they're working on the theory that a couple of navvies had a bit too much beer and . . .'

'Beer?' said Lady Maud with a strange look on her face. 'Did I hear you say "Beer"?'

'My dear lady,' said the General apologetically, 'I only mentioned beer because I believe that is what these fellows drink. I wasn't for one moment imputing . . .'

'As a matter of fact I believe it was vodka,' said Colonel Chapman tactfully. 'In fact I'm sure it was. They found a bottle.'

But the damage had already been done. Lady Maud was looking quite distraught.

*

In the pinetum Sir Giles was desperately trying to make up his mind. From his tree he had watched General Burnett and Colonel Chapman and Miss Percival arrive. They had come in one car – Miss Percival had left her car outside the main gates and had joined the General in his – and their coming seemed to offer Sir Giles an opportunity to escape if only he could reach the house. Maud could hardly shoot him down in cold blood in front of her neighbours. There might be a nasty scene. She might accuse him of arson, of blackmail and bribery. She might expose him to ridicule but he was prepared to run these risks to get out of the Park alive. On the other hand he wasn't sure that he was prepared to run the gauntlet of the lions who had sauntered away from their last meal and were lying about on the lawn in front of the terrace. Then again he was now extremely hungry and the lions on the contrary weren't. They had just eaten their fill of giraffe.

At least Sir Giles hoped they had. It was a risk he had to take. If he stayed in the tree he would starve to death and sooner or later he would have to come down. Better sooner, he thought, than later. Sir Giles climbed down and got over the railings. Perhaps if he walked confidently ... He didn't feel confident. He hesitated and then moved cautiously forward. If only he could reach the terrace. And as he moved across the grass he was conscious that he was increasing the distance between himself and the safety of the tree while decreasing that between himself and the lions. He reached the point of no return.

*

In the sitting-room General Burnett was lamenting Sir Giles' absence. 'I've tried ringing his flat in London and his office but nobody seems to know where he's got to,' he said. 'If only we could get in touch with him, I'm convinced we could bring pressure to bear on the Minister to call a halt to the motorway. I'm the last one to complain, but it's at a time like this that a constituency needs its MP.'

'I'm afraid my husband tends to let his business interests get in the way of his Parliamentary duties,' Lady Maud agreed.

'Of course, of course,' said Colonel Chapman. 'He's bound to have a lot of irons in the fire. Wouldn't have got where he has if he hadn't.'

'I think ...' said Miss Percival nervously staring out of the window.

'All I'm saying is that it's about time he made his presence felt,' said the General.

'I really do think you ought to . . .' Miss Percival began.

'It's at times like this he ought to raise his voice . . . Good God! What the hell was that?'

There was a ghastly scream from the garden.

'I think it was Sir Giles raising his voice,' said Miss Percival, and fainted. The General and Colonel Chapman turned and looked out of the window in horror. Sir Giles was visible for a moment and then he disappeared beneath a lion. Lady Maud seized a poker and opened the french windows.

'How dare you?' she shouted charging across the terrace. 'Shoo, Shoo.'

But it was too late. The General and Colonel Chapman rushed out and dragged her back still waving the poker and shooing.

*

'Damned plucky little woman,' said the General as they drove home. Colonel Chapman said nothing. He was trying to rid his mind of the memory of those gumboots, and besides, he found the General's description of Lady Maud a little inappropriate even in these distressing circumstances. His left ear was still ringing from the blow she had given him for telling her she mustn't blame herself for what had happened.

'Mind you, I'm afraid it's put an end to the Wildlife Park,' continued the General. 'Pity really.'

'It's also put an end to Sir Giles,' said Colonel Chapman, who felt that General Burnett was taking the whole affair too calmly.

'There is that to be said for it,' said the General. 'Never could stomach the fellow.'

In the back seat Miss Percival fainted for the sixth time.

*

At Handyman Hall the Superintendent explained to Lady Maud as tactfully as possible that there would have to be a coroner's inquest.

'An inquest? But it's perfectly obvious what happened. General Burnett and Colonel Chapman were here.'

'Just a formality, I assure you,' said the Superintendent. 'And now I'll be getting along.'

He went out to his car with the gumboots and drove off. In the Park the lions were licking their paws and wiping their whiskers. Lady Maud stared out of the window at them. They would have to go of course. Sir Giles might not have been a nice man but Lady Maud's sense of social propriety wouldn't allow her to keep animals that couldn't be trusted not to eat people. And then there was Blott. Blott and the events of the previous evening in Guildstead Carbonell. It was all too obvious what he had wanted Very Special for and it was all her fault. And to think she had invited Ivy Bullett-Finch to come and stay. Well, at least she had a good excuse for cancelling the invitation now. She went through the kitchen and was about to go out when it occurred to her that having tasted human flesh once the lions might not succumb quite so readily to her fear-lessness. She ought really to carry some sort of weapon. Lady Maud hesitated and then went on regardless. She owed it to her conscience to take some risks. She went down the path and into the kitchen garden.

'Blott,' she said, 'I want a word with you. Do you realize what you have done?'

Blott shrugged. 'He got what was coming to him,' he said.

'I'm not talking about him,' said Lady Maud, 'I'm talking about Mr Bullett-Finch.'

'What about him?'

'He's dead. He was killed last night when his house was demolished.'

Blott took off his hat and scratched his head. 'That's a pity,' he said thoughtfully.

'A pity? Is that all you've got to say?' said Lady Maud sternly.

'I don't know what else I can say. I didn't know he was in the house any more than you knew he was going to go and get eaten by those lions.' He picked a caterpillar off a cabbage and squashed it absent-mindedly.

'I must say if I had known what you were going to do I would never have given you the day off,' said Lady Maud and went back into the house.

Blott went on with his weeding. Women were odd things, he thought. You did what they wanted and all the thanks you got for it was a telling off. A telling off. That was an odd expression too, come to think of it. But then the world was full of mysteries.

*

In London Mrs Forthby woke with a vague sense that something was missing. She rolled over in bed, switched on the light and looked at the clock. It said eleven forty-eight and since it was dark it must be nearly midnight. On the other hand it didn't feel like midnight. She felt as though she had been asleep a lot longer than four hours, and where was Giles? She got out of bed and looked in the kitchen, the bathroom, but he wasn't in the flat. Oh well, he had probably gone out. She went back to the kitchen and made herself some tea. She was feeling very hungry too. That was strange because she had had a big dinner. She made some toast and boiled an egg. And all the time she had the nagging feeling that something was wrong. She had gone to bed at eight o'clock and here she was at midnight wide awake and famished. To while away the time she picked up a book but she didn't feel like reading. She turned on the radio and caught the news headlines. '. . . Lynchwood, Member of Parliament for South Worfordshire, who was killed at his home Handyman Hall near Worford by a lion. In Arizona a freak whirlwind destroyed . . .' Mrs Forthby switched off the radio and poured herself another cup of tea before remembering what the announcer had just said. 'Oh dear,' she said, 'this afternoon? But . . .' She went through to the sitting-room and looked at the date on the clock. It read Friday the 20th. But yesterday was Wednesday. Giles had said so. She had said it was Tuesday and he had said Wednesday. And now it was Friday morning and Giles had been killed by a lion. What was a lion doing at Handyman Hall? What was Sir Giles doing there, come to that? They had been going to Brighton together for the weekend. It was all too awfully perplexing and horrible. It couldn't be true. Mrs Forthby dialled the nice lady who told the time. 'At the third stroke it will be twelve ten and twenty seconds.'

'But what's the date? What day is it?' Mrs Forthby asked.

'At the third stroke it will be twelve ten and thirty seconds.'

'Oh dear, you really aren't being very helpful,' said Mrs Forthby, and began to cry. Giles hadn't been a very nice man but she had been fond of him and it was all her fault.

'If I hadn't been so forgetful and had remembered to wake up he would still be alive,' she murmured.

*

At his Mobile HQ Dundridge greeted the news next morning jubilantly.

'That'll teach the stupid bitch to build a bloody Wildlife Park,' he told Hoskins.

'I don't see how you can say that,' said Hoskins. 'All it's done is to create another vacancy in Parliament. There will have to be a bye-election and you know what happened last time.'

'All the more reason for pressing ahead as quickly as possible.'

'What? With Maud Lynchwood in mourning? The poor woman has just lost her husband under the most tragic circumstances and you—'

'Don't give me that bull,' said Dundridge. 'If you ask me she's probably delighted. Wouldn't surprise me to learn she'd arranged the whole thing just to stop us.'

'That's bloody libel, that is,' said Hoskins. 'She may be a bit of a tartar but . . .'

'Listen,' said Dundridge, 'she didn't give a tuppenny damn about her husband, I know.'

'You know?'

'Yes I do know as a matter of fact. I'll tell you something. That old cow tried to seduce me one night and when I wouldn't play ball she took a potshot at me with a twelve-bore. So don't come that crap about a sorrowing widow. We're going ahead, and fast.'

'Well all I can say is that you're flying in the face of public opinion,' said Hoskins, stunned by Dundridge's story of his attempted seduction. 'There's Bullett-Finch dead and now Sir Giles. There's bound to be a public outcry. I should have thought now was the time to lie doggo.'

'Now is the time to establish ourselves at the Park itself,' said Dundridge. 'I'm going to move two bulldozers and a base camp up by that arch of hers. If she wants to squawk let her squawk.'

*

But Lady Maud didn't squawk. She had been more shocked by Sir Giles' death than she would have expected and she felt personally responsible for what had happened to Mr Bullett-Finch. She went about her duties automatically but with an abstracted air, occupied with the moral dilemma in which she found herself. On the one hand she was faced with the destruction of everything she loved, the Hall, the Gorge, the wild landscape, the garden, the world her ancestors had fought for and created. All this would go, to be replaced by a motorway which would be a useless, obsolescent eyesore in fifty years when fossil fuel ran out. It wasn't as if the motorway was needed. It had been concocted by Giles to make himself a paltry sum of money, a mean, cruel gesture to hurt her. Well Giles had got his comeuppance but the legacy of the motorway remained and the methods she had had to use had degraded her. She had fought fire with fire and other people had been burnt, Bertie Bullett-Finch and – quite literally – the poor man who had put the paraffin lamp in front of Mr Dugdale's garage.

It was in this mood of self-recrimination that she attended the coroner's inquest which returned a verdict of accidental death on Sir Giles Lynchwood and commended his widow on her bravery while pointing out the unforeseen dangers of keeping undomesticated animals on domestic premises. It was in the same mood that she superintended the removal of the lions, the last giraffe and the ostriches, before going off to a Memorial Service at Worford Abbey. All this time she avoided Blott, who stuck to the kitchen garden in low dudgeon. It was

only when, on her return from the Abbey, she saw the bulldozers parked near the iron suspension bridge opposite the
Lodge that she felt a pang of remorse for the way she had
upbraided him. She found him sulking among the black-
currants.

'Blott, I'm sorry,' she said. 'I feel I owe you an apology. We
all make mistakes from time to time and I've come to say how
grateful I am to you for all the sacrifices you've made on my
behalf.'

Blott blushed under his tanned complexion. 'It was nothing,'
he mumbled.

'That's just not true,' said Lady Maud graciously, 'I don't
know how I would have managed without you.'

'You don't have to thank me,' said Blott.

'I just wanted you to know that I appreciate it,' said Lady
Maud. 'By the way as I came in I noticed the bulldozers by the
Lodge . . .'

'You want them stopped, I suppose?'

'Well, now that you come to mention it . . .' Lady Maud
began.

'Leave it to me,' said Blott, 'I'll stop them.'

Lady Maud hesitated. This was the moment of decision. She
chose her words carefully.

'I wouldn't like to think that you were going to do anything
violent.'

'Violent? Me?' said Blott sounding almost convincingly aggrieved at the suggestion.

'Yes, you,' said Lady Maud. 'Now, I don't mind spending
money if it's needed. You can have what you want but I won't
have anyone else getting hurt. There's been quite enough of
that already.'

'Your forefathers fought for . . .'

'I think I'm a rather better authority on what my ancestors
did than you are,' said Lady Maud. 'I don't need telling. That
was quite different. For one thing they were agents of the
Crown and acting within the law and for another the only
people to get hurt were the Welsh and they were savages.

Besides, I'm a Justice of the Peace and I can't condone anything illegal. Whatever you do must be lawful.'

'But . . .' began Blott.

Lady Maud interrupted him. 'I don't want to hear any more. What you do is your own affair. I want no part of it.'

She strode away and left Blott to consider her words.

'No violence,' he muttered. It was going to make things a little difficult but he would think of something. Women, even the best of them, were illogical creatures. He walked out of the garden and down the drive to the Lodge. On the far side of the suspension bridge two bulldozers, symbols of Dundridge's task force, stood under the trees. It would have been so easy to disable them with the PIAT or even to put sugar in their fuel tanks but if Maud said he must stay within the law . . . Stay within the law? That was another strange expression. As if the law was some sort of fortress. Blott looked up at the great arch towering above him.

He had just had an idea.

25

In spite of his intention to act swiftly the Controller Motorways Midlands found it difficult to act at all. Work on the motorway came to a virtual standstill while the various authorities responsible for the preservation of Guildstead Carbonell and law and order on the one hand wrangled with those responsible for the construction of the motorway and the destruction of the village on the other. To make matters worse there was a walk-out by dumper drivers who claimed they were being victimized by being barred from the Royal George for the damage done to the bar-billiards table by the clog-dancing of the bulldozer men, and a work-to-rule by the demolition experts who asserted that the arrest of Mr Edwards constituted a threat to their basic rights as Trade Unionists. To end the dispute Dundridge paid for the bar-billiards table out of incidental expenses and interceded with the police to release Mr Edwards on bail pending a psychiatrist's report. In the middle of the confusion he was summoned to London to explain remarks he had made in a television interview filmed in front of the ruins of Finch Grove.

'Couldn't you have thought of something better than "That is the way the cookie crumbles"?' Mr Rees demanded. 'And what in God's name did you mean by "There's many a slip twixt cup and lip"?'

'All I meant was that accidents do happen,' Dundridge explained. 'I was being bombarded with—'

'Bombarded? What do you think we've been since then? How many letters have we had?'

Mr Joynson consulted his list. 'Three thousand four hundred and eighty-two to date, not including postcards.'

'And what about "We all have to make sacrifices"? What sort of impression do you think that makes on three million viewers?' shouted Mr Rees. 'A man living peacefully in a quiet corner of rural England minding his own business is battered to death in the middle of the night by some fucking idiot with an iron ball weighing two tons and you talk about making sacrifices!'

'As a matter of fact he wasn't minding his own business,' Dundridge protested, 'he was continually ringing up to—'

'And I suppose you think that justifies . . . I give up.'

'I think we have to look at it from the point of view of the potential housebuyer,' said Mr Joynson tactfully. 'It's difficult enough for the average wage-earner to get a mortgage these days. We don't want to give people the idea that they run the risk of having their houses demolished without the slightest warning.'

'But the house wasn't even scheduled for demolition,' Mr Rees pointed out.

'Quite,' said Mr Joynson. 'The point I'm trying to make is that Dundridge here must adopt a more tactful approach. He should use persuasion.'

But Dundridge had had enough. 'Persuasion?' he snarled. 'You don't seem to understand what I'm up against. You seem to think all I've got to do is serve a compulsory purchase order and people simply get out of their houses and everything is hunky-dory. Well let me tell you it isn't that simple. I'm supposed to be in charge of building a motorway through a house and park belonging to a woman whose idea of persuasion is to take potshots at me with a twelve-bore.'

'And evidently missing,' sighed Mr Rees.

'Why didn't you inform the police?' Mr Joynson asked more practically.

'The police? She *is* the police,' said Dundridge. 'They eat out of her hand.'

'Like those lions I suppose,' said Mr Rees.

'And what do you think she built that Wildlife Park for?' Dundridge asked.

'I suppose you're going to tell us next that she wanted to find a way of disposing of her husband,' Mr Rees said wearily.

'To stop the motorway. She intended to whip up public support, gain sympathy and generally cause as much confusion as possible.'

'I should have thought she could have safely left that to you,' said Mr Rees.

Dundridge looked at him balefully. It was obvious that he did not enjoy the confidence of his superiors.

'If that's the way you feel I can only resign my position as Controller Motorways Midlands and return to London,' he said. Mr Rees looked at Mr Joynson. This was the ultimatum they had feared. Mr Joynson shook his head.

'My dear Dundridge, there is absolutely no need for you to do that,' said Mr Rees with forced affability. 'All we ask is that you try to avoid any more unfavourable publicity.'

'In that case I look to you to give me your full support,' said Dundridge. 'I can't be expected to overcome the sort of opposition I'm faced with unless the Ministry is prepared to throw its weight behind my efforts.'

'Anything we can do,' said Mr Rees, 'to help, we will certainly do.'

Dundridge left the office mollified and with the feeling that his authority had been enhanced after all.

'Give the swine enough rope and I daresay he'll hang himself,' said Mr Rees when he had gone. 'And frankly I wish Lady Maud the best of British luck.'

'Must be a terrible thing to lose a husband like that,' said Mr Joynson. 'No wonder the poor woman is upset.'

*

But it was less the loss of her husband that was upsetting Lady Maud than the bills she was receiving from various shops in Worford.

'One hundred and fifty tins of frankfurters? One thousand candles? Sixty tons of cement? Two hundred yards of barbed-wire? Forty six-foot reinforcing rods?' she muttered as she went through the bills. 'What on earth can Blott be thinking of?' But she paid the bills without question and kept herself to herself. Whatever Blott was up to she wanted to know as little about it as possible. 'Ignorance is bliss,' she thought, demonstrating a lack of understanding of the law which did her little credit as a magistrate.

*

And Blott was busy. He had spent the lull provided by Dundridge's troubles in preparing his defence. Lady Maud had specified that there must be no violence on his part and as far as he was concerned there would be no necessity for it. The Lodge was practically impregnable to anything short of a full-scale assault by tanks and artillery. He had filled all the rooms on either side of the archway with bits of old iron and cement and had sealed the stairway with concrete. He had covered the roof with sharpened iron rods embedded in concrete and entangled with barbed-wire. To secure an independent water supply he had run a plastic pipe down to the river before the concrete was poured into the rooms below and to ensure that he could withstand a prolonged siege he had laid in enough foodstuffs to last him for two years. If his electricity was cut off he had a thousand candles and several dozen containers of bottled gas and finally, to prevent any attempt to drive him out with tear gas, he had unearthed an old army gas-mask from his cache in the forest. Just in case the mask was no longer proof against the latest gases he had turned his library into an air-tight room to which he could retreat. All in all he had converted the Lodge from a very large ornamental arch into a fortress. The only entrance was through a hatch in the roof under the barbed-wire and spikes, and to enable him to leave when he wanted Blott had constructed a rope ladder which he could let down. Finally and just in case things did get violent he had collected a rifle, a Bren gun, a two-inch mortar, several cases of ammunition and hand-grenades with which to deter boarders. 'Of course, I'll only fire over their heads,' he told himself. But there would be no need. Blott knew the British too well to suppose they would do anything to endanger life. And yet without endangering life, and Blott's life in particular, there was no way of building the motorway on through the Park and Handyman Hall. The Lodge, now Festung Blott, stood directly in the path of the motorway. On either side the cliffs rose steeply. Before anything could be done the Lodge would have to be demolished and since Blott was encased within it, demolishing the arch would mean demolishing him. They couldn't even use dynamite to blast the cliffs on either side without seriously risking his life and threatening the collapse of the arch. Finally to ensure that no one could even drive through the gateway he erected a series of concrete blocks in the middle of the archway. It was this last that forced Lady Maud to ask him what the hell he thought he was doing.

'How do you expect me to do my shopping if I can't drive in and out?' she demanded.

Blott pointed to the Bentley and the Land-Rover parked beside the two bulldozers on the other side of the suspension bridge.

'Good Lord,' said Lady Maud, 'do you mean to say you moved them without my permission?'

'You said you didn't want to know what I was doing so I

didn't tell you,' Blott told her. Lady Maud had to admit the logic of the answer.

'It's going to be very inconvenient,' she said. She looked up at the Lodge. Apart from the spikes and the barbed-wire on the roof it looked as it had always looked. 'I just hope you know what you're doing,' she said and made her way through the concrete blocks and across the bridge to her car. She drove into Worford to see Mr Ganglion about Sir Giles' will. From what she had been able to ascertain she had been left a widow of very considerable means, and Lady Maud intended to put those means to good use.

*

'A fortune, my dear lady,' said Mr Ganglion, 'an absolute fortune even by today's standards. Properly invested, you should be able to live quite royally.' He looked at her appreciatively. Now that he came to think of it she had every right to live royally. There was that business of Edward the Seventh. 'And as a widower myself . . .' He looked at her even more appreciatively. She might not be to every man's taste but then he wasn't up to much himself and he was getting on in years. And ten million pounds in property was an inducement. So too were those photographs of Mr Dundridge.

'I intend to re-marry as soon as possible,' said Lady Maud. 'Sir Giles may have left me well provided for but he did not fulfil his proper functions as a husband.'

'Quite so. Quite so,' said Mr Ganglion, his mind busily considering Dundridge's accusation of blackmail. It might be worth his while to try a little expeditious blackmail himself. He turned to his safe and twiddled the knob.

'Besides, it's not good for you to have to live alone in that great house,' he continued. 'You need company. Someone to look after you.'

'I have already seen to that,' said Lady Maud. 'I have invited Mrs Forthby to come and make it her home.'

'Mrs Forthby? Mrs Forthby? Do I know her?'

'No,' said Lady Maud, 'I don't suppose you do. She was Giles' . . . er . . . governess in London.'

'Really?' said Mr Ganglion glancing at her over the top of his glasses. 'Now that you come to mention it I did hear something . . .'

'Well never mind that,' said Lady Maud, 'there's no point in flogging a dead horse. The thing is that from what I have seen of the will he had made no provision for the poor woman. I intend to make good the deficiency.'

'Very generous of you. Magnanimous,' said Mr Ganglion and took an envelope from the safe. 'And while we're on the subject of human frailties, I wonder if you would mind glancing at these photographs and telling me if you have seen them before.' He opened the envelope and spread them out before her. Lady Maud stared at them intently. It was obvious she had seen them before.

'Where did you get those?' she shouted.

'Ah,' said Mr Ganglion, 'now I'm afraid that would be telling.'

'Of course it would,' snarled Lady Maud, 'what do you think I asked you for?'

'Well,' said Mr Ganglion, putting the photographs back into the envelope, 'a certain person, let us say a prospective client, consulted me . . .'

'Dundridge. I knew it. Dundridge,' said Lady Maud.

'Your guess is as good as mine, my dear Lady Maud,' said Mr Ganglion. 'Well this client did suggest that you had been using these . . . er . . . rather revealing pictures to . . . er . . . blackmail him.'

'My God,' shouted Lady Maud, 'the filthy little beast!'

'Of course I did my best to assure him that such a thing was out of the question. However he remained unconvinced . . .' But Lady Maud had heard enough. She rose to her feet and seized the envelope. 'Now if you feel that we should institute proceedings for slander . . .'

'Accused me of blackmail? By God I'll make him regret the day he was born,' Lady Maud snarled and stumped out of the room with the photographs.

Dundridge was in his Mobile HQ drawing up plans for his next move against Handyman Hall when Lady Maud drove up. Now that he was assured that the Ministry would throw their full weight behind his efforts he viewed the future with renewed confidence. He had spoken to the Chief Constable and had demanded full police co-operation should Lady Maud refuse to comply with the order to move out of Handyman Hall and the Chief Constable had reluctantly agreed. He was just giving Hoskins his instructions to move into the Park when Lady Maud stormed through the door.

'You filthy little swine,' she shouted and tossed the photographs on to his desk. 'Take a good look at yourself.' Dundridge did. So did Hoskins.

'Well?' continued Lady Maud. 'And what have you got to say now?'

Dundridge stared up at her and tried to think of words to match his feelings. It was impossible.

'If you think you can get away with this you're mistaken,' bawled Lady Maud.

Dundridge clutched the telephone. The filthy bitch had come back to haunt him with those horrible photographs and this time there was no mistaking who was playing the main role in these obscene contortions and this time too Hoskins was present. The look of horror on Hoskins' face decided him. There was no way of avoiding a scandal. Dundridge dialled the police.

'Don't think you can wriggle out of this by calling a lawyer,' Lady Maud yelled.

'I'm not,' said Dundridge finding his voice at last, 'I am calling the police.'

'The police?' said Lady Maud.

'The police?' whispered Hoskins.

'I intend to have you charged with attempted blackmail,' said Dundridge.

Lady Maud launched herself across the desk at him. 'Why, you filthy little bastard,' she screamed. Dundridge lurched off his chair and ran for the door. Lady Maud turned and raced after him. Behind them Hoskins replaced the telephone and picked up the photographs. He went into the lavatory and shut the door. When he came out Dundridge was cowering behind a bulldozer, Lady Maud was being restrained by six bulldozer drivers and the photographs had been reduced to ashes and flushed down the pan. Hoskins sat down and wiped his face with a handkerchief. It had been a near thing.

'Don't think you're going to get away with this,' Lady Maud shouted as she was escorted back to her car. 'I'll sue you for slander. I'll take every penny you've got.' She drove away and Dundridge staggered back to the caravan.

'You heard her,' he said to Hoskins slumping into his chair. 'You heard her attempt to blackmail me.' He looked around for the photographs.

'I burnt them,' said Hoskins. 'I didn't think you'd want them lying around.'

Dundridge looked at him gratefully. He certainly didn't want them lying around. On the other hand the evidence of an attempted crime had been destroyed. There was no point in calling in the police now.

'Well at least if she does sue me you were a witness,' he said finally.

'Definitely,' said Hoskins. 'But she'll never dare.'

'I wouldn't put anything past that bitch,' said Dundridge recovering his confidence now that both Lady Maud and the photographs were out of the way. 'But I'll tell you one thing. We're going to move into Handyman Hall now. I'll teach her to threaten me.'

*

'Without the photographs I'm afraid you would have no case,' said Mr Ganglion when Lady Maud returned to his office.

'But he told you that I was blackmailing him. You told me so yourself,' said Lady Maud.

Mr Ganglion shook his head sadly. 'What he said to me, my dear Lady Maud, was by way of being a confidential communication. He was after all consulting me as a solicitor and since I represent you in any case my evidence would never be accepted by a court. Now if we could get Hoskins to testify that he had heard him accuse you of blackmail . . .' He phoned the Regional Planning Board and was put through to Hoskins at the Mobile HQ.

'Certainly not. I never heard anything of the sort,' said Hoskins. 'Photographs? I don't know what you're talking about.' The last thing he wanted to do was to appear in court to testify about those bloody photographs.

'Peculiar,' said Mr Ganglion. 'Most peculiar, but there it is. Hoskins won't testify.'

'That just goes to show you can't trust anyone these days,' said Lady Maud.

She drove home in a filthy temper which wasn't improved by having to park the Bentley outside the Lodge and walk up the drive.

26

If her temper was bad when she returned to the Hall that afternoon it was ten times worse the next morning. She woke to the sound of lorries driving down the Gorge road and men shouting outside the Lodge. Lady Maud picked up the phone and called Blott.

'What the devil is going on down there?' she asked.

'It's started,' said Blott.

'Started? What's started?'

'They've come to begin work.'

Lady Maud dressed and hurried down the drive to find Dundridge, Hoskins and the Chief Constable and a group of policemen standing looking at the concrete blocks under the archway.

'What's the meaning of this?' she demanded.

'We have come to begin work here,' said Dundridge keeping close to the Chief Constable. 'You are in receipt of a compulsory purchase order served on you on the 25th of June and . . .'

'This is private property,' said Lady Maud. 'Kindly leave.'

'My dear Lady Maud,' said the Chief Constable, 'I'm afraid these gentlemen are within their rights . . .'

'They are within my property,' said Lady Maud. 'And I want them off it.'

The Chief Constable shook his head sorrowfully. 'I'm sorry to have to say this . . .'

'Then don't,' said Lady Maud.

'But they are fully entitled to act in accordance with their instructions and begin work on the motorway through the Park. I am here to see that they are not hindered in any way. Now if you would be so good as to order your gardener to vacate these . . . er . . . premises.'

'Order him yourself.'

'We have attempted to serve an eviction order on him but he refuses to come down. He appears to have barricaded the door. Now we don't want to have to use force but unless he is prepared to come out I'm afraid we will have to make a forcible entry.'

'Well, I'm not stopping you,' said Lady Maud. 'If that's what you have to do, go ahead and do it.'

She stood to one side while the policemen went round the side of the Lodge and hammered at the door. Lady Maud sat on a concrete block and watched them.

The police battered at the door for ten minutes and finally broke it down only to find themselves confronted by a wall of concrete. Dundridge sent for a sledgehammer but it was quite clear that something more than a sledgehammer would be required to make an entry.

'The bastard has cemented himself in,' said Dundridge.

'I can see that for myself,' said the Chief Constable. 'What are you going to do now?'

Dundridge considered the problem and consulted Hoskins. Together they walked back to the bridge and looked up at the arch. In the circumstances it had assumed a new and quite daunting stature.

'There's no way round it,' said Hoskins, indicating the cliffs. 'We would have to move thousands of tons of rock.'

'Can't we blast a way round?'

Hoskins looked up at the cliffs and shook his head. 'Could do but we'd probably kill the stupid bugger in that arch in the process.'

'So what?' said Dundridge. 'If he won't come down it's his own fault if he gets hurt.' He didn't say it very convincingly. It was quite clear that killing Blott would come under the heading of very unfavourable publicity at the Ministry of the Environment.

'In any case,' Hoskins pointed out, 'the authorized route runs through the Gorge, not round it.'

'What about the blasting we did back at the entrance?'

'We were authorized to widen the Gorge there because of the river and besides that section doesn't come within the area designated as of natural beauty.'

'Fuck,' said Dundridge. 'I knew that old bitch would come up with something like this.'

They went back to the arch where the Chief Constable was arguing with Lady Maud.

'Are you seriously suggesting that I ordered my gardener to cement himself into the Lodge?'

'Yes,' said the Chief Constable.

'In that case, Percival Henry,' said Lady Maud, 'you're a bigger fool than I took you for.'

The Chief Constable winced. 'Listen, Maud,' he said, 'you know as well as I do he wouldn't have done this without your permission.'

'Nonsense,' said Lady Maud, 'I told him he could do what he wanted with the Lodge. He's been living there for thirty years. It's his home. If he chooses to fill the place with cement that's his business. I refuse to accept any responsibility for his actions.'

'In that case I shall have no option but to arrest you,' said the Chief Constable.

'On what grounds?'

'For obstruction.'

'Codswallop,' said Lady Maud. She got down from the block and walked round to the back of the arch and looked up at the window.

'Blott,' she called. Blott's head appeared at the circular window.

'Yes.'

'Blott, come down this instant and let these men get on with their work.'

'Won't,' said Blott.

'Blott,' shouted Lady Maud, 'I am ordering you to come down.'

'No,' said Blott and shut the window.

Lady Maud turned to the Chief Constable. 'There you are. I have told him to come down and he won't. Now then, are you still going to have me arrested for obstruction?'

The Chief Constable shook his head. He knew when he was beaten. Lady Maud strode back up the drive to the Hall. He turned to Dundridge. 'Well, what do you suggest now?'

'There must be something we can do,' said Dundridge.

'If you've got any bright ideas, just let me know,' said the Chief Constable.

'What happens if we just go ahead and demolish the arch with him in it?'

'The question is,' said the Chief Constable, 'what would happen to him if you did that?'

'That's his problem,' said Dundridge. 'We've got a legal right to remove that arch and if he's in it when we do we're not responsible for what happens to him.'

The Chief Constable shook his head. 'You try telling that to the judge when they try you for manslaughter. I should have thought you'd have learnt your lesson from what happened at Guildstead Carbonell.' He got into his car and drove away.

218

Dundridge walked back across the bridge and spoke to the foreman of the demolition gang.

'Is there any way of taking that arch down without injuring the man inside?' he asked.

The foreman looked at him doubtfully. 'Not if he doesn't want us to.'

As if to give added weight to his argument Blott appeared on the roof. He was carrying a shotgun.

'You see what I mean,' said the foreman.

Blott looked expectantly over their heads, raised his gun and fired. A wood pigeon plummeted out of the sky. Dundridge could see exactly what he meant.

'There's nothing in our contract to say we've got to take unnecessary risks,' said the foreman, 'and a bloke who cements himself into an arch and shoots pigeons on the wing constitutes more than an unnecessary risk. He's a bloody loony, and a crack shot into the bargain.'

Dundridge thought wistfully of Mr Edwards. He turned to Hoskins.

'I think,' said Hoskins, 'that we ought to contact the Ministry in London. This thing's too big for us.'

*

At the Hall Lady Maud heard the shot and picked up a pair of binoculars. Through them she could see Blott on the roof with the shotgun. She telephoned the Lodge.

'They're not shooting at you, are they?' she asked hopefully.

'No,' said Blott, 'I was just shooting a pigeon. They're still talking.'

'Remember what I said about violence,' Lady Maud told him. 'We must keep public sympathy on our side. I am going to get in touch with the BBC and ITV and all the national newspapers. I think we can make a big song and dance about this business.'

Blott put down the phone. Song and dance. The English language was *most* expressive. Song and dance.

*

At his Mobile HQ Dundridge was on the phone to London.

'Are you seriously trying to tell me that Lady Lynchwood's

gardener has cemented himself into an ornamental arch?' said Mr Rees incredulously. 'It doesn't sound possible.'

'The arch in question happens to be eighty feet high,' Dundridge explained. 'It has rooms inside. He's filled all the bottom ones with concrete. There's barbed-wire on the roof and short of blowing the place up there's no way of getting him out.'

'I should try the local fire brigade,' Mr Rees suggested. 'They use them to get cats out of trees.'

'I have tried the fire brigade,' said Dundridge.

'Well, what do they say?'

'They say their business is putting out fires, not storming fortresses.'

Mr Rees considered the problem. 'I imagine he'll have to come out sometime,' he said finally.

'Why?'

'Well, to eat for one thing.'

'Eat?' shouted Dundridge. 'Eat? He doesn't have to come out to eat. I've got a list here of the things he ordered from the local supermarket. Four hundred tins of baked beans, seven hundred cans of corned beef, one hundred and fifty tins of frankfurters. Need I go on?'

'No,' said Mr Rees hastily, 'the fellow must have a constitution like an ox. You would have thought he would have chosen something a little more appetizing.'

'Is that all you've got to say?' said Dundridge.

'Well I must admit that it does sound as if he intends to make a long stay of it,' Mr Rees agreed.

'And what are we going to do? Cancel the motorway for a couple of years while he munches his way through that little lot?'

Mr Rees tried to think. 'Can't you talk him down?' he asked. 'That's what they usually do with people threatening to commit suicide.'

'But he isn't threatening suicide,' Dundridge pointed out.

'It amounts to the same thing,' said Mr Rees. 'A diet of corned beef, baked beans and frankfurters in the quantities you've mentioned would certainly kill me. Still, I see what you mean. A man who can even contemplate living off that muck obviously means business. Have you any ideas on the subject?'

'As a matter of fact I have,' said Dundridge.

'Not another ball and crane job I hope,' said Mr Rees anxiously. 'We can't have another little episode of that sort so shortly after the last one.'

'I was thinking of using the army,' said Dundridge.

'The army? My dear fellow, this is a free country. We can't possibly ask the army to blast a perfectly innocent Englishman out of his own home with tanks and artillery.'

'To be precise,' said Dundridge, 'he doesn't happen to be an Englishman and I wasn't thinking of blasting him out with tanks and artillery.'

'I should think not. The public would never stand for it,' Mr Rees said. 'But if he's not an Englishman what is he?'

'An Italian.'

'An Italian? Are you sure? It doesn't sound like them to go in for this sort of thing,' said Mr Rees.

'He's naturalized,' said Dundridge.

'That explains it,' said Mr Rees. 'In that case I can't see any objection to using the army. They're used to dealing with foreigners. What precisely did you have in mind?'

Dundridge explained his plan.

'Well I'll see what I can do,' said Mr Rees. 'I'll call you back when I've had a word with the Minister.'

In Whitehall the wires buzzed. Mr Rees spoke to the Minister of the Environment and the Minister spoke to Defence. By five o'clock Army Command had agreed to supply a team of commandos trained in rock climbing on the explicit understanding that they were to be used simply in a police support role and would not use firearms. As the Minister of the Environment explained, the essence of the operation was to occupy the Lodge and hold Blott until the police could evict him in a lawful fashion. 'The great thing is that the media haven't got on to the story yet. If we can get him out of there before the newsmen start nosing around we can hush the whole thing up. The essence of the thing must be speed.'

*

It was a point that Dundridge made to the commandos when they arrived for briefing that night at his Mobile HQ. 'I have here a number of photographs taken this afternoon of the target,' he said handing them round. 'As you can see it is amply provided with handholds and there are two means of access. The two circular windows on either side and the hatch in the roof. I should have thought the best method of attack would be a diversionary move to the rear and a frontal assault—'

'I think you can leave the tactical details of the exercise to us,' said the Major in charge who didn't like being told his business by a civvy.

'I was only trying to help,' said Dundridge.

'Now then,' said the Major. 'We'll rendezvous at the Gibbet at twenty-four hundred hours and proceed on foot ...' Dundridge left them to it and went into the other office.

'Well, for once we're getting things done,' he told Hoskins. 'That old bitch isn't going to know what's hit her.'

Hoskins nodded doubtfully. He had been in the army himself and he didn't have Dundridge's faith in the efficiency of the military machine.

*

Blott spent the evening reading Sir Arthur Bryant but his mind was not on the past. He was considering the immediate future. They would either act quickly or try to wear him down psychologically by sending a succession of well-meaning people to talk to him. Blott had seen the sort of visitor he could expect on the television. Social workers, psychiatrists, priests and policemen, all of them imbued with an invincible faith in the possibility of compromise. They would argue and cajole (Blott looked the word up in his dictionary to see if it meant what he thought and found he was right) and do their best to make him see the error of his ways and they would fail, fail hopelessly because their assumptions were all wrong. They would assume he was an Italian whereas he wasn't. They would think he was acting on instructions or that he was simply being loyal, whereas he was in love. They would think a compromise was possible ... With a motorway? Blott smiled to himself at the stupidity of the idea. The motorway would either go through the Park and Handyman Hall or it wouldn't. Nothing they could tell him would alter that fact. But above all the people who came to talk to him would be city-dwellers for whom talk was currency and words were coins. An Englishman's word is his bond, Blott thought, but then he had never had much time for stocks and shares. 'Word merchants' old Lord Handyman had called such people, with contempt in his voice, and Blott agreed with him. Well they could talk themselves blue in the face but they wouldn't shift him. Everything that he cared for and loved and was lay there in the Park and the Garden and the Hall. Handyman Hall. And Blott was the handyman. He would die rather than give up the right to be needed. He undressed and climbed into bed and lay listening to the river tumbling by and the wind in the trees. Through his window he could see the light on in Lady Maud's bedroom. Blott watched it until it went out and then he fell asleep.

*

He was woken at one o'clock by a noise outside. It was a very slight noise but it awoke in him some instinct, an early-warning system that told him that there were people outside. He got out of bed and went to the window and peered into the darkness below. There was someone at the foot of the left-hand column. Blott went across the room to the other window. There was someone in the Park too. They must have climbed the fence to get in. Blott listened and presently he heard someone moving below. They were climbing up the side of the Lodge. Climbing? In the dark? Interesting.

He crossed to a cupboard and took out the Leica and the flash gun and went back to the window and leant out. The next moment the entire side of the Lodge was a brilliant white. There was a cry and a thud. Blott went to the other window and took another photograph. This time whoever it was who was clinging to the side of the arch shut his eyes and clung on. Blott put the camera down. Something stronger was needed. What would make climbing difficult? Something greasy. He went into his kitchen and came out with a gallon can of cooking oil and climbed the ladder in the corner of the room to the hatch in the roof. Then he crawled to the edge and began pouring the oil down the wall. There was a curse from below, the sound of slithering and another thud followed by a cry. Blott emptied the rest of the can down the back wall and went down the ladder into his room and shone a torch out of the window. There was no one on the side of the arch now. At the foot a number of men in army uniforms stared up at him angrily. They had blackened faces and one of them was lying on the ground.

'Is there anything I can do for you?' Blott asked.

'Wait till we get hold of you, you bastard,' shouted the Major. 'You've broken his leg.'

'Not me,' said Blott, 'I never touched him. He broke it himself. I didn't ask him to climb up my wall in the middle of the night.'

He was interrupted by a sound from the other side of the Lodge. The sods were coming up there too. He went into the kitchen and fetched two cans of cooking oil and repeated the process. By the time he was finished the sides of the Lodge were streaked with oil and two more climbers had fallen.

Down below there was a muttered conference.

'We'll use the grappling irons,' said the Major.

Blott peered out of the window and shone his torch on them. There was an explosion and a three-pronged hook shot past him on to the roof and stuck in the barbed-wire. It was followed by another. Blott raced into the kitchen and grabbed a knife. A moment later he was on the roof and had cut through one rope. He crawled under the wire and cut another. There was another thud and a yell. Blott peered over.

'Anyone else coming up?' he asked. But the army was already in retreat. As they carried their wounded back across the suspension bridge and up the road Blott watched them wistfully. He rather regretted their going. A full-scale battle would have been marvellous publicity. A full-scale battle? Blott went to the cupboard where he kept his armoury. He would have to act quickly. Then he climbed up on the roof and let down the rope ladder. Ten minutes later he was standing on the suspension bridge with the Bren gun.

As the commandos trudged back up the road towards their transport at the Gibbet they were startled to hear the sound of automatic fire behind them. It lasted for several seconds and was repeated again and again. They stood still and listened. It stopped. A few moments later there was a much larger thump and it was followed by a second. Blott had tried out the PIAT and it still worked.

*

At the Hall Lady Maud sat up in bed and struggled to find the light switch. She was used to the occasional shot in the night but this was something entirely different. A positive bombardment. She reached for the phone and rang the Lodge. There was no reply.

'Oh my God,' she moaned, 'they've killed him.' She got out of bed and dressed hurriedly. The firing had stopped now. She phoned the Lodge again and still there was no reply. She put the phone down and called the Chief Constable.

'They've murdered him,' she shouted, 'they've attacked the Lodge and killed him!'

'Killed who?' asked the Chief Constable.

'Blott,' yelled Lady Maud.

'No?' said the Chief Constable.

'I tell you they have. They've been using machine-guns and something much bigger.'

'Oh my goodness gracious me,' said the Chief Constable. 'Are you sure? I mean couldn't there be some mistake?'

'Percival Henry,' screamed Lady Maud, 'you know me well enough to know that when I say something I mean it. Remember what happened to Bertie Bullett-Finch.'

The Chief Constable remembered all too well. Midnight assassinations were becoming a commonplace occurrence in South Worfordshire and besides Lady Maud's tone had the ring of sincere hysteria about it. And Lady Maud, whatever else she might be was not a woman who got hysterical for nothing.

'I'll get every available patrol car there as soon as possible,' he promised.

'And an ambulance too,' screamed Lady Maud.

Within minutes every police car in South Worfordshire was converging on the Gorge. At the Gibbet twelve men of the 41st Marine Commando, two of them with broken legs, were detained for questioning as they were about to leave in their transport. They were driven to Worford Police Station loudly protesting that they had been acting under the orders of the Area Commander and that the police had no legal authority to hold them.

'We'll see about that in the morning,' said the Inspector as they were herded into their cells.

*

At the Lodge Blott climbed up his rope ladder and hauled it up behind him. He was delighted with his experiment. All the weapons had worked splendidly and, while it was impossible in the darkness to tell what damage they had done to the Lodge, the sound of splintering stonework had suggested that there was plenty of evidence to show that the army had carried out its assault with undue force and quite unwarranted violence. It was only when he was back in his room that he could see how effective the Projectiles Infantry Anti-Tank had been. They had blown two substantial holes in the frieze and the room was littered with bits of stone. Both windows had been blown out by the blast and there were holes in the ceiling. He was just wondering what to do next when he heard footsteps running down the drive. Blott switched off his torch and went to the window. It was Lady Maud.

'Don't come any nearer,' he shouted, to lend verisimilitude to his recent ordeal and to tell her that he was unhurt. 'Lie down. They may start firing again.'

Lady Maud stopped in her tracks. 'Oh thank Heavens, you're all right, Blott,' she shouted. 'I thought you'd been killed.'

'Me? Killed?' said Blott. 'It would take more than that to kill me.'

'Who was it? Did you get a good look at them?'

'It was the army,' Blott told her. 'I've got photographs to prove it.'

27

By next morning Blott was famous. The news of the attack came too late to be carried by the early editions but the later ones all bore his name in their headlines. The BBC broadcast news of the atrocity and its legal implications were discussed on the *Today* programme. At one o'clock there were further developments when it was announced that twelve Marine Commandos were helping the police in their enquiries. During the afternoon questions were asked in the House and the Home Secretary promised a full Enquiry. And all day reporters and cameramen swarmed into the Gorge to interview Blott and Lady Maud and to photograph the damage. It was clearly visible and extensive. Bullet holes pockmarked the entire arch, suggesting that the army's fire had been quite extraordinarily wild. The heads of several figures in the frieze were missing and the PIATs had torn gaping holes in the wall. Even hardened correspondents used to the tactics adopted against the urban guerrillas in Belfast were astonished by the extent of the damage.

'I've never seen anything like this,' the BBC correspondent told his audience from the top of a ladder before interviewing Blott at the window. 'This might be Vietnam or the Lebanon but this is a quiet corner of rural England. I can only say that I am horrified that this could happen. And now Mr Blott, could you tell us first what you know about this attack?'

Blott looked out of the window into the camera.

'It must have been about one o'clock in the morning. I was asleep and I heard a noise outside. I got up and went to the window and looked out. There appeared to be men climbing up the wall. Well I didn't want that so I poured oil down the wall.'

'You poured oil down the wall to stop them?'

'Yes,' said Blott, 'olive oil. They slipped down and then the firing began.'

'The firing?'

'It sounded like machine-gun fire,' said Blott, 'so I ran into the kitchen and lay on the floor. Then a minute or two later there was an explosion and things flew around the room and a few seconds afterwards there came another explosion. After that there was nothing.'

'I see,' said the interviewer. 'Now at any time during the attack did you fire back? I understand you have a shotgun.'

Blott shook his head. 'It all happened too suddenly,' he said. 'I was all shook up.'

'Quite understandably. It must have been a terrifying experience for you. Just one more question. Was the oil you poured down the wall hot?'

'Hot?' said Blott. 'How could it be hot? I poured it out of the can. I hadn't got time to heat it up.'

'Well thank you very much,' said the interviewer and climbed down the ladder. 'I think we'll cut that last remark out,' he told the sound man. 'It made him sound as if he would have liked to have poured hot oil on them.'

'I can't say I blame him after what he's been through,' said the sound man. 'The buggers deserve boiling oil.'

*

It was an opinion shared by the Chief Constable.

'What do you mean, a police support role?' he shouted at the Colonel from the Commando Base who came up to explain that he had been ordered by the Ministry of Defence to send a team of rock-climbers to assist the police. 'There weren't any of my men within miles of the place. You send your killers in armed with rockets and machine-guns and blow hell out of . . .'

'My men were without any weapons,' said the Colonel.

The Chief Constable looked at him incredulously. 'Your men were without weapons? You can stand there and tell me to my face that your men were unarmed when I've seen what they did to that building. You'll be telling me next that they had nothing to do with the incident.'

'That's what they say,' said the Colonel. 'They all swear blue they had left and were on their way back to their transport when the firing occurred.'

'I'm not bloody surprised,' said the Chief Constable. 'If I had just bombarded somebody's private house in the middle of the night I'd say I hadn't been near the place. That doesn't mean anyone with any sense is going to believe them.'

'They weren't carrying weapons when you arrested them.'

'Probably ditched the damned things,' said the Chief Constable. 'And in any case for all I know there were others who got away before my men arrived.'

'I can assure you—' the Colonel began.

'Damn your assurances!' shouted the Chief Constable. 'I don't want assurances. I've got the evidence of the attack itself and I have twelve men trained in the use of the weapons needed for that attack who admit that they attempted to force an entry into the Lodge last night. What more do I need? They'll appear before a magistrate in the morning.'

The Colonel had to admit that the circumstantial evidence . . .

'Circumstantial evidence, my foot,' snarled the Chief Constable, 'they're as guilty as hell and you know it.'

'I still think you ought to look into the business of the civil servant who gave them their instructions,' said the Colonel despondently as he left. 'I believe his name is Dundridge.'

'I have already attended to that,' the Chief Constable told him. 'He is in London at the moment but I have sent two officers down to bring him back for questioning.'

*

But Dundridge had already spent five hours being questioned by Mr Rees and Mr Joynson and finally by the Minister himself.

'All I did was tell them to climb into the arch and hold Blott till the police could come and evict him legally,' he explained over and over again. 'I didn't know they were going to use guns and things.'

Neither Mr Rees nor the Minister was impressed.

'Let us just look at your record,' said the Minister as calmly as he could. 'You were appointed Controller Motorways Midlands with specific instructions to insure that the construction of the M101 went through with the minimum of fuss and bother, that local opinion felt that local interests were being looked after and that the environment was being protected. Now can you honestly say that the terms of reference of your appointment have been fulfilled in any single particular?'

'Well . . .' said Dundridge.

'No you can't,' snarled the Minister. 'Since you went to Worford there have been a series of appalling disasters. A Rotarian has been beaten to a pulp in his own house by a demented demolition expert who claims he was incited . . .'

'I didn't know Mr Bullett-Finch was a Rotarian,' said Dundridge desperately trying to divert the floodwaters of the Minister's mounting fury.

'You didn't know . . .' The Minister counted to ten and took a sip of water. 'Next, an entire village has been wrecked . . .'

'Not an entire village,' said Dundridge. 'It was only the High Street.'

The Minister stared at him maniacally. 'Mr Dundridge,' he said finally, 'you may be able to make these fine distinctions between Rotarians and human beings and entire villages which consist only of High Streets and the High Streets themselves but I am not prepared to. An entire village was wrecked, a pedestrian was incinerated and twenty persons injured, some of them seriously. And this village, mark you, was over a mile away from the route of the proposed motorway. A Member of Parliament has been devoured by lions . . .'

'That had absolutely nothing to do with me,' Dundridge protested. 'I didn't suggest he fill his ruddy garden with lions.'

'I wonder,' said the Minister, 'I wonder. Still, I shall reserve judgement on that question until the full facts have been ascertained. And finally at your instigation the army has been called in to evict an Italian gardener . . . No, don't say it . . . an Italian gardener from his home by bombarding it with machine-guns and anti-tank weapons.'

'But I didn't tell them—'

'Shut up,' roared the Minister. 'You're fired, you're sacked . . .'

*

'You're under arrest,' said the detective who was waiting outside Mr Rees' office when Dundridge finally staggered out. Dundridge went down in the lift between two police officers.

Mr Rees sat down at his desk with a sigh.

'I told you that stupid bastard would hang himself,' he said with quiet satisfaction.

'What about the motorway?' asked Mr Hoskins.

'What about it?'

'Do you think we can continue with it?'

'God alone knows,' said Mr Rees, 'but frankly I doubt it. You seem to forget there's another bye-election due in South Worfordshire.'

*

It was not a point that had escaped Lady Maud's attention. While the reporters and cameramen still swarmed about the Lodge, photographing it from all angles and interviewing Blott from the tops of ladders hired for the purpose, she had been applying her mind to the question of a successor to Sir Giles. A meeting of the Save the Gorge Committee was held at General Burnett's house to discuss the next move.

'Stout fellow, Blott,' said the General, 'for an Eyetie. Remarkable, standing up to a bombardment like that. They used to run like rabbits in the desert.'

'I think we all owe him a debt of gratitude for his sense of duty and self-sacrifice,' Colonel Chapman agreed. 'Frankly I think this latest episode has put the kybosh on the motorway. They'll never be able to carry on with it now. I hear there's a proposal for a sit-in of conservationists from all over the country outside the Lodge to see that there's no repetition of this disgraceful action.'

'I must say I was most impressed by Mr Blott's command of the English language on television the other night,' said Miss Percival. 'He handled the interview quite wonderfully. I particularly liked what he had to say about English traditions.'

'That bit about an Englishman's home being his castle. Couldn't agree with him more,' the General said.

'I was thinking rather about what he said about England being the home of freedom and the need for Englishmen to stand up for their traditional values.'

Lady Maud looked at them all contemptuously. 'I must say I think it is a poor show when we have to rely on Italians to look after our interests for us,' she said.

The General shifted in his seat. 'I wouldn't go so far as to say that,' he murmured.

'I would,' said Lady Maud. 'Without him we would have all lost our homes.'

'As it is Miss Percival's lost hers already,' said Colonel Chapman.

'You can hardly blame Blott for that.'

Miss Percival took out a handkerchief and wiped her eyes. 'It was such a pretty cottage,' she sighed.

'The point I am trying to make,' Lady Maud continued, 'is that I think the best way we can demonstrate our gratitude and support for Blott is by proposing him as the candidate for South Worfordshire in the forthcoming bye-election.'

The Committee stared at her in astonishment.

'An Italian standing for South Worfordshire?' said the General. 'I hardly think . . .'

'So I've noticed,' said Lady Maud brusquely. 'And Blott is not an Italian. He is a nationalized Englishman.'

'Surely you mean naturalized,' said Colonel Chapman. 'Nationalized means state-controlled. I would have thought he was the exact opposite.'

'I stand corrected,' said Lady Maud magnanimously. 'Then we are agreed that Blott should represent the party at the bye-election?'

She looked round the table. Miss Percival was the first to agree. 'I second the proposal,' she murmured.

'Motion,' Lady Maud corrected her, 'the motion. The proposal comes later. All those in favour.'

The General and Colonel Chapman raised their hands in surrender, and since the Save the Gorge Committee was the party in South Worfordshire Blott's candidacy was ensured.

*

Lady Maud announced their decision to the press outside the Lodge. As the newsmen dispersed to their cars she climbed the ladder to the window in the Lodge.

'Blott,' she called through the broken panes, 'I have something to tell you.'

Blott opened the window and leant out. 'Yes,' he said.

'I want you to prepare yourself for a shock,' she told him. Blott looked at her uncertainly. He had been prepared for a shock for some time. The British army didn't use 303 ammunition nowadays and PIATs had been scrapped years ago. It was a point he had overlooked at the time.

'I have decided that you are to succeed Sir Giles,' said Lady Maud gazing into his face.

Blott gaped at her. 'Succeed Sir Giles? Gott in Himmel,' he muttered.

'I very much doubt it,' said Lady Maud.

'You mean . . .'

'Yes,' said Lady Maud, 'from now on you will be the master of Handyman Hall. You can come out now.'

'But . . .' Blott began.

'If you'll hand me the machine-gun and whatever else it was you used I'll take them down with me and we'll bury them in the pinetum.'

As they walked back up the drive with the PIAT and the Bren gun, Blott's mind was in a state of confusion. 'How did you know?' he asked.

'How did I know? I telephoned you of course as soon as I heard the firing,' said Lady Maud with a smile. 'I'm not as green as I'm cabbage-looking.'

'Meine Liebling,' said Blott and took what he could of her in his arms.

*

At Worford magistrates court Dundridge was charged with being party to a conspiracy to commit a breach of the peace, attempted murder, malicious damage to property, and obstruction of the police in the course of their duty.

It was the last charge that particularly infuriated him.

'Obstruction?' he shouted at the bench. 'Obstruction? Who's talking about obstruction?'

'Remanded in custody for a week,' said Colonel Chapman. Dundridge was still shouting abuse as he was dragged out to the Black Maria. In the cells he was interviewed by Mr Ganglion, who had been appointed by the court to conduct his defence.

'I should plead guilty to all charges,' he advised him.

'Guilty? I haven't done anything wrong. It's all a pack of lies!' Dundridge shouted.

'I understand how you feel,' Mr Ganglion said, 'but I understand the police are considering additional charges.'

'Additional charges? But they've charged me with everything under the sun already.'

'There's just that little business of blackmail to be attended to. Now I know you wouldn't want those photographs to be produced in court. You could get life for that, you know.'

Dundridge stared at him despairingly. 'For blackmail?' he asked. 'But I was the one being blackmailed.'

'For what you were doing in those photographs.'

Dundridge considered the prospect and shook his head. Life for something that had been done to him. He had been blackmailed, obstructed, shot at and here he was being charged with these offences. If there was any conspiracy it was directed against him.

'I don't know what to say,' he mumbled.

'Just stick to "Guilty",' Mr Ganglion advised. 'It will save a lot of time and the court will appreciate it.'

'Time?' said Dundridge. 'How long do you think I'll get?'

'Difficult to say really. Seven or eight years I should imagine, but you'll probably be out in five.'

He gathered up his papers and left the cell. As he walked back to his chambers he smiled to himself. It was always nice to combine business with pleasure. He found Lady Maud and Blott waiting for him to discuss the marriage settlement.

'My fiancé has decided to change his name,' Lady Maud announced. 'From now on he wants to be known as Handyman. I want you to make the necessary arrangements.'

'I see,' said Mr Ganglion. 'Well there shouldn't be any difficulties. And what Christian name would he like?'

'I think we'll just stick to Blott. I'm used to it and all the men in the family have been Bs.'

'True,' said Mr Ganglion, with the private thought that some of the women had been too. 'And when is the happy day?'

'We are going to wait until after the election. I wouldn't want it to be thought that I was trying to influence the outcome.'

*

Mr Ganglion went out to lunch with Mr Turnbull.

'Amazing woman, Maud Lynchwood,' he said as they walked across to the Handyman Arms. 'I wouldn't put anything past her. Marrying her damned gardener and putting him up for Parliament.'

They went into the bar.

'What'll you have?' said Mr Turnbull.

'I feel like a large whisky,' said Mr Ganglion. 'I know it's prohibitively expensive but I need it.'

'Have you heard, sir?' said the barman. 'There's fivepence off a tot of whisky and tuppence off a pint of beer. Lady Maud's instructions. Seems she can afford to be generous now.'

'Good Lord,' said Mr Turnbull, 'you don't think it has anything to do with this election, do you?'

But Mr Ganglion wasn't listening. He was thinking how little things had changed since he was a boy. What was it his father had said? Something about Mr Gladstone being swept out of office on a tide of ale. And that was in '74.

28

It was a white wedding. Lady Maud with her customary frankness had prevailed over the Vicar.

'I can damned well prove it if you insist,' she had told him when he had raised one or two minor objections but the Vicar had surrendered meekly. Wilfrid's Castle Church was packed. Half the county was there as Lady Maud strode through the pinetum with Mrs Forthby as her bridesmaid. Blott, now Blott Handyman, MP, was waiting at the church in top-hat and tails. As the organist broke into 'Rule Britannia', which Blott had chosen, Lady Maud Lynchwood went down the aisle beside General Burnett, emerging half an hour later Lady Maud Handyman. They posed for photographs and then led the way down the path and across the footbridge to the Hall. The place was resplendent. Flags flew from the turrets; there was a striped marquee on the lawn and the conservatory was a blaze of colour. Everything that Sir Giles' fortune afforded had been provided. Champagne, caviar, smoked salmon, jellied eels for those that liked them, cucumber sandwiches, trifle. Mrs Forthby had seen to them all. Only the cake was missing. 'I knew I had forgotten something,' she wept but even that was found eventually in the pantry. It was a perfect replica of the Lodge.

'It seems a pity to spoil it,' said Blott as he and Maud stood poised with Busby Handyman's old sword.

'You should have thought of that before,' Maud whispered in his ear. They cut the cake and the photographs were taken. Even Blott's speech, authentically English in its inarticulacy, went down well. He thanked everyone for coming and Mrs Forthby for her catering and made everyone laugh and Lady Maud blush by saying that it wasn't every man who had either the opportunity or the good fortune to be able to marry his mistress.

'Extraordinary fellow,' General Burnett told Mrs Forthby, who rather appealed to him, 'got a multitude of talents. They say there's talk of him becoming a Whip.'

Mrs Forthby shook her head. 'I do hope not,' she said. 'It's so degrading.'

*

Mr Ganglion and Mr Turnbull took a bottle of champagne into the garden.

'They say that the occasion produces the man,' said Mr Turnbull philosophically. 'I must admit he's turned out better than I ever expected. Talk about silk purses out of sows' ears.'

'My dear fellow, you've got it quite wrong,' said Mr Ganglion. 'It takes a sow's ear to know a silk purse when she's got one.'

'What on earth do you mean by that?'

Mr Ganglion sat down on a wrought-iron bench. 'I was just considering Sir Giles. Remarkable how conveniently he timed his death. Have you ever thought about that? I have. What do you suppose he was doing in gumboots in August? It hadn't rained for weeks. Driest summer we've had for years and he dies with his gumboots on.'

'You're surely not suggesting . . .'

Mr Ganglion chuckled. 'I'm not suggesting anything. Merely cogitating. These old families. They haven't survived by relying on chance. They know their onions.'

'You're just being cynical,' said Mr Turnbull.

'Nonsense, I'm being realistic. They survive, my God, how they survive, and thank Heavens they do. Where would we be without them?' His head nodded. Mr Ganglion fell asleep.

*

In bed that night the Handymans lay in one another's arms, blissfully happy. Blott was himself at last, the possessor of a new past and a perfect present. There was no railway station waiting-room in Dresden, no orphanage, no youth, no uncertainties or doubts. Above all no motorway. He was an Englishman whose family had lived in the Gorge for five hundred years and if Blott had anything to do with it they would be living there still five hundred years hence. He had said as much in his maiden speech in the House on membership of the Common Market.

'What do we need Europe for?' he had asked. 'Ah, but you say "Europe needs us". And so she does. As an example, as a pole-star, as a haven. I speak from experience . . .'

It was a remarkable speech and too reminiscent of Churchill and the younger Pitt and of Burke to give the front bench much comfort.

'We've got to shut him up,' said the Prime Minister and Blott had been offered the Whip.

'You're not going to take it, are you?' Lady Maud had asked anxiously.

'Certainly not,' said Blott. 'There is a tide in the affairs of men . . .'

'Oh darling,' said Maud, 'how wonderful you are.'

'Which taken at its flood leads on to families.'

Lady Maud sighed with happiness. It was so good to be married to a man who had his priorities right.

*

In Ottertown Prison Dundridge began his sentence.

'Behave yourself properly and you'll be transferred to an open prison,' the Governor told him. 'With remission for good behaviour you should be out in nine months.'

'I don't want to go to an open prison,' said Dundridge. 'I like it here.'

And it was true. There was a logic about prison life that appealed to him. Everything was in its place and there were no unforeseen occurrences to upset him. Each day was exactly the same as the day before and each cell identical to its neighbour. Best of all, Dundridge had a number. It was what he had always wanted. He was 58295 and perfectly satisfied with it. Working in the prison library he felt safe. Nature played no part in prison life. Trees, woods, and all the gross aberrations of the landscape lay beyond the prison walls. Dundridge had no time for them. He was too busy cataloguing the prison library. He had discovered a far more numerate system than the Dewey Decimal.

It was called the Dundridge Digit.

Tom Sharpe
Riotous Assembly 60p

Riotously funny, savage and shocking ...

A crime of passion committed with a multi-barrelled elephant gun ... A drunken bishop attacked by a pack of Alsatians in a swimming pool ... Transvestite variations in a distinguished lady's rubber-furnished bedroom ... Famous battles re-enacted by five hundred schizophrenic Zulus and an equal number of (equally mad) whites.

'Crackling, spitting, murderously funny' DAILY TELEGRAPH

Indecent Exposure 60p

The brilliant follow-up to *Riotous Assembly* ... another of Tom Sharpe's hilarious and savage satires on South Africa ...

'Explosively funny, fiendishly inventive' SUNDAY TIMES

'A lusty and delightfully lunatic fantasy' SUNDAY EXPRESS

'All good, dirty fun' DAILY TELEGRAPH

Porterhouse Blue 60p

To Porterhouse College, Cambridge, famous for rowing, low academic standards and a proud cuisine, comes a new Master, an ex-grammar-school boy, demanding Firsts, women students, a self-service canteen and a slot-machine for contraceptives, to challenge the established order – with catastrophic results ...

Ralph Hoover
Jabberwocky 60p

Read for yourself the amazing story of the Jabberwocky – the monster so terrifying that people caught the plague to avoid it . . .

Set in the filthiest period of history, as the Middle Ages were collapsing round the well-dandruffed head of King Bruno the Questionable, it is the story of the King's attempts to save a cast of thousands from the threat of the Jabberwocky. He is helped by Dennis Cooper (a peasant's peasant) who, enflamed by undying love for 19-stone Griselda Fishfinger, gives up a quiet country life for the fleshpots of the city.

Billy Connolly The Authorized Version 75p

Compiled and introduced by Duncan Campbell

See inside for Marx and Lenin in Paris . . . McGlumpher the Lavvie Attendant . . . Topless in Biafra . . . A Half-brick Neatly Aimed . . . The Lucky Midden . . . How Adolf Hitler Died in Aberdeen . . .

Drunks and football, twisting for Scotland and the Wee Neds, Margaret Thatcher and Mary, Queen of Scots, folk music and deadly piranha, the Hare Krishna Saffron Tractor and the Six Commandments . . . the one and only book featuring the one and only Billy Connolly!